The Man Who Lost His Wife

Gilbert Welton had a charming wife and a
beautiful house, and although his publishing
business was declining it would obviously last his
time. He thought of himself as a happy man, and
believed that his wife Virginia was happy too. It
was a shock when Virginia, without explanation,
said she had to get away, a greater shock when
Gilbert made up his mind that she was having an
affair with his partner Max. She flew off to
Yugoslavia. And then she disappeared.

What has Virginia done, what will Gilbert do,
what has really happened? This is a story of
suspense and excitement, moving from London to
Yugoslavia, where Gilbert goes to search for his
wife. It is also a novel about jealousy and about a
man who tries to change his way of life, a book
which is sharply funny about half a dozen subjects,
including publishing, modern art movements and
London life in general. It will be a gloomy reader
who does not laugh at Jake Bunce's TV interview
or Coldharbour's sexual problems. For that matter,
Gilbert has his own emotional problems in the
form of a love affair with a girl who is not quite
what she seems . . .

Hard to find a label for a book which has so
many different elements. We hesitate to call it a
new kind of crime story. Mr Symons himself
calls it "a novel of suspicion". That seems a good
description.

by the same author

THE NARROWING CIRCLE
THE PAPER CHASE
THE COLOUR OF MURDER
THE GIGANTIC SHADOW
THE PROGRESS OF A CRIME
THE KILLING OF FRANCIE LAKE
THE END OF SOLOMON GRUNDY
THE BELTING INHERITANCE
THE MAN WHO KILLED HIMSELF
THE MAN WHOSE DREAMS CAME TRUE

The Man Who Lost His Wife

Julian Symons

The Crime Club
Collins, 14 St. James's Place, London

The lines on page 109 from "No Orpheus
No Eurydice" in Stephen Spender's *Ruins
and Visions*, are used by permission of the
poet's publishers, Messrs Faber and Faber.

ISBN 0 00 231521 1

Printed in Great Britain
Collins Clear-Type Press
London and Glasgow

Contents

CONTENTS

PART III: WIFE FOUND

PART I

Wife Going

CHAPTER ONE

Breakfast Conversation

A JUNE MORNING, the sky blue. If anybody had asked Gilbert Welton *are you happy* and if he could have been persuaded to answer (which is unlikely, because the question would not have seemed to him meaningful) he would have said *yes*. The most serious problem confronting him seemed to be the buying of a new hat. Yet happiness is often the thinnest of veneers, and Virginia's words slightly scratched its surface. His coffee cup was raised to his lips when she spoke.

'I think I should go away.'

For a moment he did not properly hear the words, and when he heard he did not understand them. He drank some coffee, dabbed his lips with his napkin. 'What was that?'

'I said, I ought to go away.' She amended this, although with an air rather of amplifying it. 'I mean, have a holiday. To think things out.'

He pushed his plate with a half-eaten piece of toast on it firmly away from him. 'What are you talking about?'

'You heard me. I've said it twice. Just for a time.'

It occurred to him that she was ill, and had been keeping the fact from him. 'Is there something wrong? Have you been to a doctor?'

Virginia gave the question her serious consideration. 'No, I haven't. There's nothing *wrong*. Not in that way.'

Gilbert did not think of himself as an impatient man,

7

but the conversation irritated him. 'Then I don't understand you.'

'I need to find out things. About myself. About us.'

He felt relief at the words. Virginia was a great reader of glossy magazines, and obviously her words sprang from an article in one of them. 'Do You Need a Holiday From Your Husband? . . . The Strain of Being Happily Married . . . Are You a Robot Wife?', he could see the headlines. He did not say this, but instead stared down at the things on the table, the blue and green cups, toast precisely cut in triangles, home-made marmalade, butter in its dish. Then he looked up and out into the garden, a St John's Wood garden, small and neat, with rose-bushes and clematis trailing up the end wall. Last night Virginia had been putting fertilizer on the roses.

'Last night you were doing the roses.' It seemed a sufficient contradiction of her words.

She offered him a cigarette, but he shook his head. He never smoked before midday. She lighted one herself and blew out smoke. 'What was I doing to them?' He hesitated —had it been fertilizer, or had she been digging about with a trowel? She smiled faintly. 'You see?'

'What difference does it make what you were doing?'

'If you don't see that—'

'I don't. You're being ridiculous.'

'You think so?'

With conscious patience he went on. 'You must have a reason. What things do you want to think out?'

She blew out more smoke. 'I like marriage to be hills and valleys, a sort of switchback ride. You want to live on a plateau. But do I want that, that's what I have to find out.'

Hills, valleys, plateaux, what was she talking about? It occurred to him that if he took the conversation seriously this should be an emotional moment, one or other of them ought to be excited, throw something, burst into tears. In-

8

stead Virginia sat in her flowered dressing-gown, neat, dark, elegant, perfectly composed. They were two composed people. He took refuge in irony.

'Not immediately, I hope. We've got people coming to dinner. Max is bringing that American novelist.'

A smile curled the edges of her mouth. 'I'll be here. Everything's laid on. I thought I might go next week.'

Irritation swelled in him like a balloon, but he kept his voice down. 'Virginia, I'm a rational person—'

'Oh, so am I. I mean, you've taught me.'

'You're not making sense. You tell me you have to go away because you want to live on hills instead of plateaux. It can't be the truth.' He snatched at the packet of cigarettes which she had left on the table, took one out and lighted it.

'Would it make more sense if I said I'd been considering it for some time?'

'No.' He said what he had not intended. 'This all comes from something you've been reading.'

She did not comment on this, but stood up. The impression of delicacy given by her features was rather belied by her figure which was strong, coarse, with shapely but powerful peasant legs. 'I've got to get dressed, I'm having my hair done at ten.'

'You told me this when there was no time to talk,' he said, although there was nothing he wanted less than to talk about it.

'There'll be plenty of time for that.' She paused at the door and added reflectively, 'Though I'm not sure there's anything to say.'

He sat at the table after she had gone, touching things with his fingers, the coffee and milk jugs, the toast-rack. He reflected that some people would have gone upstairs now and as the phrase went *had it out with her*, but he was Gilbert Welton and that was not possible for him. He believed, as he often said in the office, that if you let a difficult situation alone it generally changed into an easier one. And as he listened to Virginia talking with her usual cheerfulness to their daily, Mrs Park, it was hard to believe that any 'situation' existed at all.

'I'm off, got to rush.' She blew him a kiss. 'You'll be late for the office. See you tonight. Bye.'

As he brushed his teeth and ran the comb through his hair he told himself that the whole thing was nonsensical. He still had a lot of good thick wavy hair, and the grey wings added distinction. A touch of grey was appropriate at the age of forty-five, and he had kept his figure, his face was almost unlined. People rarely realized that Virginia was twelve years his junior. Not that he minded if they did realize it. He believed that if he took some care about his appearance it was not out of vanity, but because there was nothing more wretched than a middle-aged man who had let himself go.

By the time that he had said goodbye to Mrs Park and stepped out into a fine morning he had eliminated the breakfast conversation from his conscious mind. Virginia was—he always realized the fact with surprise—a stupid woman intellectually. At the hairdresser's she would read another magazine article and talk just as seriously about— oh, about the problems of being a second wife. Probably she would not refer again to their conversation. If she said nothing, he had no intention of mentioning it.

CHAPTER TWO

A Bad Morning At The Office

GILBERT HAD a feeling for architecture. He derived pleasure every time that he looked at the proportions of their early Victorian house, the weight and shapeliness that avoided the solemn ostentation of later Victorian building. The appearance of the office, a small eighteenth-century house just off the sleazier part of Soho, gave him pleasure too, and so did the fascia which said *E.R. and Gilbert Welton* in elegant capitals. The plate glass window beneath, which carried a display of the firm's recent publications, was not so good. Not that there was anything wrong with it, or with the books discreetly displayed there, but the very idea that a publisher should set out his wares in a shop window as if he were a butcher was faintly disagreeable. Inside, he nodded to the new switchboard girl whose name he could not remember, and went upstairs.

His office was square, with a large desk almost in the middle of it. He had no sooner sat down at the desk than Miss Pinkthorn was on him. She was a large efficient woman who had been with the firm in his father's time. She surged in like a resistless tide, and bustled about the office conveying by the sense of urgency in her movements that he was late. The clock on his desk said half past ten.

'Mr Paine would like a word. As soon as you're free.' Paine was the production manager, and his words were always technical. 'And Derek Niven rang about the design for his jacket. He asked you to ring back. I don't think he likes it.'

I don't think he likes it—what a wretched way to formulate a phrase. Why not say accurately, *I think he dislikes it*? Looking down at the mercifully small mound of correspondence on his desk and then up again at the massive body confronting him, he wondered suddenly and uncharacteristically about Miss Pinkthorn's sex life. He had a vague idea that she lived with her widowed sister, but perhaps this was not true, perhaps she had spent the previous night with a man, middle-aged to elderly, to whom she had said this morning, *I think I should go away*. Was there a man, any man at all, in Miss Pinkthorn's life?

'Yes,' he said as he turned over the letters in front of him. 'Yes. Yes.'

'Shall I get Mr Niven?'

Up with her knees and down with her head, That is the way to make good cockle bread. He averted his gaze from Miss Pinkthorn's bulk.

'Let me have a copy of the jacket drawing.'

'On the desk.' A large hand unearthed it, bulging breasts were adjacent to him. The drawing was deplorable, but it was said to be the kind of thing that sold books.

'Authors never like their jackets. I sometimes wonder why we let them see anything at all.' He exhaled, a soundless sigh. 'Get me Mr Niven. And when I've done with him, ask Paine to come up.'

The day had begun. It continued like other days, with long and tedious discussions about costing figures and sales figures and a wrangle with an agent about the advance that should be paid to an author whose contract was due for renewal. He thought suddenly—and it was the kind of thought that hardly ever received admission to his mind—that publishing of this kind was not an occupation that suited him. The production of some finely printed little pamphlet containing a dozen poems by a young writer, a limited edition of a previously unknown essay by Max Beerbohm, these would have been a different matter, but the hour to hour minutiae of a business run presumably for profit was something that seemed, if he was rash enough to consider it, almost degrading. During a long discussion with Paine and Coldharbour about the costing of a travel book which seemed certain to show a loss no matter how many or how few copies were printed, his mind drifted to the breakfast conversation. It became linked with an image of Miss Pinkthorn kicking up her bulky legs.

'At three thousand copies, with this number of plates, there's nothing in it for us if we sell them all.' Paine was a small man with a disagreeable Cockney whine in his voice. 'At five thousand—'

'We shall never sell five,' Coldharbour chimed in.

'If we cut the number of plates by half—'

'We should lose sales,' Coldharbour said. 'Besides, the number of plates is in the agreement.'

Silence. They looked at him. He said nothing.

'Lyme and Makepeace are expensive,' Paine whined. 'I could try Selvers.'

That stung him. 'Could you guarantee that Selvers would do as good a job?' He knew the answer to that. 'Very well then, it's out of the question.'

In the end they agreed to print five thousand copies and hope for the sale of sheets to America. It was a faint hope. When Paine had gone Coldharbour said, 'Have you got five minutes to spare, Gilbert?'

Denis Coldharbour was a thin nervous man who had come into the firm five years earlier, as a working director providing an infusion of fresh capital. The business Gilbert inherited from his father, E.R., had been comparatively small but flourishing. It was based upon one best-selling middlebrow novelist, several useful bread-and-butter writers, some highly successful children's books and a steady selling series called 'British Sights and Scenes'. At the time that E.R. collapsed and died while making a speech to the Publishers' Association about trade terms on single order copies, he was starting to develop a series of educational books for sale in the under-developed countries. Since Gilbert took charge the best-seller had gone elsewhere, two of the bread-and-butter writers had died, the number of British Sights and Scenes about which books could be written seemed to be exhausted, and he had abandoned the educational books as too much trouble, replacing them by an idea of his own for a finely printed series of reprints of travel classics which had proved a disastrous failure. Coldharbour's money had been welcome.

That could not quite be said of Coldharbour. He was a fussy man who sprayed his office daily with some strange insecticide, ate vegetarian food and always wore a brown paper vest for warmth. His first words now were slightly startling. 'How's Virginia?'

He repeated the name as though she were a stranger. 'Very well. Why?'

'I saw her at the Moonsight Galleries yesterday. She seemed rather—' Coldharbour sought for a word and came up with—'distrait.'

'Did you talk to her?'

'I didn't actually talk to her, no.' He moved in his chair and the brown paper crackled slightly. 'I didn't know she was interested in modern art.'

Neither did I, Gilbert refrained from saying. 'Do you mean she looked ill?'

'Not *ill*.' He spoke as if there were some area between illness and health in which he had discovered Virginia. 'Oh, certainly not ill. I didn't mean to alarm you.'

'There's no question of being alarmed,' he said with unintended sharpness. Supposing he said that Virginia had announced her intention of going away, would Coldharbour be surprised? Perhaps he had wondered for a long time why she had married a man so much older than herself. Coldharbour proceeded always by hints and suggestions. Was he saying now that there had been a man with Virginia in the gallery?

'She's a very delightful woman.' Coldharbour himself

14

lived alone in a large basement flat in Maida Vale. Gilbert was aware that he had not heard what was being said, and asked Coldharbour to repeat it.

'Johnson, Braddock, Delaney.'

'What was that?'

'And possibly Sharkey.' Coldharbour looked coy. 'Even Heenan.'

'Who is Heenan?'

'Not hard edge. And certainly not Pop.' A surprisingly masculine chuckle rumbled up from inside him. 'A long way beyond Pop.'

'Denis, I seem to have missed something.'

'They call themselves Spatial Realists, their whole concept is one of spatial flatness. After all a canvas is originally flat, isn't that so? Any attempt to deny flatness is in a sense a fake.' Coldharbour put his fingers together. 'As you know, Gilbert, I've always maintained that we've missed the boat in the past. My belief is that the time has come . . .'

Ever since he came into the firm Coldharbour had wanted to produce a number of monographs, first on Art Nouveau and its origins, then on abstract art, most recently on a movement called Pubism which so far as Gilbert could see would have landed them in court for reproducing obscene pictures. Obviously Pubism had been replaced by Spatial Realism. He felt inclined to say that the whole idea was nonsense, but that was not the way in which a civilized publisher talked to a colleague.

'You thought a series of monographs . . .'

'No. Oh no, not a series. I see it as one big book, *Spatial Realism and the Art of the Seventies*, something like that. Of course we should need an informed introductory essay by somebody who knows what's what, Bryan Robertson perhaps or David Sylvester.'

'Denis, what can I say? It's simply not on.' Out-of-date slang, no doubt, and he regretted it. Yet somehow the phrase was reassuring. 'It's outside our field. We're not equipped to

15

handle it saleswise.' Not slang now but jargon, yet again it seemed expressive.

'If we never publish any art books they'll always be out-side our field,' Coldharbour said reasonably. He crossed one knee over the other, showing an expanse of dead white leg. A curious scent was wafted across the room. Had Cold-harbour been spraying his socks? The smell stirred some memory which he could not be bothered to place. 'I know for a fact that Studio Vista are interested, and Faber too. A Tate exhibition is a real possibility.'

'You know what our commitments are. It could be a very expensive book.'

A derisive sound came through Coldharbour's nose. 'If there is a show at the Tate we could sell ten thousand.' He pulled at the trouser, showing more leg. 'Am I to under-stand that you dismiss it out of hand?'

'I don't see how we can do it.'

'Then I have to say that in my view this is a practicable and profitable piece of publishing which should be most seriously considered.' He sat up and the brown paper rustled. 'Which is more than can be said for some of Bom-berg's activities.'

As though on a signal the door opened and Max Bom-berg's round head appeared. 'Killing two birds with one stone,' he said and entered. 'Gilbert, Denis, great news.' He spread his arms, grinning.

Max Bomberg was a Hungarian who had come into the firm two years earlier on the recommendation of Virginia's Uncle Alex, who was something to do with a merchant bank. He had had no previous direct connection with book publishing, but had been managing editor of a group of magazines and then sales director of a printing house which produced technical journals mainly for the overseas market. The magazine group had been bought up by a large cor-poration at what was said to be a bargain price because they were on their last legs, and there were rumours that many

16

of the technical journals were being eaten by red ants in African warehouses, but Uncle Alex had no doubt about Bomberg's ability. The man was a business genius, he said. Had he got money? He had something better, a nose for success.

'What's your turnover?' Uncle Alex had asked, rather like a nurse asking about bowel motions, and when he heard the answer had said that Bomberg would double it within a couple of years. The business genius had been invited to dinner and under Uncle Alex's benevolent eye had talked vaguely but impressively about profitability margins and the tactics of expansion. Would he put in capital? Not exactly, but a complicated arrangement never clearly understood by Gilbert was made under which Welton's obtained a holding not in the printing house but in an allied company, and Bomberg was given what seemed to be an extremely large number of shares in Welton's. Since then—well, since then it was hard to say exactly what had happened. Certainly turnover had increased considerably, but this was because Bomberg had taken on a number of new authors, paying what were by Welton's standards enormous advances. Where was the money coming from? At such a question he would smile in a slightly pitying way.

'About this, my dear, you don't worry. It will be a bad day when Max Bomberg can't get credit for a good proposition, and this is a first-class proposition.' Max never put forward anything but first-class propositions and Gilbert, who was aware of the restraints and hesitations in his own nature, warmed to such certainties. Now Max's cherubic grin widened. He said dramatically, 'Bunce is on "People in the News" tonight. I have arranged it.'

Jake Bunce was an American novelist who had come over for the publication of his novel, *The Way They Get You Going*. He was one of Max's most dubious acquisitions. Gilbert did not see how they could recoup the advance that had been paid to lure him away from a bigger firm. When they discussed taking him on, Max had slapped a copy of *Life* on the table.

'Look there, a six-page spread, Jake Bunce on Dope, Drink and Saintliness. You see what it says, he's the hottest thing out of Brooklyn since Mailer.'

'*Brooklyn*,' Coldharbour had said, with the air of a man who has heard of the place.

They had taken Bunce on, he had arrived in England that day and was coming to dinner. Bomberg had gone to the airport to meet him, and must just have returned.

'That's very good news.' Gilbert was never able quite to convey enthusiasm.

Max pointed a finger. '*And* he has a radio interview on "World at One" in a couple of days' time. I tell you, they're falling over themselves. We've got a really hot property here.'

'Where is he now?' Coldharbour asked lugubriously. He had unhooked his leg and the scent had disappeared.

'Resting up in the hotel. Oh, I tell you he's a charmer. Can't wait to meet you.'

If Jake Bunce had really been so anxious to meet him, Gilbert reflected, he could have come to the office, but he did not say this. 'I shall see him this evening.'

'You certainly will.'

'And you'll make sure he gets to the studio.'

'You bet your life. About this evening, just one little thing.' He spoke with the casualness he always used when saying something awkward. 'Jake's brought this girl over, some kind of way out girl in films.'

'We're not paying any of her expenses, I hope.' Coldharbour spoke sharply.

'Now, Denis, would I commit us to anything like that?' Max transferred his attention back to Gilbert. 'No, the thing is this, my dear, Jake asked if he could bring Lulu along with him tonight. I said yes. He's pretty informal, you know, he's an informal kind of character, he never had

18

any doubt it would be OK.' In moments of embarrassment or excitement Max's speech was often infused with a slightly American flavour. 'I'm sorry as hell if it's going to put out Virginia. Should I give her a ring?'

'I'll speak to her myself. I'm sure she'll manage.' Who knew what extraordinary thing Virginia might say on the telephone?

He rang her after Max had bounced out and Coldharbour had reluctantly followed him, threatening to renew their discussion about Spatial Realism later on. Her voice had the composure and coolness he had always admired.

'It's a bore but we'll manage. Would you like me to rustle up another man?'

'No, don't bother.'

'I look forward to Mr Bunce and his Lulu. And Max is always fun.'

'It's good of you not to make a fuss.'

He thought of mentioning the breakfast conversation, even though earlier he had decided not to refer to it, but no words came out. Then Miss Pinkthorn sailed in with letters which she placed aggressively in front of him. He said goodbye and put back the receiver. As he did so he remembered the recollection roused by Coldharbour's scent-sprayed socks, if indeed it had been his socks that gave off that curious whiff. In the last few weeks Virginia had changed the scent she used, from one which was light, cool and only faintly discernible, to something distinctly heavier and sweeter. Somebody with a less keen sense of smell might not have noticed it, and his own awareness had been only semi-conscious. Why had she changed?

CHAPTER THREE

Lunch At The Club

THE CLUB was one of those frequented in about equal proportions by publishers, writers, lawyers, advertising and public relations men, and rather oddly a considerable number of tennis and cricket players and other athletes, who were attracted by the squash and fives courts and the large swimming-pool. Gilbert lunched there on Monday, Wednesday and Friday of each week. To do so had become part of the pattern of his life. Besides, E.R. had lunched there three days a week. 'The best club in London,' his father had said on first leading him into the long dark panelled room. 'You never know who you may meet here. Great men, little men, administrators and creators. You may sit next at table to Stephen Spender or to the Lord Chief Justice. Membership of the club is a liberal education.'

On that first occasion Gilbert had sat next to a barrister who talked about the iniquities of the builders who were putting up his new house, and he had never actually seen either Stephen Spender or the Lord Chief Justice in the club, but he appreciated the principle of what his father said. As a young man he had wanted above all to emulate E.R., his heavy oratorical flow of speech, his firmness in taking decisions and refusal ever to admit that he had been wrong. Why was he unable to acknowledge even now that he was nothing like his father? Why, he wondered as he walked up the steps and nodded in response to the hall porter's greeting and spent a minute looking at the ticker-tape which did not much interest him, and another minute in studying the details of the next club supper which interested him even less, why did he come to the club at all?

And why was Virginia using a different scent?

At the long table he sat between an actor named Peter Halding and Langridge-Wood, one of the partners in a large printing firm, and a friend of E.R. Later, as they went into the lounge, Langridge-Wood tapped his shoulder. They took their coffee to a window seat.

'Come and play a hundred up.'

'I ought to get back.' But in the office Coldharbour might be at him again, and there was a manuscript about which he had postponed making a decision for days.

'Won't take you long to beat me. Want to have a chat.'

In the billiards room, under the lights which shone down intensely on the green baize, he felt more at home than in most other places. Playing the balls up the table as they cued for break and watching his own land almost on the back cushion, a perfect stroke, he reflected that this at least was something he had done better than his father. In the hush of the semi-darkened room, where the only sounds were the slight squeak of chalk on cue tip and the click of white on red, there was a sort of placidity. That morning on his walk to the office he had been uncustomarily disturbed by the thought that he was destined to live out his days in E.R.'s shadow, doing inefficiently what his father had done well, slowly running down the firm that his father had created. But as he put side on his ball so that it shot delicately off white and into the pocket, these things took on their proper perspective. What did it matter if the firm was running down? Was it Louis XV who had said 'It will last my time'? Welton's would certainly last his time, and Matthew had made it plain that he wanted no part in it. There would be no second descension from father to son, he thought as he admired his own skill in playing a nursery cannon and keeping the balls together. The firm had given

21

him an easy life, an elegant house, Virginia. Thinking of Virginia he miscued. Langridge-Wood used the chalk.

'Just a word, young Gilbert. Wanted to say I was very glad to hear there are prospects.'

'Prospects?' What was the old fool talking about, the new authors on their lists?

Langridge-Wood's bald head shone under the lamps. He was a player who when in doubt hit the ball as hard as he could and hoped for the best. Now he banged white and red round the table and saw his optimism rewarded when the red dropped unexpectedly into a pocket. He followed this with two successful forcing shots and made a break of fifteen.

'Life in the old dog yet. Don't mind saying there are times when I've been worried.'

'Really?'

'About the firm. But it's a great country, America. Wide open. E.R. always said so. Accepters, not rejecters, he used to say. That's important.'

He must presumably have heard about Bunce. 'Yes, we're very pleased with what's been happening. You know he's over here?'

Langridge-Wood's hearing aid started to whistle. 'What's that? Didn't hear.'

'We're all very pleased. On this side of the water,' he added, and felt the inanity of a phrase which E.R. would have rolled out impressively.

From this point on he began to play badly. Mention of E.R. made him remember their games here, games which his father usually won when it came to a close finish. Nerve, E.R. had said to him, you're a better player than I am, my boy, but you just lack that little bit of nerve. And now Langridge-Wood, hitting the balls as though he hated them, playing uncouth strokes that sent them flying round the table to come together again miraculously for an easy shot

22

to follow, went ahead and punctuated his play with un-intelligible remarks.

'Africa too, that's opening up. Very shrewd,' he said at one point, and at another, 'You know what E.R. said? "Get your toe in you've got your foot in. Get your foot in and if you're tough enough they'll never get you out." Very true, that. True about Africa, I've always thought so.'

In the end Gilbert began to bang the balls as hard as Langridge-Wood, but with less success. He lost the game.

'They dropped for me.' Langridge-Wood racked his cue with some satisfaction. 'Soothing game. Always find it clears the head. Mind you, you were out of touch. Glad we've had a word.'

'Yes.'

'And just bear us in mind in the future. I see great things ahead.' He sounded like a seaside palmist.

'I'm delighted to hear it.'

'Glad for you, young Gilbert. I was a friend of your father's, remember. He was a great man.'

They parted on the steps. Langridge-Wood gave his hand a meaningful pressure, said, 'We'll be in touch,' and stepped into a cab. Gilbert walked back to the office. Coldharbour left him in peace. He looked again at the manuscript, the memoirs of a Second World War military leader, and decided to reject it. Then he went home.

CHAPTER FOUR

Dinner Party

WHEN HE turned on the set Jenny Johnson, well-known as a TV interviewer whose questions turned into speeches longer than the answers of her victims, was in full flow.

'You've written an outspoken novel about drug-taking, Mr Bunce, and another about homosexuality which shocked

23

some people over here who thought it should be banned—'

Jake Bunce had been nodding his head as though about to fall asleep, but now he interrupted her, shoulders rocking a little in soundless mirth. 'I know, yeah, banned. Banned. I heard about that, that gave me a laugh.'

It took more than such interpolations, or the fact that Bunce's gaze was directed down at her very visible thighs, to put Jenny out of her stride. 'And now your new book, out in a few days, *The Way They Get You Going*, is likely to shock a lot more people if I'm not mistaken—'

'I shouldn't wonder.' The soundless laughter was repeated, one Bunce hand moved in the direction of Jenny's leg and drew back. 'I shouldn't wonder at all.'

Virginia came and sat beside him, watching intently.

Jenny gave one of those hopelessly ineffectual tugs at her almost non-existent skirt that had helped to make her celebrated, and leaned forward to ask one of her typical questions, projected with an air of deadliness but in content slightly anodyne. 'And what would you say is the difference between your earlier books and *The Way They Get You Going*?'

Jake Bunce fingered his lower lip and actually lifted his gaze from Jenny's thighs to her face before replying. He was not the small dark hairy man Gilbert had for some reason envisaged, but fair and gangling with one of those unfinished innocent American faces in which the features seem to be wholly amorphous, the nose from one view a blob and from another a powerful organ, the mouth a sensitive blur which changed surprisingly into a lipless pair of pincers.

'The difference is,' he began slowly, 'in those other books I had the drug scene, see, or the gay boys, but here it's the whole thing, everything's there. I'm moving to something universal and that's what I've always been after, though how can you know where home is till you're there, it's like you gotta go through these other things before you get to experience total reality.'

At the welcome, intelligible word *experience* Jenny rushed in with one of her famous interruptions. 'Experience, you said, there are scenes in your book dealing with—oh, various perversions and incest—'

Jake was a match for any interrupter. 'Incest, that's no perversion. Just a social taboo, that's all.'

Jenny gave a trill of irritated laughter. 'Very well, but you'll admit that there *are* perversions in your book, sadistic and masochistic acts and so on. Do they spring from experience?'

'Everything in my books comes from life. It's all experience.' At this point Jake actually did lean forward and place his hand on Jenny's knee. 'A novelist should experience everything, all extremes. He's all of humanity. He's a white Negro or he's nothing.'

Gilbert turned off the set. 'I hope he's not going to talk like that when he's here.'

'I thought he was rather sweet. And I never expected to see anybody actually touch Jenny Johnson, most of them think she's a sacred object. It's time to change.'

In the bedroom, when she asked him to help with the zip of her dress, he placed a hand on her back. She shivered.

'Are you a sacred object too?'

She turned to face him. 'You don't want to touch me, do you? It's a kind of duty, something expected. You always do what's expected.'

'How absurd.'

'I sometimes wonder if you're basically homosexual. Don't look so disgusted, you know we all have male and female elements. Like my moustache.' It was true that she had a faint down on her lip which had to be controlled by depilation. 'I think you may have a strong female streak, that's all.'

25

The remark made him unreasonably angry. 'Who's been filling your head with this nonsense? Another man?'

'Are you jealous?' She stood looking at him with her brassière partly removed, then took it off completely. Her breasts were small, with dark nipples. 'If I said yes, would you be jealous?'

'For God's sake. First of all you say I mustn't touch you and then you stand with your breasts showing and ask me if I'm jealous.'

She looked at him with that characteristic faint hint of a smile. 'I'm going to have my bath.'

She went into the bathroom. Water ran. When it stopped he heard her singing.

The arrangement of a dinner party had not been easy because Max was divorced from his wife, and was bringing Jake without (before the mention of Lulu) any feminine accompaniment. It is easy to find unattached men to put right any disbalance between the sexes but less easy to find unattached women, and Virginia had solved the problem by asking Felicity James and her friend Arabella, who was always called Arab.

They arrived while John and Sandra Sutherland were half-way through their first gin and tonic. Felicity was one of the new school of lesbian novelists, those who do not write directly about their sexual attitude in the Radclyffe Hall manner. There were lots of men in Felicity's novels, but they were always shown clearly as the weaker sex and by the end of the book were mentally or financially dependent on women, or had been ruined by them. In person Felicity, large, bony and highly coloured in dress and appearance, filled any room she entered.

'Sherry, Gilbert. Bone dry and ice cold,' she said in response to his question. When he said that the sherry would be dry but not ice cold she raised the gold lorgnette that was her single concession to old-style lesbianism and stared at

him for a moment before pronouncing 'Whisky and soda.'
She turned to pretty, plumpish Sandra. 'And what do you
do?'

'I'm a housewife.'

'You find that adequate? I'm not a feminist but house-
work bores me. Arab likes it.' She turned away, dismissing
Sandra in favour of her husband, who was a lecturer in
sociology at London University. Phrases drifted through
their conversation: 'Balance of statistical probability . . .
basically a revolt against mechanism . . . separate Pop from
McLuhan . . .' Sutherland had large hornrims, and like
many sociologists was a compulsive talker. Although Felicity
gave him one glare through the lorgnette, she seemed upon
the whole to approve of him. Arab, who was ten years her
junior and had a soft crushed face, seemed content to sit
watching them and saying nothing.

The Sutherlands lived almost opposite, and Sandra told
Gilbert about a Swedish au pair girl up the road who had
given a party for a dozen hippies while the advertising director who employed her was away. She described in detail
and with relish the amount of drink that had been con-
sumed, the furniture that had been smashed and the orna-
ments that had been stolen. The party had ended when four
of the hippies, high on pot, had wandered naked into the
road. Gilbert found himself thinking about Virginia. She
had gone into the kitchen to superintend the cook, who had
come in specially for the evening and was talented but er-
ratic.

'You're not listening. I'm boring you.'

'Of course you're not.'

'John says I bore everybody with my tittle-tattle. Do you
like tittle-tattle?'

'I call it gossip. I like it very much. How do you think
Virginia is looking?'

'Marvellous. She always does. Not like me, bursting out
of my clothes.'

27

'I've been a little worried.' Sandra, whose plump amiability concealed a rich vein of malice, looked at him eagerly, but before he could say anything rash Virginia returned. She glanced meaningfully at Felicity's empty glass and Gilbert did some refilling. As he passed Virginia he smelled her musky scent.

Almost half an hour later things were strained. Felicity had become tired of sociology, or perhaps just tired of trying to out-talk Sutherland, and was telling Sandra, Virginia and Gilbert what was wrong with the London theatre. Sutherland, after trying to make conversation with Arab, which was almost an impossibility, had lapsed into an unusual silence. Arab, whose own silence gave her all the more time for consumption of liquor, was staring at him in a slightly glassy-eyed way. Where was Max, where was Bunce? As though in answer to the question the bell rang. There were voices in the hall. With relief Gilbert opened the door of the drawing-room to see Max's round smiling face.

'A triumph, my dear, a triumph. Did you catch it? Have you ever seen anyone deal with Jenny like that, wasn't it just terrific? Jake, this is Gilbert Welton.'

'Good to meet you. Say, Max, you call that girl tough? We got fifty in the States who'd eat her in a couple of mouthfuls and then say what's the next course.' Seen in person Bunce looked even more ingenuous, and younger, than on the TV screen. His hand seemed almost boneless.

'And this is Lulu.' Even Max's exuberance was slightly damped as he stood aside to reveal a tall dark girl with long hair, wearing a rough denim shirt and dirty-looking jeans. 'She wondered if it would be OK to come along in what she was wearing, and I said yes of course.'

The girl scowled. 'I got nothing to change into. I just wear stuff till it's finished.' Her voice sounded like a can grating over pebbles.

Max had said that it was a mistake to arrange a dinner

party for anybody like Jake Bunce, and within ten minutes of sitting down at table it was evident that he had been right. Without being in any way impolite, Bunce seemed to feel that it was his duty to keep up a continual flow of conversation, and it was conversation of the utmost freedom which he addressed to the table at large. Felicity had carried the London theatre theme with her to the dinner-table, and once set on course she took a great deal of moving, but Bunce managed it.

'Osborne, Wesker, Bowen, what the hell kind of plays do they write?' he asked genially.

Felicity put down her fork, raised her lorgnette. 'They've all been produced recently on Broadway.'

'Broadway.' Bunce chuckled. 'I crap on Broadway.'

Virginia's mouth quivered slightly. 'What kind of plays do you like, Mr Bunce?'

'I reckon the theatre as such is played out, that is the theatre as a convention, you get me? Broadway, off Broadway, I mean none of it's real, it's something a lot of actors are faking up. But off off-Broadway now, we got something there that's really going. There's this cellar called Where You Are. When you go in you're blindfolded, turned round three times and told to start moving.'

'A kind of blind man's buff,' Sandra suggested. Bunce beamed.

'Right. But there's this difference. You're groping around, see, and you touch other bodies or objects or whatever, and you don't know a thing. But in Where You Are there's a mediator, sometimes a man, sometimes a woman, and they act as guides.'

'What to?' Arab asked, and giggled suddenly. They were almost the first words she had spoken.

'That's it. They guide you *where they think you should go*. You might find yourself on a mattress with a girl or another fellow, or on the john, or they might take off your shoes and socks and put your feet in cold water, or stick a pin in your arm. Or you might get taken into a cinema, bandage whipped off and you're shown a horror film, Auschwitz or something. Just what they think you can take.'

Felicity glared. 'I don't call that theatre.'

'It's *living* theatre.' He pushed away his plate and made points on stubby fingers. 'It teaches lessons, like we all need to learn. One, there's the authority principle, in this world we don't any of us control what happens. Two, reality's lots of different things like pain, horror, love. Three, what life means is drama, it isn't just going to the office every day, the important things happen when everything's intense, that's what's crucial. Four.' He looked at his fingers and gave up. 'That's about it, I guess.'

'The moments when everything's intense,' Virginia repeated. 'I like that.'

'If that's theatre I can do without it,' Sandra Sutherland said. 'I go to the theatre to be amused, I don't mind saying it. And for something with a meaning I can understand.'

Lulu had been eating like a starved animal, head low over her plate, hair close to the food. She had a chicken leg in her fingers, gnawing it close to the bone. Now she put it down and said in a voice thick with chicken, 'You don't get the meaning? The meaning is, life is love.'

Jake beamed. 'You got it. That's the message, today and every day.'

There was silence. Then Max began to talk about the new cinema in the uncommitted or less committed Communist countries, Yugoslavia, Rumania, Bulgaria. Felicity raised her lorgnette while waiting to interrupt. Gilbert felt a nudge. It was Lulu.

'She a dyke?'

He was saved from the need to reply because Sandra on his other side spoke at the same time. He turned to her gratefully. 'What was that?'

30

'I only said I'm terribly old-fashioned, but I like to read novels with a story. That's why I read so many thrillers. John thinks they're an outdated form of pop culture, but I still enjoy them. Why don't you publish any?'

He started to explain that it was no use publishing just one or two crime stories, you had to go in for them in a big way. He was uneasily conscious that Lulu had returned to her bone and then rejected it, and that across the table Felicity was laying down the law about the limitations not only of Communist but of all other films. John Sutherland said something about Italian neo-realism, Virginia murmured the name of Antonioni, and Max who never cared for argument addressed himself to placating Felicity.

'Your books now, I find it quite amazing that they are not filmed. If you were Rumanian every one, every one would be filmed. As they appeared.'

'Two of my last three books have been sold for films,' Felicity said icily, but Max was not deterred.

'In Italy, Germany, Yugoslavia, it would have been all three. Your last novel—' He paused, at a loss for the title. Felicity frowned. Arab supplied it in a penetrating whisper.

' *A Particular Kind of Man.* '

'Of course. Magnificent. What a terrific part for Richard Burton or Paul Scofield.'

'That's the one which isn't being filmed,' Arab said. 'The others are being made in France.'

A toothpick twirled in Bunce's mouth. 'MGM are going into production of my last one, *The Gay Life*, next month. They've got a whole cast of fags.' He moved into his soundless laughter routine.

Gilbert looked at Virginia. She rose. The other women rose with her except Lulu, who remained seated. 'Hey, what is this?' She stared at them.

One of the things that Gilbert had always admired about Virginia was her refusal to be perturbed. 'We'll have our coffee in the drawing-room and leave the men here.'

'Leave the men?' It was not Lulu's clothes but her features that were dirty, Gilbert decided. And her hair could certainly do with a wash. 'We gonna have a party on our own, is that it? I don't get my kicks that way.'

Bunce leaned forward. 'Lulu, baby, it's an English custom. You go next door for a while, see, drink some coffee, we stay here, have some port and brandy, then we meet up later. Isn't that right, Gil?'

Nobody had called him Gil for years, and the name sounded surprisingly pleasant. 'That's right.'

'So you just run along, Lulu baby.'

'Balls to them,' Lulu said. 'How do I know what that bloody great dyke might try if I get left alone with her? I'm staying here.'

Felicity raised her lorgnette and raked Lulu with one final dismissive glance. 'Arab, it is time to go.'

Across Gilbert's mind there flashed the question : what would E.R. have done? Before he could find an answer, Felicity and Arab had gone.

In the drawing-room Jake and Lulu engaged in a long wrangle about her behaviour. Virginia had disappeared. Max and Gilbert provided the audience. Neither Jake nor Lulu sat on a chair. Jake was cross-legged on a pouffe and Lulu sprawled on the floor.

'So she's a dyke, what's it matter, what you got against them?'

'I just didn't want her hands on me, is all. You see the way she looked?'

'You talk about love, you say love's the meaning. You just haven't got the meaning, you're nowhere near it. And you owe something to Gil, it's his home, how do you think he's feeling?'

Max muttered something and went out. Jake seemed really upset. His flexible nose twitched like a rabbit's. 'He

32

brings you into his home and you insult his guests. What kind of way is that to behave? Gil's upset, isn't that so, Gil?'

Gilbert did not reply. Lulu said something inaudible. 'What's that, baby, don't keep it to yourself, say it so we can hear.'

'I said, go fuck yourself.'

'Is that a way to talk?' Jake spread out his arms appealingly. 'I ask you, Gil, is that a way to talk?' This time he did not stay for an answer. His features set into the mask of a gloomy thinker. 'I tell you the trouble with you, kid, is you've got nothing at all and you try to make it look like something. Me now, I've been through the whole works, pot, LSD and the hard stuff, boys and girls, the Eastern crap and the Russian crap, and I'm out on the other side. Way out and clear. Did you know I was three months in a monastery out in Nepal, did you know that, Gil?'

'Yes.' This was in fact one of the most-publicized periods of Jake's career.

'To know what's real you got to find out about yourself. That's what I was doing with those monks, and believe me it paid off.'

'In cash.' Lulu held up her glass for more brandy.

'But you, what did you ever do except come up from Deadsville to the Village and underground films, and believe me that's not much of a journey.' He shook his head mournfully. 'Not much of a journey at all. And now you come where it's civilized, the cradle of civilization you might say, and you don't know how to behave.'

Could Bunce's sales compensate for his conversation? And where was Max? He rose, and Bunce scrambled to his feet. Was he leaving? No, with a muttered apology he moved in the direction of the brandy. As Gilbert closed the door he heard Lulu say, 'I'll tell you something, Jake, you bore the tits off me.'

In the hall there was no sound. A sudden doubt, a feeling

of disaster, sent him up the stairs two at a time. He went swiftly along the passage, flung open the bedroom door. The room was empty. He heard voices. From the bedroom window figures were faintly visible in the garden, moving towards the house.

He confronted them as they came in through the garden door. Virginia's colour was high, her manner serene. Max's hair was in its usual tight curls, but then it was hair that would hardly be ruffled by a hand passing through it, and nothing would ever change his cherubic smile. He began to speak as soon as they were through the door.

'I wanted to apologize to Virginia, to tell her that I feel— I feel desolated.'

'I thought it was funny. Felicity's a first-class bitch anyway. A butch bitch.' She giggled, and that was not characteristic.

'You have a very sweet wife.' Max took Virginia's bare arm and kissed her cheek. Upon the fleshy part of her arm near the shoulder there was a small circular discoloration.

He released her. 'Jake is sweet too, the sweetest man in the world. But that girl.' He was shaking his round head when they heard the sound of breaking glass.

In the drawing-room Jake and Lulu were standing body to body, glaring at each other. Fragments of glass lay in the fireplace. They might have been figures fixed in a tableau. Then Jake raised his hand and deliberately slapped Lulu's face. She cried out something. Blood trickled from her mouth. Virginia stood beside Gilbert and he heard the indrawing of her breath.

Jake raised his hand again, lowered it. 'Max, get me out of here. I don't know what I might do to her.'

Lulu put her grubby hand to her face and looked at it wonderingly. 'The bastard's made me bleed.'

'I must apologize,' Jake said to Virginia. 'She threw her glass—your glass—at me and it broke.'

'Now then, my dears, it is time to go home.'

34

Such difficult circumstances always brought out the best in Max. He cajoled and bullied the pair of them out of the drawing-room, got them through the front door together yet kept them apart, pushed Lulu into the back seat of his car and Jake into the front. At the last moment Jake broke away, ran back to the house and clasped Virginia's hand.

'I apologize again. It was a *graceless* thing to do.' He kissed her on the lips and ran back to the car. His hand, with the ring on it that had cut Lulu's mouth, waved out of the car window.

CHAPTER FIVE

A Woman's Arm

'WHO HAS NOT felt the beauty of a woman's arm?' George Eliot asks in *The Mill on the Floss*. 'The unspeakable suggestions of tenderness that lie in the dimpled elbow, and all the varied gently-lessening curves, down to the delicate wrist, with its tiniest, almost imperceptible nicks in the firm softness.' Virginia's arms, rich and creamy, had always held a deep sexual attraction for Gilbert. He caressed and kissed them before making love, and when the sleeve of her dress fell back as it sometimes did to reveal the whole arm from wrist to elbow, white, smooth and untouched by down, he would look at it with the intensity of feeling that other men give to breasts or buttocks. When she clasped her arms round his neck or behind his back, the vision he had of their contact with him was a vital stimulus to the act of love. It was an excitement he had never mentioned to her beyond saying that she had beautiful arms.

In the bedroom, looking at the discoloration which he

35

surely would have noticed if it had been present when she came in to dinner, he saw clearly Max Bomberg's mouth move away from hers to kiss the upper part of her arm and then to nip the flesh between his teeth. It was something that he had never done, that he would have felt to be a desecration.

'What has happened to your arm?'

'What do you mean?'

He touched the spot. 'It wasn't there earlier this evening.'

'I must have knocked it,' she said indifferently.

He overcame his dislike of mentioning sexual matters. 'Somebody gripped your arm. Or bit it.'

You're being ridiculous.' With her half-smile she added, 'Anyway, bites don't show that quickly.'

'How do you know?'

She shrugged. 'You don't want me to go into details. You never liked them.' And it was true that before they married she had mentioned past affairs. She had been on the editorial staff of a fashion magazine, and from what she said almost every woman in the office had had an affair with some man or other. He had always flinched from the details, saying that what she had done in the past was not his business.

'Somebody bit your arm. Max.' He could not refrain from saying it, although the words sounded absurd.

'Oh really. Do you suppose he was biting my arm in the garden?' That was just what he did suppose, but she made it sound like a bad joke. 'I went out because I'd had enough of it, that's all.'

'He followed you out there.'

'He came out to say he was sorry. Just as he told you. Anyway, I preferred the American.'

'Bunce?' he said in astonishment.

'There's a kind of sweetness about him. He's magnetic. The moments when everything's intense, I know what he means.' She pulled her dress over her head, and as she did

36

so he saw the distinct dark hairs growing in her armpit. What was the meaning of them, why were they there when in the past she had always used depilatories to remove them? 'Why—' he began, and stopped.

'Yes?'

He put on his pyjamas. The action gave him confidence. 'Why aren't you using your cream?'

'What cream, I don't understand.'

'Under your arms.'

'Oh, that. I don't know really. Yes, I do. I read an article about men preferring women to be natural, and there's nothing more natural than letting hair grow.'

'You know I dislike it.'

'How could I know, you've never said so. Although I suppose I might have guessed.' Stretching her arms she revealed again the unsightly growth. 'Some men like it.'

'Not Englishmen.'

'If you knew what you sound like.' She turned her back as she took off her knickers and stood naked. 'I suppose you'd like it if I had no hair at all on my body. A statue, that would suit you.' She slipped a filmy nightdress over her head.

The image flashed through his mind of a statue as something indeed desirable, the body smooth and cold, no blemishes or beauty spots, the perfect arm curving upwards into the shoulder, nothing anywhere unsightly, no drop of sweat disturbing the perfection of the form.

'The years between thirty and forty are crucial for a woman, did you know that?' This comes from a magazine too, he thought, the whole thing comes from magazines. 'It's a climacteric.' He felt certain that she had read the word for the first time recently, but it was typical of her that she pronounced it with perfect ease and naturalness. 'Perhaps something to do with the change, though it would be early for that. Anyway, it's a difficult time. You ought to realize that.'

37

Relief surged over him, a conviction that she was acting out the part of a sensitive woman after reading 'A Woman in Her Thirties, The Difficult Decade'. What would be the appropriate Sunday colour supplement reaction? A brusque injunction to snap out of it and remember the duty a wife owed to her husband, or readiness to talk the whole thing over? As though to confirm his thoughts she went on, 'It's all been psychologically established, you know.'

Psychologically established! He thought of her indrawn breath as she saw the blood on Lulu's mouth and felt angry. A mirror on the wall reflected his blue-pyjamaed body as he stood beside her, gripped her and turned her to him.

'All that talk about being natural, what you mean is that you want force. Violence. Isn't that so? Bunce excited you because he hit her.'

'Whether I want it, that's not important.'

'Of course it is. You've been saying how important.'

He pushed her and, taken by surprise, she fell back on the bed. Her nightdress came up to reveal the lower half of her body. He pulled at the nightdress but failed to get it off because she was lying on it. She rolled over so that the round buttocks were visible, her body more at his mercy than when she faced him. He felt the stirring of desire and tugged at his pyjama cord, pulling the wrong end so that it came into a knot. Face down, head in the eiderdown, she muttered words which he still heard quite distinctly, her voice unwaveringly calm.

'What matters is whether you want it. Violence.'

Had she read that also in a colour supplement? Desire left him, what he was doing seemed merely distasteful. He got up off the bed. Virginia turned and without haste or primness pulled down her nightdress.

'It's a matter of establishing a relationship pattern.'

'Where did you read that?'

'In a book.' There was a slightly triumphant note in her

voice. Books were trump cards compared to magazine articles. 'If you don't establish the right pattern in the early years of marriage it's very bad.'

'Was it from this book that you got the idea about my being homosexual?'

'Yes. There are six basic relationships and ours—'

'Spare me the details.' They had separate beds, and he got into his own.

'I don't think you need me. You want a housekeeper. Or perhaps a hostess. But is that all I want? I'm going away to find out.'

'You mean that's all, the only reason?'

'Doesn't it seem enough?' She began to apply cream to her face and went on talking tranquilly. 'Five years and we don't have a relationship, we're just two people living together. People to whom nothing ever happens.'

'What do you want to happen?'

'I don't know. I want the moments when everything's intense, when you really feel things. You don't know me in that way, any more than I know you.'

'I think I know you pretty well.'

'You're wrong. You only know one Virginia, the one you've made, a person you've created. There might be half a dozen others. You might like one of them better.'

'And are there? Six other Virginias?'

'That's what I want to find out.'

'There's no other man?'

'No. Though at the climacteric there might be.'

'And if there were it would be someone like Bunce?'

'I don't know. Perhaps.' She got into bed and turned out the light. 'Gilbert.'

'Yes?'

'I think I should go as soon as possible really. To clear my mind. You can tell people I'm on the verge of a nervous breakdown.'

'Thank you.'

'It might be true. Do you understand things better now, now I've explained?'

'I don't understand anything. I think the whole thing's idiotic.'

She did not speak again. It was a long time before he fell asleep. Thinking about the conversation he decided that what she had said was just crazy enough to be true. There had been brief periods in the past when Virginia's calm had been broken. She had once bought a sauna, had it installed, and gone into it several times a day, emerging pinkish but exhausted instead of exhilarated. She had lost interest in it when a doctor said it might be damaging her health. At another time she had spent hours every day at the Zoo, taking particular interest in the caged birds. Perhaps this was something of the same kind, something that would be forgotten in a week.

Or perhaps she was lying to him. Thinking of that intrusive hair in her armpits and the bruise that flawed the classical beauty of her arm, it seemed certain to him that she had a lover.

CHAPTER SIX

The Anglo-Germanic Syndrome

'A VERITABLE shambles. My dear, I'm sorry.' Max smiled.

'Never mind. How did you get on?'

'In the car not so bad, but when we got back to the hotel they started again. In the end I took them to the Out Going.'

'What's that?'

'One of those clubs. You know.' Gilbert nodded, although

he didn't know. 'Jake is a very sweet person, but the girl is hell. I don't know why he has her along. She had a row with a waiter. I got to bed at four-thirty.'

'I'd never have known it.' And indeed Max looked his usual rosy self with the air of breezy freshness about him that marks many central Europeans. He tapped a finger on Gilbert's desk and said 'Eugene Ponti'.

'What?'

'*The Tigress.* The biggest European seller of the last ten years was his *Apes, Gods and Men.* A master novelist.' Was Max quoting reviews? It was never possible to be sure. 'Now he has completed *The Tigress.* And he is not happy with his English publisher, I know this for a fact. He hates the translation.' A man confiding a secret, Max said, 'Eugene is ready to move.'

'You know him?'

'I have contacts. An approach is possible, but it must be made now. Strike while the iron is hot,' he said with an air of originality.

'What do you want to do?'

'Go to Milan. Fly there, see him, make the arrangement, fly back. A few hours. I shall be away no more than that. All right?'

Was Max sexually attractive to women? The unusual colour on Virginia's cheeks when she came in from the garden, their conspiratorial air—but at this he checked himself, for had the air been conspiratorial? He could not really remember what they had looked like. Perhaps Max was the kind of man who could discover the Virginias neglected by Gilbert, Max the florid, Max the hand kisser, Max the arm biter.

'I suppose so, yes. We ought to discuss what we can offer.'

'Here are details of sales for his last book. Don't ask how I have obtained them.' A roll of the eye suggested some unmentionable piece of wickedness. He went on casually. 'Jake will be no trouble at all, I will tell him—'

41

'Oh no.'

'Look, my dear. This whole thing is important, I mean do we want to get hold of a European best-seller when we are on the ground floor, or not?' Max flung himself into a chair, leaned back. 'It would be possible for you to go to Milan if you wish. But not advisable. My contact is Eugene's secretary. Flavia.'

'I see.'

'That is the way things are done.' It was not the way things had been done in E.R.'s time. 'Now I can assure you Jake will be no trouble. I shall tell him that he must get in touch with you only if there is something urgently vital.'

'Perhaps Coldharbour—'

'You must be joking.' The slang sounded particularly inappropriate on his lips. 'Jake likes you, he says you are an English gentleman. Jake is a very sincere person, he wouldn't say that unless he meant it. So now let us discuss a few details and then we are all fixed.'

No sooner was Max out of the room after discussing the few details about the advance that could be offered than Miss Pinkthorn came in, her eyes gleaming with bad news.

'I've had Mr Manhood on the telephone, Mr Dexter Manhood. He hasn't received his manuscript.'

'What manuscript?'

'*A Welter of Gore.*'

'That book about a murder case? It should have gone back to him—oh, weeks ago.'

'Exactly. But it hasn't. I told him it would be looked into at once.'

'Find out who was responsible, and ask them what's happened.'

With a barely suppressed air of triumph Miss Pinkthorn said, 'I was away with influenza. Miss Steel should have sent it back.'

'Then speak to her.' Miss Steel was Max's secretary, a pretty but inefficient girl.

42

'I have done so. At first she remembered nothing about it, then she said she *thought* it had gone to the typing pool.' There were only two typists where in E.R.'s day there had been four, but it was still called the typing pool. 'Miss Clayton doesn't remember it, so it must have been Mrs Fairweather.'

'I didn't know we had a Mrs Fairweather.'

'She was a temporary from an agency.'

'Then speak to—'

'Of course I rang the agency. Mrs Fairweather is no longer on their books. She has moved from her last address.'

'If she didn't send it, the manuscript must be in the office.'

'We don't know that it was ever posted.' She administered this blow like a policewoman.

'It must be found.'

'I am instituting a thorough search,' Miss Pinkthorn said, still in the policewoman role. She glanced as she went out at the photograph of E.R. on the wall. Manuscripts had never disappeared in his time.

Left alone, he looked at some depressing sales figures and then at some equally depressing costing figures. Abandoning these he went over to the bookcase that housed the firm's publications and took down *Sexuality, Aggression and Nationality* by N. M. Sverdlov, a book they had published four years earlier in a brief phase of enthusiasm for the idea of starting a psychoanalytical library. His appointment with Sverdlov was for midday.

'Two and a half times a week. You don't reach that norm?'

'I'm afraid not. Not quite.' An apologetic note seemed inevitable.

'And whose responsibility is that?'

'I don't think I can say. I don't know.'

'No children,' Sverdlov said accusingly. 'Why not?'

'Virginia had an abortion. Before we were married. She

43

can't have children. But I don't think she wants them. I've always thought we're happy as we are.'

'You think so, but does she?' Sverdlov was a small busy man with a rumpled look. 'We have to remember that she is a second wife. The first Mrs Welton was different?'

'Yes.'

'And your relationship with her, that also was different?'

'Yes.'

'You were divorced. By whose wish?'

'I think you could say it was mutual. But it was a long time ago.'

'Your first wife, do you still see her? Has she remarried?'

'I don't see her. But I'm sure I'd know if she had re-married.'

'Your son Matthew. How do you get on with him?'

'Quite well. But we don't see much of each other. He lives in Amsterdam.'

'Does your wife get on with him?'

'When she sees him, yes, very well. But I don't see what all this has to do with Virginia wanting to leave.'

'Directly, perhaps nothing. It is an essential part of the atmosphere in which both of you live. However, I am inclined to agree. Basically I have no doubt that we have here a question of national temperament.'

'I don't quite follow you.'

'I will be frank. You are an Englishman, a very typical Englishman, reserved, shy. You don't know how to express your feelings. You have the male's normal sexual aggression, but you wish all things to remain unstated. Your wife is entirely different.' He thrust out hairy wrists from a shirt distinctly dirty at the cuffs. '*Entirely*.'

'Is she?' His impression had been that Virginia's attitude was similar to his own.

'From what you have told me, undoubtedly.'

'But Virginia is English too.'

44

'Altogether? Absolutely and completely? You said she had an Irish grandmother.'

'Yes, but—'

'Then she is part Celtic. I divide European sexual attitudes into four main groups, Slav, Latin, Celtic, and Anglo-Germanic.'

'I know. We published your book.'

'The question is why have you come to me? Perhaps it would be good for you to have children, but that is not possible. However, I am not a marriage counsellor. You wish my advice on how to put right this imbalance, how can we channel your aggression. Correct?'

'No, I don't think so.' Sverdlov looked surprised. 'We've been happily married for five years, and now she talks in this absurd way about my being homosexual.'

'You are not homosexual?'

'Of course not.'

'You have no homosexual experiences?'

'Certainly not.'

Sverdlov shook his head. 'Unusual. Significant.'

'She says she isn't in love with anybody else, she simply wants to go away. But what's happened, what's wrong?'

'*What's wrong!*' Sverdlov showed a number of discoloured teeth in a menacing way. 'My friend, we are living in a time of revolutions, that is what is wrong as you call it. The anarcho-sexual revolution is sweeping away everything that was taboo under the Anglo-Germanic code. We all have these feelings, we are all sexual revolutionaries at heart. You do not regard yourself so?'

'No, I don't.'

'Precisely. Yet there are feelings which demand release, isn't it so?'

Were there such feelings? A tight knot seemed to have formed in his stomach, he found it difficult to speak. 'I don't know of any such feelings. I am—I have been—perfectly happy.'

45

'Anglo-Germanism at its most obstinate.' Sverdlov moved one hand to a nostril, subsequently concealing it under his desk. 'And I am telling you it is no good. What is hidden must be acknowledged, brought into the light.' He produced his own hidden hand and tapped the desk. 'You have the sexual revolution up here.' The head was tapped. 'When it should be down here.' He appeared to indicate his stomach, but the reference was no doubt to a lower region.

'D. H. Lawrence said much the same thing.'

Sverdlov shrugged, indifferent to what D. H. Lawrence might have said. 'Quite frankly, sexual Anglo-Germanism makes me despair.'

'Perhaps it's just that Virginia is passing through a difficult time.'

'Not at all. It is *you* who are passing through a difficult time, as you call it, a period of Anglo-Germanic frustration.'

'Do you think she is telling the truth, or that she has a lover?'

'Quite possibly she has a lover. She is a Celt. She is not interested in politics?'

'Not at all.' Only in articles in glossy magazines, he felt inclined to add.

'The anarcho-sexual revolution can be expressed through politics. But if she is not interested, then her only expression is through sex. That is quite simple, inevitable. A general law.'

'You can't give me any advice?'

'I am telling you facts. General laws apply to particular cases. What is the point of *advice*, who takes it? You are suffering from the Anglo-Germanic syndrome. To use a term you may understand, it is an emotional block. Until it is removed you can have no genuine relationship. If you wish to consult me to that end, we can make an arrangement.'

'What sort of arrangement?'

'Nothing less than three sessions a week would be any use.'

'For how long?'

'A year. At least a year, perhaps more. Who can say?'

'I haven't got the time.'

'Very well.' Sverdlov rose behind his desk, a small man. His eyes flashed with anger. His finger pointed. 'But I must warn you. It is the Anglo-Germanic syndrome that led to the concentration camps.'

CHAPTER SEVEN

Moonsight and Coldharbour

LITTLE MR CLAPPERTON folded his hands over his round belly. 'The function of the hat, Mr Welton sir, is only partly protective. It is also ceremonial. It announces *I am that I am*, it stresses individualism and expresses a fine scorn for uniformity. It enhances and impresses.'

'Yes,' Gilbert said doubtfully. In the glass a staid middle-aged man looked at him, his head topped by a curly-brimmed dark grey bowler.

'Unquestionably. What was the object of the bear-skin shako and the tall plumed hat of the eighteenth century? To give an appearance of added height and so frighten the enemy. Not that that is necessary in your case of course, but the hat always enhances, it adds a particular flavour and style to the personality.' The bowler was whisked away and replaced by a small tweed hat which perched on the top of his head.

'No, I don't think that one.'

'This would have been your father's style.' Under the

47

plain black bowler he looked for traces of the resolution and solidity that had marked ER's appearance, and failed to find them. His features looked longer, paler and more ineffectual than they were. 'It expressed his personality, it said "I am a man who stands foursquare, I care for nobody." If you'll forgive my making so free, Mr Welton sir, that was the way I always thought of him. He had the same hat through the years, with just the tiniest change in the brim width. The British bowler stands foursquare, as you might put it.'

'It isn't for me.'

'Perhaps not.' Mr Clapperton prowled round Gilbert, looking at his front, side and even back views, and then produced a wide-brimmed dark green trilby. 'There are other colours, but the green has what I should call a freshening effect. Nothing outrageous, but just that little touch of the unusual.'

'Certainly it isn't like what I've got.' His present hat, his invariable hat, was a black Homburg. Mr Clapperton picked it up and looked at it affectionately.

'A fine hat. It symbolises the secure, the reliable, it says *you can trust me*. It is the hat of the man who knows his position in society and means to stay in it. A badge of position, as much as the Chinese imperial headdresses with their ornamentations showing the sun and moon or, at the other extreme, the wide-brimmed straw hat of the Mexican peon. In a sense, you can't better it.' He patted the Homburg. 'I should be sorry to see it relinquished altogether. But at the same time, if you want to have just that occasional extra edge of dash and style . . .'

Gilbert put down the dark green hat and picked up his own. 'I'll think about it. I'm sorry to have taken up your time, Mr Clapperton.'

'Always a pleasure to see you, my dear sir.' A bell tinkled as the door closed. The visit to *Clapperton, Hatter,* after a rubbery sandwich in a pub, had offered no solace. He dropped in at Sotheby's and looked at some first editions which at another time would have excited him. Now he felt no desire to possess them. He went out after five minutes and telephoned Virginia from a call box. There was no reply.

For Gilbert Welton serenity was identifiable with a settled pattern of life. Now that the pattern had been pulled apart by Virginia's behaviour, he was afflicted by a deep uneasiness which communicated itself to everything that surrounded him. He recognized the immediate cause of this uneasiness as jealousy, an emotion often most agonizing when it has no precise object on which to focus. He felt that if he had been told by Virginia that she was in love with Max he could have faced the situation. He would have asked whether she truly preferred this florid mid-European to him and if her answer had been yes, he would have tried to accept it. What had she said about the existence of six Virginias? As he looked into the window of a shop at a dummy apparently clothed only in a number of sashes he rehearsed a series of scenes with those other Virginias, lecherous or violent or untidy. Virginia advanced up Bond Street to meet him, deliberately placed his hand upon her breast and suggested that they should have sex in the taxi on the way home. Virginia, with a laddered stocking and food spots staining her dress, served an atrocious meal to half a dozen guests. Virginia, putting down her glossy magazine with a slow smile, revealed behind it Stendhal's *Le Rouge et le Noir*. That such Virginias might exist caused him more torment than the woman he visualized willingly crushed by Max's little arms.

He found another telephone box and rang again without result. In the house there would be silence except for the repeated *burr burr*. She had gone. Upstairs in the bedroom her cupboard would be tidily empty, the traditional note propped on a dressing-table clear of creams and lotions, addressed in her firm regular hand. He was aware of the absurdity of his feelings, their disproportion to the known facts. Such awareness seemed to make no difference.

When he put down the receiver and stepped out of the box a sandwich man confronted him. Long curling hair flowed to the man's shoulders, a row of beads drooped on his pullover. The board he carried said: 'The Realism of Space is the Opposition of Indivisibles.' Two others were behind him and they were parading up and down outside a picture gallery. The fascia of the gallery showed a small yellow moon and the word *sight* in childlike script. He went in.

The canvases on the walls seemed to be distinguished chiefly by a deliberate avoidance of perspective. The figures in them, brawny workers, round-faced women, idiotic-looking gaping children, were as flat as the electric cookers, refrigerators and motorcars beside which they stood, or which in some of the paintings they intersected. Heeney, Sharkey, Delaney, the signatures said, but they might as well have been the work of a single painter as far as Gilbert could see. He went into a second room and was stopped by a painting on the far wall. It was a picture of Virginia.

She was the only human figure. She stood naked, bisected by a dark brown chest of drawers which cut into her navel and eliminated one of her legs, and a large carton labelled Daz which obscured the back of her head and truncated one arm. A knife pointed at one of her breasts and a fork at the other. Her face was turned away to show a three-quarter profile, yet this incomplete body was unmistakably hers. He had seen the neck turned away from him like this a hundred times, had seen her standing with just such negligent ease, the body leaning slightly forward. The truncated arm was by her side, the marble shoulder blending into it, but the other arm was raised presumably to touch the missing back of her head. In the armpit there nestled an odious growth of hair.

'Interesting.'

Gilbert looked at the young man beside him. 'You're Mr Moon?'

'Alastair Moon.' He was not a round-faced Moon but a lantern-jawed one, his face encompassed with hair. He wore a corduroy suit and a string tie. 'Interesting,' he repeated, adding 'Don't you think?'

'I was looking for my wife.'

The young man glanced round with a whimsical air to indicate that they were alone. 'This is a picture of her.'

'Really?' Moon took from his pocket a pair of small spectacles, not moons but half-moons, put them on and looked again at the painting.

'She was in here the day before yesterday.' Had she come alone? 'I believe with a friend.'

'She is not here now,' Moon said gravely. 'As you see. Do please wait for her. If that's what you've arranged.'

In the studio of the Spatial Realist Virginia had stood, statuesque and beautiful. The painter walked over to her, spanned the slender wrist with his hand and raised it to reveal—a slight shudder passed through his body. He was aware that Moon had spoken.

'What?'

'Did she like the picture?'

'I don't know. I believe she may have been with my friend Coldharbour.'

'Denis Coldharbour. Of course I know him. He's most intelligent.' Gilbert agreed, although this was for him a new light on Coldharbour. 'I remember his coming along. He was most enthusiastic. Perhaps we've met at one of Denis's parties.'

'I didn't know that he gave parties.'

'Oh yes.' Within the fringe of hair Moon's mouth twitched

in a smile. 'But I don't think he came in with your wife. You'll know Jack perhaps? Jack Sharkey, who painted the picture. He's here.'

'Where?' Gilbert looked round.

'Outside.' Over the ridiculous half-moons Moon examined him as though he belonged to another species. 'The sandwich men.'

It was the one with the beads. He had narrow red-rimmed eyes, his neck was grimed with dirt, no doubt his hands also were filthy. Gilbert found it hard to know what to say.

'One of those pictures inside, one of yours—'

'Scon with your eytel.' That was what it sounded like.

'A picture of my wife. That is, she appears in it.'

Sharkey eased the board off his shoulders, rested it on the ground, said militantly, 'Grot evvy nutting.'

'I don't understand.'

'These.' He jerked a thumb at the sandwich boards and asked 'Canass four?'

'Canass four?'

'Or five?'

Gilbert spoke clearly as an elocutionist. 'I simply want to know how you came to include my wife in your picture. She is standing like this.' He raised one arm in the air and then quickly lowered it.

'Canass four. Torapic on to water room. Gotta find 'em somewhere, rile bunny honey.'

'Bunny honey?'

'Sex mechanism plus. Cut and insert. Whattawant, Whistler's mum? Playboy playgirl, get it?' Sharkey dug in his clothing, found tobacco and roller, made himself the thinnest of cigarettes. 'Your wife one? Never.'

'You're telling me—?'

'A cut out, man, a cut out.'

Gilbert stared at him, turned and hurried back into the gallery. Moon had disappeared. He stood in front of the picture. Emotion ebbed away. How could he have thought this lifeless doll, an obvious cut out from a magazine, was Virginia?

On the telephone her voice was cool as water. 'Gilbert, hallo.'

'I thought—where have you been?'

'Making arrangements.'

'To leave?'

'For my holiday, that's right. What's the matter?'

'I thought you had gone.'

'What do you take me for, I wouldn't go without telling you. But it might be a good idea if I went tomorrow, I think I'll try to arrange that.'

The relief of hearing her voice was so great that he was almost prepared to agree. Instead he said, 'You went into an art gallery the other day. The Moonsight.'

'Oh yes, I remember. There were some boys with sandwich boards outside. I thought it might be fun, but they were boring pictures. Have you been there too?'

'Yes. I'll see you this evening then?'

'Of course.'

'There are things I want to know.' But what were they, what did he want to know when it was all so unintelligible? 'And say.'

'I thought you'd said it all last night. But I'll be here.'

The office door opened and Coldharbour came in, rustling slightly. Gilbert replaced the receiver.

'We had a little unfinished business. From yesterday. We were interrupted.'

Gilbert looked at him with disfavour. He found himself blaming Coldharbour, quite unjustly, for his ludicrous mistake at the gallery. 'I'm very busy.'

Coldharbour ignored this, sidled forward. A whiff of his characteristic smell came across the desk. 'It was about the Spatial Realists.'

53

'Yes. I went to see the show today.' He paused to give the next words appropriate weight. 'I thought it was rubbish.'

Coldharbour made his nose sound, but was not deterred. He sat down and crossed his legs. 'That's a point of view, but you're not an art critic. Perhaps you don't know the way in which this show has been received. The *Observer* man talked about a new concept of space.'

'Rubbish.' He repeated the word more loudly. 'And I talked to one of the artists, if that's what you call them. To Sharkey. I couldn't understand more than one word in three of what he said.'

'With any new movement there's a difficulty in communication.'

'There's no point in talking about it. Absolutely none.'

Coldharbour pouted, which was his extreme expression of disapproval. 'I think that's an utterly unreasonable attitude.'

'You can think what you like.'

'And if I may say so it is very different from the one you adopt towards other people.' Coldharbour always if possible avoided referring to Max by name. 'Other people are allowed to do as they wish, they have a free hand, whereas my suggestions are not given a reasonable hearing. And this is so even when other people are working perhaps quite *against* the firm's best interests.'

'What are you talking about?'

'I must warn you that I'm not prepared to put up with this kind of thing.' He walked out and slammed, quite positively slammed, the door.

Half an hour later Gilbert felt sorry about the way in which he had spoken to Coldharbour, and went down the corridor to say so. But although the small office was impregnated with insecticide so that it smelled like a conservatory Coldharbour himself was not there, and apparently had gone for the day. Walking back to his own office Gilbert reproached himself. Coldharbour was a director, and his ideas ought to receive attention. The thing to do would be to go round this evening and apologize. Denis was the kind of lonely man who was warmed by any sign of friendship.

In the corridor somebody bumped into him. A small man, almost a dwarf, with one shoulder higher than the other, said 'Sorry.'

Gilbert felt immediately the shame he always experienced when in contact with somebody physically handicapped. 'I'm very sorry.'

'Mr Welton? I'm W. Jones.'

The girl with him, one of those in the typing pool, gave a small yelp of warning or alarm.

'Very pleased to meet you. This young lady thought you were out.'

In his new spirit of charity Gilbert said 'You wanted to see me? Come in.'

He led the way into his office. W. Jones sat on the other side of the desk and beamed out of exophthalmic eyes.

'About my manuscript. You wrote some nice letters.'

'I'm afraid I don't quite—'

'I use a pseudonym. Dexter Manhood. *A Welter of Gore.*'

He looked with dismay at the beaming dwarf and pressed the button that summoned Miss Pinkthorn. When she stood in the doorway, like some implacable Eastern goddess clothed by mistake in English spinster wear, he raised his eyebrows hopefully. Still in the Eastern mode she gave a slow shake of the head. W. Jones swivelled round and directed his beam at her. She went out. Gilbert gloomily contemplated the figure opposite, who now produced some grubby sheets of paper which he flattened out. Holding them close to his nose he said, 'January 18, manuscript sent to you, acknowledged by P.C.'

'P.C.?'

'Postcard. February 27, a letter. Dear Mr Manhood,

55

we have read your book *with great interest*, but there are just *one or two points* which, etcetera. Signed by your good self.' The sheet was flourished in front of Gilbert and withdrawn. 'April 19, a delay of more than six weeks you observe. Dear Mr Manhood, in reply to your letter I am afraid we have still *not reached a decision* . . .'

He ceased to listen. In the Moonsight Gallery Virginia rested quietly in the arms of Coldharbour, an odalisque with the back of her head cut off, her naked body stretched like a board upon his lap. He leaned over her, smiled, murmured, 'You must be impregnated with Kilfoulair.' Gilbert gave a short bark of laughter and W. Jones looked surprised. Evidently he was expecting some reply.

'I can assure you we've been considering it very carefully.'

'But five months, Mr Welton. Five months.'

'I have my partners to consult. It doesn't rest entirely with me. Mr Bomberg is often inaccessible.' He wagged his head over the Foggish inaccessibility of Bomberg. 'He's out of the country at present.'

'Perhaps I should have used an agent. But I never touch them, man to man is the way I like it. Isn't that the best way?'

'Very often, yes.'

'It's not unreasonable now to ask for a decision. Is it?'

'A final reading,' he said desperately. 'By a most distinguished criminological expert, I mustn't tell you his name. Just give us a few more days, Mr Jones.'

Shoulder arched, eyes popping, the dwarf considered. 'Very well. But that isn't the only reason I came in, Mr Gilbert. I came to tempt you.'

Was a sexual advance to be made? But before he had time to be thankful that a desk separated them W. Jones had produced from somewhere a packet wrapped in brown paper and was undoing it, grinning.

'The Slough slaughter.'

'I beg your pardon?'

'My next book. A whole family killed for no reason, the bodies cut up and put into plastic bags you remember?' The packet was undone. Smiling, W. Jones held up photographs of disjointed legs and torsos. 'Very special photographs of the victims. Quite unique. I have my contacts.'

He lowered his gaze and saw Virginia, a bloody torso, being embraced by Sharkey.

It took him another half-hour to get rid of W. Jones. When he had done so he rang for Miss Pinkthorn and said that he was not available if Mr Jones called again. 'And it is vital that we should find his manuscript.' Her reply made it clear that she could not be responsible for the errors of others. It was after half past five when, with the beginnings of a headache roaming round his skull, he set out for Coldharbour's flat.

He went down six dark steps to a basement area, pressed an illuminated bell. There was no sound from within, not even the sound of a bell ringing. He tapped gently on the door without result. Curtains were drawn across a window that fronted on to the basement area. Was Coldharbour out, had he made a wasted journey to Maida Vale? The irritation of the thought made his headache more distinctly perceptible. Standing at the bottom of these steps, from which the June evening light was cut away, he felt that he had been here before. On what other occasion had he stood at the bottom of steps like these, waiting with an uneasy prescience that something hateful lay behind a closed door? Before he could trace the memory the door opened a few inches and Coldharbour's body appeared.

'Oh. It's you.'

'Denis.' He essayed a smile. 'I wanted to have a word in the office, but you'd left.'

'Yes.'

'I thought I might have offended you. I didn't mean to.'

'Not at all.' Coldharbour spoke in a formal manner. Even in the dim light it was apparent that he had on some unusually bright clothing. 'I was about to take a bath. But perhaps you'd like to come in.'

'Thank you.'

Coldharbour bent down. There was the sound of a bolt and chain sliding along a groove. A dark passage led to the sitting-room. He switched on the light. 'I always keep the curtains drawn. People can look in from the street.' In the electric light he was revealed as wearing a Japanese robe in light blue and silver, embroidered with dragons. Below it his legs showed dead white.

'I'm sorry about this afternoon. I'd had a bad day.'

'Not at all,' Coldharbour said again, uncharacteristically unmelted by the words. There were bottles on a table at the end of the room, but he did not offer a drink. Why not? And why was the door bolted and chained? Looking at the small section of bare chest visible in the vee opening of the robe Gilbert knew that there was somebody else in the flat. Could it be Virginia?

'There was something else.' He sat down. Coldharbour also sat, on the edge of a chair, ready to spring up again in a moment. 'You said something about Max working against the firm's interests.'

'I didn't mention a name.'

'No, but it was obviously Max. What exactly did you mean?'

A lavatory flushed, footsteps sounded. Coldharbour looked nervously at the door. 'I can't talk about it now.'

'You've got somebody here.'

'The people upstairs use my lavatory.' The robe came open further, revealing a surprisingly hairy chest. Modestly he drew it together. 'I have reason to believe that our partner is trying to make an arrangement with another firm. But I cannot talk about it now.'

'Denis, you can't say things like that without justifying them.'

'Tomorrow,' Coldharbour said with unusual firmness. 'Excuse me.'

The door opened. A young man came into the room. He wore a white vest and tight blue jeans with a wide black belt. His arms were splendidly muscled. His hair was thick and fair. He put his hands on slim hips, stared and said nothing.

Coldharbour gulped. 'Bill, I told you—'

'You *told* me?' The young man's voice was thick.

'I asked you—I said I shouldn't be more than five minutes.'

'I got tired of waiting.' He said to Gilbert, 'Perhaps you'd like to join the party.'

A key turned in a lock. Coldharbour put a hand to his mouth. His eyes were panic-stricken.

'I thought you'd put the bolt on,' the young man said.

'I did. But then he came.'

'You clot.'

Another figure appeared in the doorway, a hulking body with a small head, beetle-browed, grizzle-haired. Coldharbour spoke shrilly. 'Stanley, I thought I'd made it clear that you are *not* welcome here any longer. I've asked you before to give back that key.'

Stanley filled the doorway. He glanced at Bill but his gaze rested longer on Gilbert. 'Who's he?'

'I'm just going.'

Stanley's voice was surprisingly quiet in such a big man. 'You're a friend of Denny's? You'll understand then. I'm a friend too, have been for a couple of years, and now he's trying to ditch me. And for what? A pin-up out of a boysie magazine.'

'Excuse me.'

Stanley courteously made way but said emphatically, 'I ask you, is it right?'

'You can have him,' Bill said. 'I met him in a club, that's all. He's nothing in my life.'

Coldharbour started after Gilbert, who had reached the passage. 'Don't go.'

Laughter came bubbling up in him, he felt his body shaking with it. 'You wanted to get rid of me. We'll talk tomorrow.'

As he closed the door and went up the steps he heard Coldharbour's voice raised after him in a depressing cat-like wail. He found a taxi in the street, and on the way home meditated upon the manifold tribulations of love.

CHAPTER EIGHT

Wife Away

WATCHING the bird move along the ground, rise and slowly disappear, he looked for her face in the tiny holes that slotted its side and of course did not see her. The image of those caged Zoo birds in which she had been so deeply interested came to his mind. One day she had insisted that he should go with her and they had watched the bright creatures flying about, making love, chattering like fools, clinging to the sides of the cage.

'They're beautiful.' He had agreed. 'What do you suppose they think about?'

'I doubt if they do think. Not in the way you mean.'

'But they communicate. I read an article that said so. They can't like this, can they? For them it's like being in prison.'

'If you let them out they'd die.'

'Perhaps they'd sooner die.'

'When it comes to the point we'd all sooner live than die. Like Jews under German occupation. Most of them tried to go on living.' As soon as the words were spoken he regretted their sententiousness. 'It's a stupid comparison, people and birds.'

'I suppose so, yes.'

The conversation came back to him now that she had flown away to Yugoslavia, a bird inside another bird. Yugoslavia, he had said last night, why Yugoslavia?

'Celia Brunner says it's beautiful. And not too hot in June. But it might have been Geneva. Or Innsbruck. I just happened to be able to book a flight to Dubrovnik.'

It seemed useless to ask whether she was going alone, or would meet somebody there. 'I can't imagine what you'll do.'

'Swim. Look around.'

'You don't even know the language.'

'And think. About me. Us. You should do that too.'

'I could fly out and join you. In a couple of days you'll be bored.'

'Then I shall go somewhere else.'

'And if you're not?'

'I told you. I shall come back in a fortnight.'

Desperately, truthfully, he said, 'I don't see the point of it.'

'And what's the point of the way we live now? Nothing happens.'

'What do you expect to happen?'

'I don't know. But you want it that way. I have to find out if I do.'

'Supposing we'd had a child. Would it have been different?'

'How do I know? What a silly question.'

'And what is it I should think about?'

'I told you. You, me, us.'

In the morning she had everything packed and labelled, talked to Mrs Park, arranged that if he ran short of anything he would leave a note. Mrs Park accepted the whole thing as commonplace. 'Do you good,' she said. 'You've been looking peaky.'

In the morning he took her to Heathrow, kissed her cheek—at the last moment she averted her mouth—saw her walk out of the passenger lounge when the flight was called. Even when the bird rose from the ground he felt that somehow a trick had been played upon him. Surely she would walk across the tarmac and say that the whole thing was a joke? But she did not.

In the office the search for the Dexter Manhood manuscript continued unabated and unsuccessful. Mrs Fairweather had been traced and knew nothing about it. Miss Pinkthorn's eyes gleamed with pleasure. Coldharbour did not put in an appearance and there were some tiresome queries about a book he was handling. Ambiguous readers' reports on two manuscripts lay on Gilbert's desk. He sent out for sand-wiches and began to read one of them himself. It was a novel purporting to be written in the first person by a deaf mute whose feelings were conveyed in an invented language which consisted of single-syllable words and exclamations. Interspersed with his narrative were extracts from a heavily ironical Report on the Sexual Customs of the Tribe sup-posedly composed by the psychologist who was handling the case of the deaf mute, and interpolated in the text of the Report were what amounted to quite separate novels about the problems of two couples mentioned in it. One couple were the parents of the deaf mute. He read a hundred pages, dictated on his tape recorder a letter of rejection, and turned to the other manuscript, which was concerned with the problems of a Negro dwarf who lived in a tree house and was perfectly happy until he fell in love with a white girl seven feet tall who took him home to her Gothic castle in Bigland. It was a relief when the telephone rang, although he flinched when the girl said it was Mr Bunce.

'Gil? Jake. How about Lord's?'

'What's that?'

'Up in North London. You're a cricket buff, right, isn't that where they play the top games?'

'Oh I see, Lord's. Middlesex play there, yes.'

'I wondered could we take in a match this afternoon? If you've got the time. Max said to ring you, but if you're too busy that's OK.'

There was something disarming in the apologetic hesitancy of Bunce's voice, and Gilbert agreed with a warmth that surprised himself to pick up Jake from his hotel. Before he left the office a cable came in. It was from Max in Milan and read: PROGRESSWISE SLOWLY ABSENTEE EUGENE TRACKING THROUGH FLAVOUR WILL KEEP IN TOUCH. Flavour was presumably the secretarial Flavia, and presumably also the cable meant that Max would be away for another day or two. Well, life would be more peaceful without him.

Jake was waiting in the hotel lobby. He wore a zipping windcheater and levis. 'Am I dressed right? I mean, is there some special gear you wear for cricket?'

'Not the spectators, only the players.' In the taxi Gilbert explained the elements of the game and Bunce said, 'Yeah, yeah, I see, got it.' He tapped the paper under his arm. 'I've been boning up a little. I see Kent set the game alight yesterday, it says here Cowdrey hit the ball all over the ground.'

'Yes. You must be prepared for—I mean, it may be rather slow by your standards. A match can take three days.'

'Sure, sure, I know. It's like English life, a ritual. I'm interested in the symbolism. And, Gil.'

'Yes?'

'I want to say again I'm sorry about your dinner party. That Lulu should be kept locked up in a bedroom. I got rid of her.'

'You did?'

63

'She's moved in with Danny Knight, you know, the actor, he likes them rough. Gil, am I shocking you?'

'No.'

'I don't want you to think I got no feelings. I do have. But not about Lulu.' He gave what Gilbert thought of as an American smile, youthful and shy.

Gilbert was a member and he took Bunce into the Long Room, where the American looked with interest at the portraits round the walls. 'Old stuff,' he said. 'Respect for the past. I like it.' They sat outside the pavilion and watched Middlesex batting. There were few people in the ground, most of them small children or old men, and the play was appropriately becalmed, the batsmen pushing the ball placidly back down the pitch, occasionally dabbing it off their legs or down to third man for a single. Virginia would be settled by now in her hotel. He would telephone her tonight. With this decision he felt his eyes closing. A ripple of applause made him open them again. One of the batsmen had hit a boundary.

Jake leaned forward watching intently, his lick of fair hair hanging down. 'What does it mean to you, Gil, all this?'

'Mean?'

'It's a dance to slow music, I get that. But there's more to it, it kind of expresses British temperament, right?'

'Yes, perhaps it does if you put it that way.'

'It gets you where you live, stands to reason it must do.'

Drowsily he wondered whether this was true, and decided that there was something in it. 'Perhaps it's what I should like life to be, leisurely, with nothing unexpected happening.' It occurred to him that this was a variation on what Virginia had said last night, and Bunce's next words seemed to flow on naturally from this thought.

'I liked your wife, admired her very much. But I guess she wouldn't be too keen about cricket.'

Gilbert felt an inclination to confide in him, but resisted it. 'That's right. She thinks it's a bore.'

'Thinks it's a bore,' Bunce repeated, and laughed in what might have been a meaningful manner. He turned to the sports page in the paper, as though reading an account of the previous day's play would provide some final answer to his questions. Gilbert closed his eyes and saw the cheek he had kissed at parting, wonderfully smooth. Why had she not kissed him on the mouth, did she now find him repulsive? Such ideas were alien to him. He was startled when Bunce said emphatically, 'Sex.'

One of the batsmen had been bowled, his middle stump knocked out of the ground. 'What?'

'That's why you get a kick from it.' He tapped the paper. 'You use the ball, see, and you try to get rid of the stump. See what it says here, Herman uprooted the middle stump and that's what just happened now, right?'

'Yes, but—'

'Boy, that bowler's uprooted his middle stump all right, it's a castration symbol, see? And those pads the batter wears, he's protecting his stump with them. He wants to hit that ball, get the damn' thing away from him to the boundary, the limit. Get that ball away, he's saying, I don't want it near my stump. You read what Melanie Klein says about bat and ball games?'

'I can't say I have.'

'They symbolize a fear of sex, keep it hidden, that's the thing, destroy it if you can. And the white clothes, what do they mean but purity? It's a hell of a funny game.' The players went into the pavilion. 'That's it then, glad to have seen it.'

'They'll be coming out again. This is the tea interval.'

'I guess I've seen enough.' With cricket satisfactorily explained Bunce rose to his feet. Gilbert got up too. 'Gil, it's been great. I appreciate it, I really do. Why not stop by my hotel around seven, I'd like to have a talk. And your wife too if she's around, let's have an evening together.'

'Virginia's gone off on a short holiday.' The reticence of his own phrase was somehow decisive, and he said yes to the invitation. Bunce ambled away. Gilbert stayed watching the cricket for another half-hour, but those remarks about sexual symbolism seemed to have taken away his pleasure. He found that he could not contemplate a return to the office and went to the club where he at once fell asleep in the reading-room.

CHAPTER NINE

A Tangible Ghost

HE SAT in the Out Going, aware that he had drunk too much whisky. Around him there was a tremendous noise, part of which came from The Worst, a group playing at the other end of the room. The Worst's vocalist, stripped to the waist, had the words *I Tangle* painted on his chest. Some words of his theme song came through :

> . . . as we jangle
> Because I . . . tangle
> . . . Want to tangle . . . angle . . .
> What is it . . . love . . . strangle . . .

The final line, which he fairly belted out, was perfectly clear : 'Because I got got got just got to tangle with you.' Everybody in the room appeared to be talking rather than listening, talking less to other people than to himself or herself. The Out Going was the last in a succession of similar establishments that they had visited in a group that had grown steadily larger and now numbered a dozen people. Jenny Johnson was with them, and so were Felix Perkins the photographer, who had been drinking with them at the hotel and a film producer named Lefty Leftwell. In their presence Bunce seemed a different person from the young man who had sat beside Gilbert at Lord's. In the same gangling body this other Bunce appeared, at once aggressive and self-pitying. It might have been said that he was playing to an audience, but if so he was obviously dissatisfied with his performance. Greeting Gilbert in the hotel with a kind of melancholy warmth, he had talked almost the whole evening about his own genius, and the way in which America made him suffer. At one point Jenny, rather in her televisual incarnation, had asked why he lived in the United States if he hated it that much. Bunce's mouth quivered, he looked as if he were about to cry.

'Because it turns me on, baby, the whole show turns me on, because I love the goddam place, that's why.' He waved an arm, struck Felix Perkins on the chest, smiled apologetically. 'It's a great country, but it makes you suffer.'

They were all sitting round two small tables, and Jenny's thigh was pressed close against Gilbert's. 'He's a genius,' she said. 'You must be proud to publish him.'

He started to tell her that Jake was really his partner's responsibility, but she rose, slipped past him and joined a risen Bunce in the crowd of figures swaying in the centre of the room. *Why did you wear that bangle?* The Worst's vocalist asked. *Made me want to tangle.* The words became hopelessly lost.

Perkins said, 'They've got something, don't you think? A *reverberant* quality.'

'I don't know, have they?'

The photographer was thin, long-fingered, hollow-cheeked. He wore a frilled lace shirt with ruffles at the neck.

'It's a song for sad men. Like me. My wife's left me. Do you know what she said? "We're not cohering any more, and when you're not cohering what's the good." I have these rages. Do you have them?'

'I don't think so. No, I don't have rages.'

'You wouldn't think I did, would you? Once she seemed to like them. But not now. I had a card from her the other day. From Istanbul. It broke my heart.'

'Rages,' a voice said jeeringly. It came from a broad-faced ruddy man. 'Tantrums!'

'Oh Richard, please,' Perkins said.

Richard jerked a finger. 'That cow, he's on the box with Jenny, she asks him something, he has one of his tantrums and cuts loose with a load of dirty talk. And my old mum's listening, she's disgusted. "Is that the sort of thing your friends say, son?" she asks me.' He leaned across, took hold of Perkins's shirt front. 'You know what you are, don't you? A cow, a bloody liberal cow.'

'Richard, don't be fierce.'

'Don't be fierce,' Richard mimicked. 'You ought to be ashamed, using that language when old ladies are listening. You know what? They think photographers are a crowd of yobs, they think we're all like you.'

'You're tearing my shirt.' Perkins seemed rather pleased than distressed.

'You're a photographer too?' Gilbert asked.

'Too right I am.' Richard glared, released Perkins's shirt. 'You another liberal cow?'

'I don't think I'm anything at all.'

'That's right, boy, don't you be anything at all. Don't talk dirty on the box. Mind you, she asks for it.' He gestured at Jenny, who was clinging to Bunce on the floor. 'You know what my mum says about her?'

'Richard. Felix. Darlings!' A small blonde pushed her way through the crush and became visible in the dimness as an actress with a familiar face. 'Fay,' everybody cried,

68

'It's Fay.' The men got up and kissed her. Bunce returned sweating from his dance and kissed her too.

'Lovely,' she cried. 'But do I know you?'

'Everyone knows me, Jake Bunce.' She squealed with pleasure. 'And you're Fay. I got to prove something to myself, Fay.'

'What's that?'

'You going to bed with me tonight?'

Fay squealed again, turned to Gilbert who sat pressed within his chair and kissed him warmly. 'What do you think about that?'

'I don't know.'

She ran a hand through his hair. Behind her another woman hovered, taller, bigger. What seemed an irresistible press of bodies from behind moved Fay forward and she gently dropped into Gilbert's chair and placed an arm round his neck. The taller woman stood looking down, spoke his name.

'Gilbert, what in Christ's kind of a name is that?' Fay cried. 'That's Georgie Drake, you know Georgie.'

'I know Georgie.' He pushed Fay away, stood and faced her. He had not seen her for seven years, but she was the most tangible of ghosts. She was immediately recognizable, yet the missing years had wrecked her. The broad flat face was coarsened, the body thickened by drink, there was about her an air of bursting over-ripeness. Only the eyes of distinctive delicate blue looked at him with the openness that he remembered. It was more than seven years ago, it was ten, that he had gone down the basement steps similar to Coldharbour's and thundered on the door and pushed past the man who opened it and found her on the bed, drunk and giggling. Her mouth had wavered as it always did when she was unsure of her reception, as it was wavering now.

'Georgie,' he repeated and then said 'Mary,' and her wavering mouth smiled. His pleasure at seeing her was so great that he could have laughed or cried. He took her hands and said with perfect simplicity, as though the desert years between them did not exist, 'Mary, let's go.'

CHAPTER TEN

The Past

'WHAT DO I THINK?' E.R. had asked, chalking his cue and standing beside it with his large head raised like that of a Roman senator about to pronounce sentence on an erring centurion. He bent down and played a stroke with his customary care, just missing a difficult cannon. 'It is one more absurdity added to the long list. What else is there to think? And what is the point of asking me? You are twenty-four years old. If you choose to marry a chemist's daughter from Camden Town it is your affair, not mine.'

He was intimidated, as always, by the way in which E.R. put it. Before the war his mother had been there to protect him from such weighty sarcasm, to laugh at E.R. and make him laugh too. The bit of shrapnel that killed her outright while she was making her way to a shelter after shopping had seemed unreal to him at the time, a telegram received in Africa, some words of sympathy from the Colonel. Even if it had been possible he would not have wished to go home, and in a way the fact that he did not return cushioned him from the reality of his mother's death, so that when he did come back to England he expected to find her waiting to greet him in the Chelsea house where they had lived since his childhood. Instead there was simply his father, installed there with a housekeeper to whom his manner was one of ferocious formality. Gilbert had missed university when he was called up for Army service in 1941, and four years later he felt little inclination to go. E.R. had always assumed that he would enter the business, and he did not openly question this assumption. Within a few weeks of living at home, however, he had rebelled to the point at which he said that he wanted a place of his own. E.R. had raised no objection. He got rid of the housekeeper, sold the house, and moved into a service flat in Kensington. The departure from home had been the outward mark of an estrangement that had deepened in the three years before this announcement of marriage.

Now he said, 'I don't see that Mary's father being a chemist has anything to do with it.'

'Ha.'

They played a few more strokes. 'I want to leave the firm.'

'Very well.'

'I'm going to start a bookshop somewhere in the country. In Gloucestershire perhaps. And set up a small private printing-press.'

With careful savagery E.R. potted the red, playing the ball so hard that it almost bounced out of the pocket. 'The New Life.' The phrase referred to the group of which Gilbert was a member.

'Yes, as a matter of fact there will be a New Life community starting near Gloucester.' What he had to say next required an effort. 'There's the matter of money.'

E.R. finished his break. 'My game.' He racked his cue and stood glaring from under great grey brows. 'I hope you don't expect me to provide it.'

'There's the money Mother left. If you approve—'

'Very well. You have my approval.'

He felt immense relief. Of course they would have got married anyway, but the money made it that much easier. 'And your blessing, I hope.'

'My blessing.' E.R. contemplated the words as he

71

switched off the lights above the table. He hardly ever raised his voice and now his words were all the more effective for their measured weight. 'You know I wanted you to carry on the firm. Now you will not be doing so. You have involved yourself with a group of ridiculous nonentities, you propose to marry a chit of a chemist's daughter and to embark on a scheme that is as certain of failure as anything can be in this life. I am willing for you to have the money left by your mother because it is properly yours, but I should be condoning your stupidity in an unpardonable way if I gave you my blessing.' He paused and said with the sense of timing that rarely forsook him, 'Shall we go down to the bar?'

He had been right, of course, he had been dismally and painfully right in everything except in the description of Mary as a chit. In the taxi, with his arm round her ampleness, he reflected that even as a girl Mary had been heavy-boned and brawny. Now, with her head rolling on his shoulder, she murmured something that he failed to hear. She repeated it.

'Nothing is lost.'

'What do you mean?'

'Do you remember saying that to me? Nothing we do, think, feel together is lost, it always remains somewhere in our personalities, when people love each other it makes a link that can never be broken. Do you remember?'

'Yes,' he said untruthfully. He had said many similar things at that time. When the war ended and he came out of the Army with the rank of captain he had been sure of nothing except that the world was totally changed and that his life ought to change with it. He had seen men killed because they obeyed his orders, had glimpsed later as a staff captain something of the confusion and pettiness that marks every bureaucratic organization, and he had no intention

72

of spending the rest of his life propping up such organizations. In the 1945 General Election a political party named Common Wealth fought using the slogan, 'What is morally wrong cannot be politically right,' and although Gilbert was not interested in politics he shared the Common Wealth feeling that a new and better society was coming into existence. Entering the firm had been understood, at least by him, as a breathing space while he discovered the nature of that society. He saw a New Life meeting advertised in a weekly paper, went to it, and joined.

The New Life group had been founded a few months before the end of the war by a dynamic bald man in his forties named George Riddiatt. The group believed in freedom. 'We must be free to share with others all that we hold most sacred in life itself,' Riddiatt would say, his dark eyes gleaming. 'What do I mean by sacred? Every one of us has his own answer to that, the sacred things are locked up here.' He would strike his barrel chest and his hearers understood that the sacred things were impalpable, it was the glimmering web of human feelings that those who lived the New Life would be sharing in a world remote from envy, jealousy and greed. Corporeal possessions were comparatively unimportant but these too would be shared in the New Life communities that were springing up all over Europe and America.

Had it all been as ridiculous as it seemed now, an old tune played to the credulous by a bald Pied Piper? It had fitted his personal needs at the time, and he had taken part with enthusiasm in the formation of the Literary, Dramatic and Psycho-Dynamic Groups and in the plans for transforming the farm which Riddiatt owned, and where he had worked during the whole of the War, into the first New Life community. He had met Mary in Psycho-Dynamics, and had been attracted at once by her rebellious innocence. The decisions that he had reached by painful effort, in making up his mind to live alone and to leave the firm, seemed to pose no problems at all for her. She regarded her parents as ignorant ogres, and agreed without any hesitation at all to come and live with him. After they had slept together at his flat she took him to see her mother and father. Gilbert was surprised to find them rather meek little people.

'I'm leaving here, we're going to live together.' Mary looked at them defiantly.

Mr Drake coughed. 'I don't know why you've thought it necessary to bring Mr Welton along—'

'His name's Gilbert.'

'Pleased to meet you, Gilbert.' They shook hands.

'Of course we should like it if you got married,' his wife said, later. They were so acquiescent that there was nothing to rebel against, as it seemed to Gilbert.

'You don't understand. They've tried to keep me down. Always. Now they can't, that's all.'

'It might be a good idea to get married.'

She disagreed. Was not marriage a negation of freedom, a completely artificial attempt to bind people together socially? Gilbert, who had in mind the effect on E.R., replied that since the ceremony was unimportant it didn't matter whether or not they conformed to it. They took the question to Riddiatt, who agreed with Gilbert. Had the question of getting his mother's money anything to do with it? Looking back years later he feared that it had. In the end they compromised by getting married in a register office with witnesses called in from the street, and announcing the fact afterwards. They bought the bookshop before marrying, and spent their honeymoon getting it straight and putting the old printing-press in the cellar in order. George Riddiatt's former farm, now the New Life centre, was only a couple of miles away, and New Lifers came in every day to chat, help, drink coffee. Within a few weeks Mary was pregnant. Broad and beaming, an image of sturdy health, she sat in the shop talking to members of the group, while Gilbert worked downstairs printing pamphlets.

When was the New Life over, when did the dream fade? Its fading had a connection, in some way that he did not understand, with the surprisingly difficult birth of Matthew, who was more than a week late. Riddiatt had said that he should be present at the birth, Mary had wanted him there, and he had sat watching horrified while she shrieked, moaned, arched her body as though bitten by a snake, and eventually excreted the messy red howling creature. And in more material terms it was of course linked to the evident failure of the bookshop to attract many people except the New Lifers, and to Gilbert's realization that George Riddiatt was not a prophet but a windbag with both eyes on the main chance.

And yet perhaps the basic reason was just the fact that Mary and he had deceived each other when they married. Slowly he understood that her broad-beamed solidity concealed a wildly romantic nature in rebellion not only against her parents but against almost every aspect of conventional society. Twenty years later Mary would have been a pot-smoking hippie with different problems. At the end of the nineteen forties she was a high flying romantic who expected him to lead her into always wilder and more imaginative areas of freedom. Were they making losses on the bookshop, was there little prospect of being paid for the New Life pamphlets? She found it impossible to feel any interest in such material matters, and used to take Matthew up to the New Life centre, leaving Gilbert to look after the shop. Sometimes she would stay there all day, these visits being succeeded by storms of remorse in which she would cling to him and assure him that he was the only man she could possibly love. This meant, as he ought to have known, that she was going to bed with Riddiatt. When he discovered

75

this he found it impossible to blame her. She was only carrying out the principles of the group, as she pointed out to him, and any pain he felt sprang from the envious feelings that they had both forsworn. But other wives also carried out the principles, other husbands were less tolerant. Within a year the group broke up in furious dissension. Riddiatt went to the United States with a rich American girl who had recently joined, married her, and when Gilbert had last heard of him was running a School of Metaphysical Drama in California.

A few months later Gilbert sold the bookshop for less than half the price he had paid for it, and went back to work in the family firm. E.R. did not comment on what had happened beyond saying that he was glad Gilbert had come to his senses. He never came to see them in the flat that Gilbert bought with the money from the sale of the bookshop.

His arm was developing pins and needles and he withdrew it from behind her back. She turned to look at him.

'Where are we going, to your house?'

'Yes.'

'What's happened to your wife, to Vir-Virginia? Or is she there?' He had almost forgotten her occasional slight attractive stammer.

'She's away.'

'Away.' Her laugh, throaty and full of sexual promise, had not changed. 'I still love you, that's funny, isn't it, after all these years. Nothing is lost, I remember that. I remember everything.'

'Nobody remembers everything. Just what they want to remember.'

'That isn't true,' she cried with the earnestness that had always impressed him because it obviously welled up from a nature whose feelings went so much deeper than his own.

'I remember Starting Again, did you think I'd have forgotten that?'

Starting Again. It was what they had said hopefully when they moved into the flat and for two years, perhaps three, *Starting Again* had remained their motto. Then Matthew stopped being a baby and went to school, and Mary took drama classes to fill in the time and began to come back late in the evenings and Starting Again was over. How was it possible that he had endured the drink and quarrels and unfaithfulness for five years after that? There must have been a strong link, he thought now wonderingly, the link between them must have been very powerful to last so long. Now Mary sat upright on the seat, away from him.

'How's Matt?'

'Well. I had a letter a couple of weeks ago.'

'He hasn't written to me in months. No reason why he should, I expect you say. But it wasn't all my fault. I did the wrong things, but it wasn't all my f-fault.'

'I never said it was.'

'I never got anywhere near to you. Except at the b-beginning perhaps. I don't know what you want from women, and I don't think you know either. That was always the t-trouble.'

'What are you doing now?'

'This and that. Telly mostly. When they want a fat middle-aged tart they think of me.' She paused. 'It would be p-polite to laugh.'

'I've seen you once or twice. And thought about you.'

'Thank you very much. To tell the truth it's absolute bloody hell. I'm through with the telly or it's through with me. I'm living with Fay.'

'Fay? Oh yes.'

'You'd never have thought I was a lizzie, would you? And butch at that. And the thing is I'm not really. Anyway I think that's finished too, Fay's bored with me, I'll be moving out before long.'

'Did you find it satisfactory?'

'Of course I bloody didn't. I told you I'm not a lizzie. Only when you're—'

'What?'

'Nothing.'

The taxi stopped. She went ahead, opening the gate while he paid the driver. As he caught up with her she looked at him.

'Why have you brought me here? Some sort of re-revenge. Is that it? It would be like you.'

The remark stung him. 'When did I ever take revenge on you?'

'Not me. Yourself.'

He opened the door and switched on the hall lights. She looked around her with the inquisitiveness of a woman entering the house where a man she knows well is living with another woman. In the drawing-room she took in the striped settees, the polished tables, the pictures, the careful arrangement of everything. She turned to him with the wide trustful smile he remembered. 'She's not much like me, is she, that's for sure.'

And he remembered too—there was, after all, a great deal he had not forgotten—the chaos in which Mary lived for preference, the bits of butter left on tables and adhering to newspapers dropped on top of them, the gravy from a week-old meal gathering fur on a shelf, the bedroom's invariable disorder. He had said during one of their quarrels, 'I suppose you think you've got more important things to do than making the bed,' and she had answered, 'Yes, lying on it.' He had laughed without being appeased. For Mary order and neatness were incompatible not only with the New Life, but with everything in her nature. Outward chaos symbolized inner rebellion.

'Whisky?'

'And a drinks cupboard. Whisky, yes, with soda. I'll bet she's the kind of woman who never runs out of soda.'

'Yes. Is it a good thing to run out of soda?'

'I su-suppose not.' She sat down, crossed her legs, licked a finger and ran it over a stocking. 'A ladder, bugger it. I saw you once together. In a restaurant, you didn't see me. Pretty, but not your style I'd have thought. Though perhaps it was me who wasn't your st-style.'

'Perhaps.' He stood looking down at her, contemplating the face which retained some of the wide artlessness of youth, the body gone to seed.

'I don't see what the hell you brought me here for. Where is she, isn't she coming back?'

The words clanged in his head. He had to telephone Virginia.

'Or are we going to bed, is that it? It's been a long time. And it was never what it might have been, was it?'

'I don't know.'

'This is everything, this is what life means. Do you remember I used to say that to you. But it was never true. I had it better.'

'With a dozen others, I daresay.'

'Oh Christ, you are a bastard. All I wanted—' She gave up the sentence, drank.

In the hotel bedroom at Dubrovnik Virginia moved in a torment of pleasure beneath a body lean, brown, covered with hair, whose face was indiscernible. 'Yes. What did you want?'

'What does it matter, I shall never get it now.' With dismay he saw her take off her shoes, put her feet up on the sofa. 'Did it all mean nothing, then?'

'Did what mean nothing?'

'The things we said. Not just you and me, the Group. It can't all have been wasted, can it?' Her eyes stared at or through him, blue and innocent, asking as she had always asked for some reassurance about life or the world. 'I kept all your letters, you know that? Sentimental.'

'Yes.'

79

'All right then, I'm sen-sentimental. Let's go to bed.'

As she spoke the words his revulsion from her became complete, the need to speak to Virginia physically urgent. 'I'm sorry. You'll have to go.'

'She's coming back?' Again with her wide smile she said, 'I'd like to meet her. You did ask me in.'

'I've got to make a telephone call.'

'Go ahead. I'm happy here.' She held out her empty glass. 'Though I could do with another drink.'

Her presence in the house was intolerable to him. He went to the sofa, pulled her up so that she stood beside him, slapped her face. The sound was unpleasant. As he saw the look of the innocent eyes change to wonder and dismay he felt that he had done some terrible injury to an animal.

'I'm sorry.'

'Don't be sorry.' She swayed a little and he realized that she was drunk. 'You've said it too often. Where's my coat, did I have one?'

'Virginia won't be back. You can stay here. In the spare room.'

She shook her head. 'In the spare room. No, thanks.'

'Are you all right? Let me ring for a taxi.'

She shook her head again. At the door she touched her face where the mark of his fingers showed, and then touched his gently. 'Goodbye, Gilbert.'

'I'm very sorry,' he repeated inanely, like a head waiter apologizing for some failure of service.

'I don't know what you want, but it's not me. It was never me. You ought to find out. It's upsetting for women when men don't know what they want. I feel sorry for Vir-Virginia.'

She walked down the steps and then up the road, a bulky middle-aged woman.

Back in the drawing-room he found himself shivering, poured more whisky and drank half of it at a gulp, then looked at his watch. The time was half past eleven. Too late to telephone? The question was unreal, because his need was so urgent that the consideration of time did not enter into it. He dialled the operator and asked for the number.

'Yugoslavia,' a friendly man's voice said. 'That's a long way away. There'll be a delay. I'll call you back.'

He wandered round the room, putting straight the cushion on which Mary had sat, taking out her glass to the kitchen and washing it, obliterating the traces of her visit. What unbelievable stupidity it had been to bring her back here, why had he done it? And what had she meant by saying that he didn't know what he wanted? The two of them were utterly unsuited and it had taken a long time to find out, that was all.

The telephone rang.

The friendly operator said, 'Your call to Yugoslavia should be through now. Hold on a moment.' There was a series of clicks, then a tapping sound.

'Is that the Hotel Splendid?' The tapping continued, then there was an ear-splitting noise followed by a volley of what he assumed to be Serbo-Croat. 'Is that the Hotel Splendid?' More Serbo-Croat. He said loudly and slowly, 'Is there anybody who speaks English?'

A woman's voice intervened, evidently expostulating with somebody. With him? Apparently not, for the volleyer returned and spoke sharply, with rising excitement. Gilbert tried to get above them both with a shout. 'I want to speak to Madame Welton.' Silence. 'Get Madame Welton for me please.'

The two decided to ignore him and began to argue again. The operator came on, cutting them out.

'Don't seem to be doing too well, do we? Got a line crossed out there from the sound of it. Did you get any sense at all?'

'None whatever.'

'I'll try again.' He heard the same two voices, then the operator cut them out. 'I can try and get hold of Dubrovnik exchange again.'

'Thank you.'

'But that means breaking the connection. Is it urgent?'

'Yes.'

'See what I can do. Hold on.' More clicks, then a different voice. The operator, more resourceful than Gilbert had expected, spoke slowly in an unintelligible language. There was a good deal of conversation which ended with laughter on both sides.

'Look, I'm sorry, old man—'

'Please don't call me old man. We don't know each other.'

The operator became curt and formal. 'I'm sorry, subscriber, Dubrovnik say that all lines to the Hotel Splendid are engaged.'

'That's absurd. They can't be at this time of night.'

'I can only tell you what Dubrovnik reports.'

'Is that why you were laughing?'

'He made a joke about the length of time people spend on the telephone. I agreed.'

'Is he going to ring back?'

'I can ask him to do so if you wish. I couldn't guarantee that he will.'

'What do you advise?'

'If it's very urgent I should try again in half an hour. I'm going off at midnight. That's in five minutes.' A click and he was back with the dialling tone.

The idea of telephoning seemed absurd. What would he say if he spoke? 'I just rang to see if you were all right . . . having a good time . . . met anybody interesting . . . is somebody in the room with you?' It was a stupid idea, of a piece with his behaviour during the evening. He brushed his teeth and went to bed, staring at Virginia's untouched coverlet.

He was unable to sleep. Was Bunce in bed with Jenny Johnson or with Fay, talking to her about the sexual symbolism of cricket? And what about Mary? The words were repeated in his head with tom-tom rhythm. It had been wrong to bring her back to the house, an act of deep insensitiveness. Tottering slightly, never too steady on her pins, Mary returned to the flat she shared with the actress Fay, and found it empty. From a drawer in a dressing-table she took a small packet of letters done up in pink ribbon and began to read them, her tears dropping on to the sheets. What did the letters say? They were in his writing and he strained to make out the words but was unable to do so. Mary looked up at him. 'Starting Again,' she said. She was smiling not at him but at somebody behind him, and turning he saw Virginia advancing towards her. 'Starting Again,' Virginia repeated and then bent over Mary and kissed her upturned face while he watched in horror, wanting to protest but unable to cry out. 'No,' he was able to manage at last. 'No.'

He woke shivering, his pyjamas damp with sweat, went down to the kitchen and made himself a cup of tea, returned to bed. A phrase of Scott Fitzgerald's, changed and no doubt debased, was repeated in his mind. 'When you wake and remember the past you never go back to sleep.'

It was after three o'clock when he slept. In his dreams the telephone seemed to be ringing.

CHAPTER ELEVEN

Telephone, Newspaper, Cable

THE AGONIES and terrors of the night vanish in the light of morning. Gilbert Welton woke, bathed, shaved, dressed, made himself toast and coffee, spoke to Mrs Park, walked to the office in bright sunshine. Over the toast and coffee he skimmed through a letter from Amsterdam in Matthew's round hand. 'How are you both? Very sorry I haven't written recently but we've been very busy, however better busy than slack . . .' Matthew was a stolid, pleasant, rather boring young man, not bright enough for university, who had gone into an Anglo-Dutch engineering combine as a trainee and had then come out of it to start a firm for the sale of some gadget used in the operation of concrete mixers. His partner was the inventor of the gadget and, surprisingly to Gilbert, they seemed to be doing very well.

Surprisingly also, Matthew got on very well with Virginia, who had adapted herself easily to the idea of having a grown-up stepson. Something about this humdrum letter helped to set the preceding night into perspective. He had drunk too much and behaved foolishly, but nothing had been done that could not be undone, and his need to telephone now seemed incomprehensible. You were married, your wife had gone away for a while because she was feeling the sort of strain that all married couples suffered from time to time. To make a telephone call in the middle of the night was just about the worst possible course of action. He decided that he would stop behaving stupidly. He would not telephone Virginia, but would wait for her to get in touch with him. It was Friday. No doubt he would hear from her before the week-end was over.

He spent the next seventy-two hours in the semi-anaesthetised condition of a man waiting for an operation. The office on Friday was somnolent. There was no word from Max. He left at three o'clock, went to the Zoo and watched the sea-lions being fed. They positioned themselves on rocks and caught in their mouths the fishes thrown to them. Later he found himself standing in front of the aviary and contemplating the birds in a fixed meaningless way. On Saturday he went to the club and played squash, on Sunday the Sutherlands invited him to lunch. He told them that Virginia had gone away for a short holiday, and that pressure of work prevented him from going with her. Sandra said nothing further about her departure, but started to talk about the attractiveness of Bunce. What food had they given him, what else had been said? Half an hour after leaving them he could not remember.

He went home and began to turn out old clothes from his bedroom drawers and then to throw away papers. Then he tried to open the small desk in which Virginia kept her correspondence. It was locked. He tried several keys without success and eventually forced the lock with a chisel, searching in it with an eagerness he could not explain. He found nothing but bills, cheque book stubs and half a dozen old letters of his own.

The telephone did not ring. That night he drank a good deal of whisky, and on Monday morning woke with a headache. There was no letter from Virginia. Well, she had left on Thursday so she would hardly have had time to write, but he decided to ring her at midday. As he entered his office on Monday morning the telephone was ringing.

'Mel Branksom.' The voice on the telephone was American, deep and warm. 'Branksom Associates. I don't know whether Max told you we'd had a chat.'

'As a matter of fact he didn't. He's in Italy at the moment.'

'That's too bad.' The voice was slightly ruffled, velvet

85

rubbed the wrong way. 'I guess he left in a hurry. I was putting, you know, a little idea to Max that he thought would interest you, and I wondered if you'd do me the honour of having lunch one day. Just to discuss it.'

'Can you give me some idea—' He paused as Coldharbour's face, with a bruise showing on one cheek, appeared at the door. He beckoned to the face before completting the sentence. '—what it's all about.'

'Well now, I'd sooner not do that on the telephone. I'd sooner put it face to face.'

What had Max been up to? Remembering that conversation with Langridge-Wood he became suddenly anxious to know. His diary pad was blank for the day. He suggested that Branksom should have lunch with him at the club. The voice became richer and warmer.

'I'd enjoy that, I really would. I look forward to meeting you.'

He put down the telephone and said to Coldharbour, 'Branksom Associates. Something to do with Max.'

Coldharbour shifted in his chair. 'Precisely. You remember I mentioned it.'

'I can't say I do.'

'I heard in a roundabout way that our friend had been discussing matters with them. Behind our backs. It is *not* the sort of thing that inspires confidence. I mean, are Branksom the sort of firm we want to get mixed up with?'

Gilbert nodded in a placatory manner. Branksom Associates were an American firm who had recently set up in England as publishers of sensational non-fiction books dealing with sex, crime and prison camp atrocities. They were said to have made a good deal of money. 'You don't know what they've got in mind?'

'Certainly not. If I had known I should have told you.'

'We may as well find out. There's no harm in talking.'

Coldharbour's sniff said that there might be harm in anything connected with Branksom. He moved one leg restlessly.

'About the other night. I don't want you to have the wrong idea.'

'Please, Denis.' The embarrassment he always felt at any suggestion of admission to the private lives of other people operated immediately. 'It had nothing to do with me.'

'That's perfectly true. I just wanted you to understand. Life is not always easy.' He suddenly scratched his neck. 'Stanley *was* a good friend of mine, but we had rather fallen out.' He seemed to find the phrase reassuring enough for repetition.

'I'm sorry to hear it.'

'However, our difference of opinion was only temporary. Bill proved to be very much what Stanley suggested, I'm afraid. Not a very agreeable fellow.'

'Denis, I must insist. I don't want to know anything more about it.'

He was surprised by the look Coldharbour gave him. 'You never want to know, do you?'

'What?'

'About other people.'

'I don't know what you mean.'

'That's all right,' Coldharbour said obscurely. He stood up. 'I take it your mind is quite made up. About the Spatial Realists.'

'The Spatial Realists?' For a moment he failed to make the connection. 'I'm sorry I put it so strongly, but—well, yes. It's outside our field.'

'Very well.' A hand strayed to his bruised cheek. 'Since you're completely opposed there's no point in discussing it further. No doubt you'll keep me apprised of any developments in connection with Branksom.' With a bob of the head he was gone.

The intercom buzzed. Miss Pinkthorn said with relish, 'I have Mr Manhood on the line.'

'I'm out.'

'I have told him. He says that he wants a decision in the

next week, otherwise he must ask for the return of the manuscript.'

'Say you'll speak to me about it. And Miss Pinkthorn—'

'Yes.'

'That manuscript must be found, do you understand?'

Between the understanding and the discovery falls the shadow. It was possible to admit frankly to W. Jones that his manuscript had been lost, but such an admission was repugnant, and what if he said that he had no carbon copy? And hadn't a set of lurid pictures been sent along with it? His early morning euphoria had disappeared and it was with a sensation of deepening gloom that he settled down to a session with Coldharbour and Trevallion, the sales manager, about the weekly figures. These were not often encouraging, and the only bright spot in this particular week was a rush of orders for Bunce's novel. Coldharbour, no doubt nursing his Spatial Realist grievance, hardly spoke. Trevallion, a cherubic pipe-smoking figure, was on the other hand only too eloquently full of praise for the persistence of the sales staff. 'That's a difficult book,' he said of a novel which had received long reviews but sold a derisorily small number of copies. 'You gave us a tough one there, but the boys are really getting down to brass tacks.'

'I don't see much sign of it.'

'It's no good expecting miracles with a book like that. I tried it myself. Hard going.' Removing his pipe, Trevallion showed his teeth as though the toughness were a literal matter of digestion.

This weekly conference was usually enlivened by the presence of Max, who could conjure up miraculous possibilities out of the most unlikely books. In his absence it was a dull affair. Half-way through it the receptionist came in with a cable. Gilbert tore it open and read: MISSED TIGRESS HERE BY HOURS STILL STALKING PROBABLY GENEVA HUNT WORTH WHILE MAX.

The cable had been sent from Salzburg. He read it to them. Coldharbour sniffed and rustled. Trevallion said, 'He's a live wire, Mr Bomberg, a real live wire.'

'Live wires cause short circuits,' Coldharbour commented with gloomy wit. Upon this note the conference ended.

Looking again at the cable he realized he had expected it to be from Virginia. He put through a call to Yugoslavia and was told that there would be an hour's delay. Should they keep the call in? He said that he would try again. Was there a connection between Max's tigress hunt and Virginia's holiday. 'Ridiculous,' he said aloud. 'Simply ridiculous.' The words did not banish the thought, which stayed with him like an ulcer pain until he went out to lunch.

'This is a real pleasure, Mr Welton.' Mel Branksom was tall and fresh-faced, his eyes solemn behind rimless spectacles. 'You know what I admire most about England? You're a people who know how to live.'

Gilbert smiled and handed his guest the menu. Branksom nodded as though it confirmed his view, and expanded on the statement.

'A place like this, it's got that blend of informality and what I can only call, you know, stateliness, that we don't seem able to manage in the States. It's friendly, it's relaxed, but it still says keep your distance, let's not be too familiar.'

He remembered Coldharbour's wounding words. 'Some people would say we keep our distance too much.'

'That isn't true. English tradition, that's something very valuable. Don't ever lose it.' The words were spoken seriously, as though tradition might be stolen like a diamond ring. 'I always say there are just two cities where I feel completely at home. One's New York and the other's London.'

Through the prawn cocktail and the steak Branksom expanded on his love for Britain and his respect for tradition. In what Gilbert had come to recognize as one American style he left a good deal of food on his plate while saying that it had been wonderful, refused pudding and cheese and asked, 'How's my good friend Max?'

'I think I told you. In Italy. Or Geneva.'

'A dynamic figure. A man who gets things done. I have a great respect for him. If I may say so you made an inspired choice when you took him in as a partner.'

'Not exactly a partner, a director. We're a family firm. My father founded Welton's.'

'Indeed I know that. Yours is a name we hold in the highest respect. A true independent British publishing house. That's what interests me.'

'What is, Mr Branksom?'

'Mel is what my friends call me. Or is that being too informal? I don't want to say anything that's, you know, out of line. I wish Max was here, he's got all that at his fingertips.' It occurred to Gilbert that anybody who thought Max had English manners at his fingertips must have an odd view of them, but he did not comment. 'What do you think about Africa?'

'The colour problem?'

'I mean as a market. The underdeveloped countries. But I needn't ask, it's a field you've explored already.' Gilbert still said nothing. He had no idea what Branksom was talking about. 'That series of educational textbooks you produced for Africa was really something.'

'Oh yes, I see what you mean.'

'You were one of the first in the field. A pity it was dropped, but still your name is known, you've got contacts. Now look, Gilbert, I'm a straightforward man, I like all the cards to be on the table, you know, face up. Then we know where we are, agreed?' It seemed safe to say that he agreed. 'Branksom, what do you think about when you hear the

name? Don't tell me, I know. *Love Slaves of the Camps,
How I Fooled the FBI, A Geisha Girl's Story.* That's not
all we publish, mind. But it's not good enough.' This time
it seemed safe not to say agreed. 'And I know it's not good
enough. That's a bad image, I said to the Board, and we're
going to change it.' Behind the rimless spectacles his eyes
gleamed with determination. 'We're going into the educational field, and we're going into it in a big way. That's
where you come in.'

'I see.'

'You've got a foothold in Africa. We haven't. I admit it.
I'm playing the cards face up.'

'Yes.'

'Now the lines I'm thinking on are these. You've got the
foothold, we've got the know how. You produce a line of
textbooks covering the whole educational field. We back
them. Welton name, Branksom money. And we really push
them, which, you know, I don't think you were able to do.
How does it sound?'

'Very interesting.'

'I like that.' Branksom slapped his knee and almost upset
his coffee cup. 'There's your traditional British reserve.
We've carried out market research, and believe me it's a
wide-open market. There's room for everybody.'

'I should like to think about it.'

'Just what Max said your reaction would be. Of course
we'd reckon to buy into Welton's.'

'You mean you'd want a majority shareholding?'

'Not necessarily.' He said vaguely, 'Leave it to the lawyers, all that. But this is the point. Whatever arrangement
was made wouldn't affect the books you publish. Welton's
stands for something that's entirely and absolutely British
and I hope I've shown my respect for that.' Langridge-
Wood passed their table, looked meaningfully at Branksom,
smiled. No doubt knowledge of his interest was responsible
for those cryptic phrases the other day. The American went

on expressing his admiration of tradition for another twenty minutes. When they parted his handshake had the firmness of a partner sealing a verbal agreement to a gold claim.

Gilbert walked meditatively back to the office. This was the fate of British publishing houses no doubt, to be taken over by rimless-spectacled Americans who talked about tradition but would turn the Welton list into a blend of pornography and vulgar adventure. Or was Branksom genuinely interested in the export market and the profits to be made from it? In any case, what should he do? Obviously Max was in favour of considering the idea, and what Coldharbour thought was neither here nor there. Should he sell out, take the cash in hand and waive the rest? The rest, after all, was E.R.'s creation and had never been truly his own concern.

'Got you.' Where had the words come from? He was thirty yards from the office and the pavements seemed empty. The wild thought occurred to him that messages were being sent to his brain by remote control. Then W. Jones stepped out of a doorway, grinning. 'This morning they said you were out.'

'Quite right, I was.'

'So I came back after lunch. I waited.' He had difficulty in keeping pace with Gilbert and did so by means of hurried little steps alternating with an occasional leap. 'But you were in this morning. Come on, Mr Gilbert, admit it.'

'No.'

'Never mind.' He tapped with his left hand the briefcase that swung in his right. 'This will interest you.'

They were in front of the office. Reluctantly he faced W. Jones.

'Look, Mr Jones, I'm extremely sorry we've kept your manuscript so long. You'll have a decision on it quite positively in the next week. You have a carbon copy, of course?'

'Never mind. Let me show you this. It will make your hair stand on end.'

92

'I'm sorry. We can't consider any other manuscript until we've decided on this one.' He went through the door. W. Jones was at his heels, like some two-legged terrier. 'You'll have to take that as final.'

'I'm disappointed, Mr Gilbert. I thought at least you'd look at these.' Faithful Fido rejected, W. Jones turned away, then brightened. 'I shall come every day for news of my book. Every day. Five months, you know.'

Gilbert made his way furiously into the room where Miss Pinkthorn ruled the roost.

'I've just been pestered again by that man Jones. Has his manuscript been found?' She shook her head. 'This is intolerable. It must be in the office.'

'Since I was not here I can't express an opinion.'

'There's no need to look so pleased about it.' Miss Pinkthorn looked startled by these harsh words, worthy of E.R. himself, and responded by a faint simper. 'Type out a memo to everybody saying they're to make a thorough search through the whole of their files, in every desk and cupboard and so on. They're to drop everything except the most urgent work and then report personally to me. I'll sign it at once.'

In the office he again put through the call to Yugoslavia. Max's secretary brought in the evening paper and put it on his desk. He drew the paper towards him and leafed through the pages while listening to the small explosions and fragments of switchboard conversation that seemed inseparable from an overseas call. In less than a minute the operator said, 'Your number is ringing.'

Burr burr burr. The burring stopped.

'Is that the Hotel Splendid? Do you speak English?'

A pause. A voice said carefully, 'I speak English.'

'I want to speak to Mrs Welton. She is staying in your hotel.'

Another pause. Heavy breathing. 'Do you understand?'

'I am writing down. Now I go away.'

93

He nodded and turned another page of the paper. There was something that might have caught his attention, but it had not done so and he could not be bothered to turn back and look for it. He began to read a paragraph about the American political situation. The writer seemed to think it was pretty gloomy.

'Hallo. Reception, Hotel Splendid.' This was a different voice, a woman's. Had he not been speaking to reception earlier?

'I wish to speak to my wife, Mrs Welton.'

'Veltin, Mrs Veltin?'

'Welton. W-e-l-t-o-n.'

'A moment.' He read the paragraph about America again. The voice said, 'No.'

'What's that?'

'No. Mrs Veltin. Not staying.'

'But that's impossible. She came last Thursday.' I remember the baggage, he wanted to say, it was clearly labelled. 'There must be some mistake.'

'I do not think so. A moment.'

She was replaced by a man's voice, hard and vigorous, which blasted away at him in French. He caught a phrase or two, which seemed to be to the effect that Virginia was not staying there, but most of it was unintelligible. He broke in, in English. 'I'm sorry, I haven't understood. Can you tell me in English?'

Pips sounded. The operator asked, 'Are you still connected?'

'Yes, yes, of course. In English,' he pleaded.

'Not so good.' A deprecating laugh. 'My English not so good. Name is Kornaro. Manager.'

'Mr Kornaro, listen. Is my wife staying at your hotel?'

'Yes.'

'Then can you fetch her to the telephone?'

'No. Not possible.'

94

'You mean she's out, on the beach or something.'

'I do not think so. Not on beach, I think.'

'Never mind then, if she's in the town. Ask her to ring me when she comes in. I'll give you the number.'

'Not in the town, I do not think.'

'Mr Kornaro, what are you telling me?'

'I beg your pardon.'

With what he felt to be conscious restraint he asked, 'Is my wife staying at your hotel or not?'

'She is staying.' Gilbert sighed with relief. 'But is not present now, I do not think.'

What the hell did the man mean? 'Do you mean she's left?'

Carefully explanatory, the voice said, 'She is here, but was not.'

'Don't you mean she was here but is not?' he said, with the feeling of playing an idiotic verbal game.

'I beg your pardon?'

There was a sputter of Serbo-Croat, succeeded by pips and severe crackling on the line. Then the dialling tone. He looked at the instrument in despair and returned it to the cradle. What was the piece in the paper that had not quite caught his attention, like a latch that just fails to engage? He turned back a page and then another without finding anything, then saw a heading and read the paragraph beneath it :

ACTRESS'S FLAT-MATE DIES FROM OVERDOSE

Fay Percival, well-known stage and TV actress, returned to her flat in Gayhill Gardens, Chelsea, early this morning to discover Georgie Drake, a friend sharing the flat with her, in an unconscious condition. She was suffering from barbiturate poisoning and died three hours later without recovering consciousness. Miss Drake had also appeared on TV and will be remembered as the landlady Mrs Potter in the long-running series 'Down Our Street.'

He closed his eyes. He saw not blackness but colours zigzagging across from left to right, blue, red, yellow. A voice said 'Mr Welton.'

He looked at the formidable bosom of Miss Pinkthorn. 'Are you feeling ill?'

'I'm all right. What do you want?'

'These are the memos you asked for. And here is a cable.'

From Virginia? He tore it open and read: STALKING OVER HOPE TO RIDE THAT TIGRESS TOMORROW MAX. He looked at the place of despatch. It had been sent from Zagreb in Yugoslavia. He made his decision.

'I want you to book me a flight to Dubrovnik. Tonight if there is one, if not as early as possible tomorrow.'

Raised eyebrows showed Miss Pinkthorn's disapproval. 'How long will you be away?'

'I'm not sure. Not more than two or three days. I'll arrange the return flight myself.'

'Mr Bomberg is also away. Will he be back tomorrow?'

'I'm not sure.'

'That leaves Mr Coldharbour.' She spoke with the air of one saying that left nothing at all. 'Shall I tell him?'

'I'll do it myself.' He signed the memos.

CHAPTER TWELVE

The Departure

'HELLO,' Fay Percival said. She was wearing skin-tight red pants and a man's jersey which flapped over her wrists. 'You're—'

'Gilbert Welton. I was married to Mary. Georgie.'

96

She stood staring at him, then said, 'Come in.'

He followed her into an untidy living-room where, without much surprise, he saw Bunce sitting cross-legged on the floor reading a book. He raised a hand without speaking and returned to the book. Looking at the cover Gilbert saw that it was a translation of the Koran.

Fay splashed whisky into a glass, handed it to him. 'We've been drinking. I wanted to smoke a little pot, but Jake said no. So what's on your mind, love? Why come to the wake?'

'I saw her on Thursday night.' Fay stared at him. 'We were talking at my house until, I don't know, after eleven. I think perhaps she rang me during the night.'

'Maybe she did. What about it?'

'I just wondered—' He could not have said what he wondered. 'Was she trying to get in touch with me?'

'Not that I know of.'

'Did she leave anything, any message?'

Fay plucked at the folds of the pullover. Her face was angry. 'No note, nothing. She'd been drinking ever since— for days.' Had she been about to say, since Thursday night? 'Yesterday the doctor says she drank herself silly, then took the pills. The phone was off the hook. Poor fat cow.' She poured more whisky into her own glass. 'It was about seven this morning when I found her. This stuff does nothing for me, you know that?'

Bunce closed the Koran. The lock of hair hung down. He looked serious and youthful. 'Interesting book. We ought to find an Arab priest.'

'Georgie had this idea she wanted to become a Muslim,' Fay said. 'It was a lot of crap.'

'You can't say that, Fay, how do you know? It might have changed her life.' Bunce was at his quietest and most reasonable.

'Darling, she'd been with me a long time. She's been a scientologist, a priestess of a lot called Heaven on Earth and a member of something called the Order of St Bridget where they all used to beat each other with wet towels.'

'Nevertheless,' Bunce said mildly.

'Darling, you know *nothing* about it. She was a poor fat cow, that's all. And she's dead.' Fay burst into tears and ran from the room.

'Guilt,' Bunce said. 'We were at a party. Supposing we'd been here and all that.'

'And supposing I'd answered the telephone that night.'

'It was Thursday, you said? If she'd wanted, she could have rung you on Friday. Or at the week-end. If she'd wanted to.'

'I suppose so.' But he did not suppose so at all. Remembering that question, *did it all mean nothing?*, he could not doubt that she was asking for his help. From the New Life you could take steps in a dozen different directions, but all of them led downwards as you looked for instant ecstasy through loving your own sex or moving into a non-corporeal world or being beaten with wet towels. And the end of it was that you were laid out flat, hands folded, the whole thing was over and it had meant nothing. He was led to say, 'She wasn't a believer, you know. She expected heaven here, not somewhere else. It would be absurd to look for that Arab priest.'

'If you say so, Gil.' Bunce stretched out his hand towards the Koran.

'She's not here?'

'Gil, get a hold on yourself. They took her away to the hospital and then the morgue.'

'I see.'

'And I wouldn't go around talking about seeing her that night and her calling you. It can't have anything to do with anything, but once the cops get to asking questions.' Bunce, a youthful father-confessor, shook a sage head. Fay appeared in the doorway. 'She has to hold the shitty end of the stick, the inquest and all that. You don't.'

The picture of Mary blended with that of Virginia. Wave-washed, the face bloated, body rolled up on foreign shingle. Had Mary looked peaceful, or had the pills blown up and distorted her features? Had she gone willingly or was there a moment when she wanted desperately to be saved? He longed to be away from the untidy room that somehow reeked of Mary, from the red-eyed actress in her floppy pullover and solemn pragmatical Bunce. Feeble rational good manners took over.

'If you're sure there's nothing I can do—'

Fay's laughter was raucous. 'Do, what did you ever do? You should hear the things Georgie told me. We had some good laughs. What kind of man is he, I'd say? And she'd answer, I only wish I knew. Poor bloody Georgie.'

'I came in because I have to go away. To join my wife. She's on holiday in Yugoslavia.'

'Virginia is certainly a lovely woman,' Bunce said.

With conscious pomposity he addressed a vacant space between them. 'I don't think there's any point in delaying my flight.'

'No point!' A great deal of laughter came out of Fay's small body. 'Darling, whatever you do there's no point.'

'Shut it, Fay.' New-style father figure Bunce did not speak unkindly. His unmade features had coalesced into a portrait of the Serious Young American, the one who understands that other people in the world have troubles and wants to help out. 'You can't do any good here, Gil. Forget you ever saw her that night, it didn't mean anything. And say hallo to your wife for me.' The Serious Young American shook hands, English-style. Fay gave him a bark of despairing laughter.

Forget you ever saw her that night : excellent advice, but how could he follow it? Hate, love, anger, ecstasy, are regarded as irrational states of feeling, but there is nothing more rational about remorse. On the way back to the office,

99

to which he returned because of a compulsive need to clear
his desk, he recalled in detail Mary's visit to the house. It
was he who had taken her there quite deliberately, had
exposed her to the sight of the apparently settled life he
had made with another woman. That now seemed terrible.
Perhaps the hour in his house had, on top of everything
else, finally broken the small grip she still kept on life. Perhaps if he had gone to bed with her (but that would have
been useless), if he had let her stay in the house, she would
not have taken the pills. What had she said at the end?
You've said sorry too often, and then *Goodbye, Gilbert.*
Those last two words seemed now intensely meaningful, yet
they had meant nothing at the time.

When he got out of the taxi it was raining. It was nearly
six o'clock and his footsteps rang in the hall with the dead
sound particular to empty offices. He went upstairs, switched
on the light in his office, which already had the musty smell
of evening. On his desk was the ticket for his flight at eight
o'clock on the following morning and a memo from Miss
Pinkthorn, with the points neatly tabulated :

(i) Here is ticket.

(ii) You have no hotel booking. Will you please in-
form me of whereabouts, so that you can be reached if
urgent.

(iii) Hope you have a good trip.

At the bottom was her clerically neat signature and a p.s.
Here is my home number in case you want it. It occurred to
him again that he knew nothing about Miss Pinkthorn. He
could not believe that she existed as a person outside the
office, living with the widowed sister. Or was she alone in
a bedsitter, cooking supper each evening and then sitting
in the room's single easy chair to watch life on the tele-
vision screen? How much had E.R. known about Miss
Pinkthorn, would he have known her telephone number?

In a calligraphy as neat as her own he wrote a reply saying that he would be at the Hotel Splendid, Dubrovnik, but that he expected to be back within forty-eight hours. He added details about two or three letters to be written, and then paused. It seemed that he should leave a message addressed to the unknown Miss Pinkthorn, but he found nothing to say.

He telephoned Coldharbour, but got no reply. No doubt he was gallivanting with Stanley. This meant another note, which he left on Coldharbour's desk. Then there was nothing to do but go home and pack.

Entering the empty house, choosing clothes with care and packing them neatly into the travelling wardrobe, he was aware of loneliness. It came on him as a physical sensation, an aching in the stomach, as influenza may be preceded by a tickling in the throat and slight pains in the limbs which are warnings of the fever to come. The ache was associated with Mary, but it was much more deeply linked with the idea that he had lost Virginia and would never see her again. As he thought about her words and actions they seemed explicable only upon the basis that she had gone to meet a lover, but this disturbed him less than his inability to summon up the physical details of her appearance. Quite simply, he could not remember what she looked like.

He rummaged in a cupboard and found some photographs, one taken on holiday when she had her head thrown back laughing, another in a group at a publisher's cocktail party, but they were no help in explaining the discoloured arm that had so much disturbed him, the cold cheek he had kissed at parting. Among the pile of photographs he came upon one of Mary in the bookshop days, hands on hips, broadly smiling. Then there was another picture of her looking down with no particular pleasure at Matthew, a small bundle in her arms.

He had not written to Matthew. Drawing a sheet of

paper out of the pigeon-hole in his desk he sat down to do so, and was conscious of overwhelming distaste and weariness. 'Dear Matthew,' he wrote, and stopped. What did you say? 'Your mother, whom you never much cared about, is dead, and your stepmother has disappeared?' Was it true that Matthew had never cared much about Mary and that she really hadn't wanted him? In Gilbert's recollection the stolid young man had been originally a stolid baby and then a stolid child, eating greedily everything put before him, crying rarely under the stresses of the New Life and Starting Again, accepting separation from his mother without many questions, asking about her only occasionally and showing affection for Virginia. Yet could all that really be true, and was it true that the only too vulnerable Mary had not cared about her son? He crumpled up the sheet of paper, threw it away, telephoned the club and found that they had a room free for the night. Before leaving the house he ran his hands over the sofa, then looked at the fingertips. It seemed to him that they tingled with some vibration from Mary's body.

He wrote ten lines to Matthew on the club paper, telling him about Mary, ordered an early morning call, played a game of snooker and then went to bed. He slept uneasily. At seven-fifteen in the morning he was at London Airport and at eight o'clock precisely the plane rose into the air.

PART II

Wife Lost

CHAPTER ONE

Dubrovnik

THE PLANE was no more than half full. Gilbert sat on the aisle. Beyond the empty seat next to him a thin faced beaky nosed man smiled encouragingly. He did not answer the smile but looked away over the aisle where a turbaned Sikh stared straight in front of him. A feeling that something terrible was waiting at the end of this journey oppressed him, like potential sickness. He considered the idea of going to the lavatory and rejected it.

'I am engaged on a quest as endless as that for the Holy Grail,' he said. 'If Virginia is in Dubrovnik she may not be pleased to see me and my journey will have been useless. It will be equally useless if she is deceiving me. I shall either learn nothing or I shall find out something I do not want to know.' As he spoke these words aloud one of the stewardesses passed by and flashed a smile at him, yet it did not seem that she heard him. Was something wrong with his vocal cords? He coughed experimentally, and was alarmed to hear no sound. Listening for the airplane engines he was met by blank silence. His hearing must have been affected by the height at which they were flying, even though the cabin was pressurised.

The Sikh across the aisle slowly turned his head and smiled, offering a gaping red mouth, then spoke. The words were not audible. He leaned across interrogatively and the

Sikh bent over too so that their faces were almost touching. Two words came from the smiling lips : 'Only connect.'

Staring astonished at the face that grinned into his own he was aware of the body of the stewardess, navy blue thighs pressed against his leaning head, hand holding out a piece of paper. The Sikh jerked his own head back, returned to his eyes front position, and now it was the stewardess who bent over him and whose mouth opened to show pink gum, white teeth. She was saying, what was it she was saying? He strove to understand the ribbons of words in her mouth but then she closed it with a snap and her fingers significantly touched his palm as she pressed into it the piece of paper she held. It was a cable and as he read the words SCREWING YOUR WIFE HERE WHAT A TIGRESS his throat protested, choking him as he tried to speak, to protest to the stewardess who said nothing but put her hand on his shoulder. Is it from Dubrovnik? was what he wanted to say, but the pressure of her hand distracted him. Why was he unable to speak?

'All right, old boy?' It was the beaky nosed man. He removed his hand from Gilbert's shoulder.

'Thank you.' He sat up. He had fallen over sideways and had a crick in his neck.

'Feeling a bit Harry groggers? You sounded desperate. Funny noises.' He put his head to one side and made gurgling sounds.

'I apologize.'

'Not to worry. Name's Painter, Jerry Painter. Not that I paint jerries, mind you.'

'Gilbert Welton.'

'Business or pleasure bound?'

'A little of both, I suppose.'

'Business for me.' He whipped out a card and handed it over. Gilbert read : *G. R. Painter, Topline Car Hire.* 'Started up a few months ago out there and something's rotten in the state of Denmark. Touch of the old Slav temperament I expect. Painter the troubleshooter, here I come. Sure you're all right?'

'Thank you.'

'Just have a zizz myself.' He nodded, closed his eyes. Within five minutes his mouth was slightly open, he looked like a dead man. On the other side of the gangway the Sikh stared expressionlessly ahead of him.

Heat shimmered on the tarmac as he walked across it with Painter. Gilbert's ears were tuned, as always at airports and railway stations, to catch a message for him on the Tannoy, a message that never came.

'Where are you staying, old boy?'

'The Splendid.'

'I'm at the Imperial. What about painting the old place a bit red tonight?' He laughed heartily. 'Joke. But I hear they've got a casino.'

'I'm afraid I can't manage that. I'm meeting my wife.'

'Oh well. Here's my bus and there's yours. See you around.'

He got into the bus labelled *Hotel Splendid*. As they moved out of the forecourt and jolted along the road to the city his journey seemed totally absurd. Two clear, different but equally embarrassing pictures came into his mind. In the first he went up to Virginia's room, entered and found her tussling on the bed with a man. In the second she lay on the beach wearing dark glasses which she slowly removed. The most disturbing thing about these encounters was that when she stared at him from the bed or took off the dark glasses she showed no sign of recognition.

As they rounded a bend he had a glimpse of the walled city, looking like a bit of a film set. The Splendid Hotel, however, proved to be a few hundred yards short of the old city, a modern slab overlooking the sea. His bus companions murmured their approval as they drove into the entrance.

The place had the reassuring anonymity of an international hotel. There was nothing too offensively Yugoslav about it.

In the foyer he was plunged at once into a tourist holiday world. Men and women wearing briefs and bikinis, sometimes covered by gay dressing-gowns, came up the steps from the beach, stalking over to the lift. All German or English, bronzed and with an air of suppressed energy, they seemed of a different species from the pallid bus passengers, who looked at them enviously. A travel courier, a bronzed girl with long dark hair and some organizational badge pinned on her, marshalled them over to the reception desk behind which two girls allotted rooms, handing out keys as though they were performing a conjuring trick. When his time came a small dark girl said, 'Your passport, please.'

'I don't have a reservation. My name is Welton. My wife is staying here.'

'Please, your passport.'

'If you can just tell me the number of her room.'

'Your passport.'

Furiously he slapped his passport on the counter. A disapproving murmur rose from those behind him at this display of petulance. The girl took it and pushed a pad towards him. 'You will please to complete this.'

'No no.' He shoved back the pad. 'Look, let me speak to Mr Kornaro. We've talked already on the telephone.'

'Telephone.' She pointed across the hall. He snatched back the passport, relinquished his place in the queue and followed the direction of her finger to find that she had directed him to a telephone kiosk. With an awareness of his own inanity he entered the box and ruffled the pages of the directory it contained, then came out and stood on the steps, looking down at the small iron tables where groups of men and women sat in the sun. He did not see Virginia. He returned to the desk when the last of the party had gone. The girl said, 'Your passport, please.'

'All I want is the number of Mrs Welton's room.'

'You do not have a reservation, then I must have your passport.'

Playing the next move in this repeated gambit, but omitting mention of the telephone, he said 'I want to speak to Mr Kornaro.'

'Mr Kornaro.' She appeared to be assessing his qualifications for an interview, then lifted the flap of the reception counter and emerged from behind it. 'Come.'

He followed her down a corridor. She knocked on a door filled with frosted glass and went in. Then she came out and opened the door. As Gilbert passed her she gave him a hostile look.

Mr Kornaro shook hands warmly. His smile showed three gold teeth. 'I understand you have a complaint about our hotel. I am sorry.'

'No, no, I have no complaint.'

'I am glad.' His smile broadened. 'This is the finest hotel in Yugoslavia.'

'Mr Kornaro, I don't think the receptionist understood—'

'A very fine lady, very efficient. Is that word correct?'

'Quite correct. We talked on the telephone. I rang you up from London.'

Mr Kornaro, one admonitory finger lifted, walked round to a cupboard behind his desk. A key from the bunch at his waist opened it and he produced a bottle of colourless liquid and two glasses which he carefully filled to the brim. He handed over one of these glasses with an inclination of the head that was almost a bow. Gilbert recognized the faint oiliness of slivovitz.

'Cheers. Down the hatch.' He drank half the glassful in one swallow. Gilbert sipped and felt the liquid run over his tongue and burn his gullet. 'You like our beautiful city of Dubrovnik,' the manager stated rather than asked. 'It is the most beautiful city in Yugoslavia.'

'Mr Kornaro.' He spoke desperately and with unusual

107

speed. 'I'm pleased to be here, but I want to talk to my wife. Mrs Welton, Virginia Welton. She's staying in this hotel. I talked to you about it yesterday. That's all I want, I have no complaints of any kind. I'm sure the Hotel Splendid is—splendid,' he finished feebly.

'Ah *ha*.' Mr Kornaro threw back his head and laughed. 'You make a joke. Very good.'

'What's that?'

'The Hotel Splendid is—splendid. Very good, I shall not forget.' He drank the rest of his slivovitz, poured a refill. 'And we spoke before, I remember it well.' He patted the telephone on his desk affectionately, it might have been an old friend. 'Mrs Welton, your wife, she was a very beautiful woman.'

'If you'll just give me her room number.' He stopped. Mr Kornaro was shaking his head. 'What's wrong?'

'I have told you on the telephone. She was not here.'

'What do you mean?'

'She has no complaints. But she is left.'

'That's impossible.' He knew that it was not at all impossible.

'She stays here three days. Then she goes. But not with complaints. I think she is not knowing that you come here, wasn't it so? So perhaps she is sad.'

'She didn't know, that's right. My plans were changed. What forwarding address did she leave?'

'I am sorry, English is not good.' Was there something inimical about the manager's stare?

'Where did she go to?'

'Ah yes. I think she is going to Mostar. A beautiful city, very Turkish. Perhaps then on to Sarajevo.'

The change in Gilbert Welton could have been timed from this moment. As he continued to ask Kornaro questions, about the best way of reaching Mostar and the hotels Virginia might have stayed at there, about the precise details of her departure (but he learned nothing more except

that on Saturday she had said that she was tired of staying
in one place, she was going to wander around), he was conscious that he had acquired the kind of knowledge that
brings with it freedom. He knew now that Virginia had
left him. She had gone to meet somebody in Mostar,
in Sarajevo, what did it matter? She was lost to him, and
he was able to accept the fact of loss. He remembered lines
from a poem read long ago :

> For he is no Orpheus,
> She no Eurydice.
> She has truly packed and gone
> To live with someone
> Else, in pleasures of the sun,
> Far from his kingdoms of despair
> Here, there, or anywhere.

But the emotion he felt in a strange city, a new country, was
not despair but relief.

'Today you look at our beautiful city of Dubrovnik,'
Kornaro said masterfully. 'Tomorrow you take the bus at
eleven hundred hours, arrive Mostar fifteen thirty hours,
find your wife, very good.' Gilbert agreed, although he was
not sure that he would go to Mostar. *He is no Orpheus, she
no Eurydice.* He lacked the will for pursuit of her into
those underground regions of the heart. He went up to the
small neat room provided for him, which had a balcony
overlooking the sea, unpacked his travelling wardrobe, lay
down on the bed and fell asleep. He woke an hour later re-
freshed, changed into sleeveless shirt and thin trousers and
went to look at Mr Kornaro's beautiful city of Dubrovnik.

It was in fact a beautiful place. He walked through the
Ploce gate into the carless city and was aware at once of
the friendly buzzing sound which comes from a group of
human beings together, when it is not overlaid by the noise
of vehicles. The prevailing colour was grey, everything was

or looked old. He stood outside a café staring down the long central Placa filled with human beings and empty of traffic, then walked slowly down the street looking into the shop windows that seemed to be selling almost exactly the same hats, scarves and blouses, silverware, wooden trays and salad bowls. The sun was hot on his head and seemed to be burning his eyes. He entered a building on his right to get away from the glare and found himself in a cloister. In the middle of it was a small garden with a fountain playing. The coupled columns were surmounted with stone heads and curious animal figures.

When he married Virginia they had taken a car across the Channel and spent their honeymoon touring Brittany. Somewhere, in a small town the name of which he could not remember, they had walked hand in hand down a street like the Placa and entered a small cloister garden like this one, with a central fountain. Thinking themselves alone they had embraced and kissed passionately, to see a moment later that they were being watched by a withered old woman who carried a basket of flowers. As he thought of this there was a movement at the end of the cloister. Two monks in brown habits appeared and walked slowly past him. '*Dobro veche*,' they said, and bared their heads. It occurred to him that he was able to think about this memory without emotion. A small but vital operation had been performed, the surgeon's scissors had said *snip* and removed suffering.

On the hotel terrace the pallid passengers had gathered round the travel girl, who flashed leaflets at them. Phrases came over to the table where he sat with eyes half closed looking out across the sea. 'Half day on Lokrum . . . caves of Kotor . . . lobster for lunch . . .' There were murmurs of delighted laughter.

'Will you come with us, Lucy?' one of the men asked.

'Of course. I am here to show you the ropes.'

'I'd love to see them. If my wife weren't here, that is. How about it, Helen, is it all right for Lucy to show me the ropes?' Loud laughter. This was what they had paid for, the holiday spirit. He closed his eyes completely. His body seemed light, even empty. Perhaps this was the way women felt after having a baby.

There was the sound of chairs scraping back. Feet moved past him. A voice said 'Hallo.'

He opened his eyes. The courier was standing beside his chair. The badge on her shirt said *Paradise Travel*. 'Hope I didn't wake you up.' He shook his head. 'You were on the bus. Are you with Paradise? No, well, I thought you might be. Some people don't like to crowd round. You're independent?'

The phrase amused him. 'Yes.'

'You looked a bit out of things. But perhaps you don't like being organized.'

Something decisive about the way she spoke appealed to him. 'Why don't you sit down? Have a drink.'

She considered the idea, and ordered Cinzano and soda. 'It's the Yugo substitute really, but drinkable.'

She was dark with lots of long hair, and what he could see of her body was completely brown. It was almost too much of an effort to speak to her, but he managed it. 'Lucy, that's a very English name, you don't look English.'

'Basically I'm Israeli. No, that's wrong, basically I'm Australian but I was born in Israel, lived there till I was sixteen.'

'Not now?' He heard his distant voice asking, although he did not care about the answer.

'I got away. I'll never go back.' Something about the tone startled him. He looked at her. In the gaze of her blue eyes staring at him from under thick brows there seemed to be a sexual invitation. He asked whether she lived in England.

'Sometimes. I'm going to change and swim. Coming?'

She cut the water with firm attacking strokes, so that he had a job to keep up with her. Later they lay side by side on the concrete stage belonging to the hotel that pushed out into the water.

'You don't look as if you're here on holiday.'

Should he say *I came to look for my wife but have given up the search*? 'I'm a publisher.'

'Yes?'

'I came out to look for a colleague.' The effort of constructing a reasonable story defeated him.

'I don't care, you know. There's no need to tell me lies.'

'I'm not.' He raised himself on one arm to deny it. Her navel winked at him. 'You might say I'm at a loose end. It's hard to explain.'

'Then don't.' Her eyes were remarkably fine, a piercing blue. 'You're going to burn. I'll oil you. Turn over.'

As her hands moved on his back and shoulders, then along his legs, he felt the stirring of desire. With the decisiveness that marked her most trivial actions she put back the top on the bottle. 'My father looked like you. That withdrawn look. It says don't come too near. Is that what you're like?'

'I suppose it is, in a way. Do you think it's a bad way to be?'

'I think perhaps I do. He's dead, my father. Five years ago.'

'I'm sorry.'

'Why be sorry, why should you care? Though he was a good man in lots of ways. A super person, they said at my English school.'

'You went to school in England?'

'For a bit. When I said I wouldn't stay in the kibbutz. All the girls said *super* and *I fancy him*.' She looked at him fiercely. 'I expect they do still.'

'It can't be that long ago.'

'Five years. I'm twenty-two.' A voice said 'Lucy.' She got up. 'Do you think I'm father-fixated?'

'I shouldn't think it likely.'

'Because I fancy you, you know that don't you?'

'Lucy.' A large bouncing girl stood beside them. She wore an incongruous pinafore dress with a badge that said *Irma, Goethe Travel*. Her blonde hair burst out from a yachting cap. 'Lucy, it is about the trip to Lokrum. Some people who want tickets, they say you promised. Hallo,' she said to Gilbert who scrambled up.

'My name's Gilbert Welton.'

'English manners, I love them. We shake hands, isn't that right?' They shook hands.

He felt that he should say something to Lucy, but she waved an arm, said that she would see him around and was gone. He watched the two girls going along the concrete and up the steps, then sank back on to his cushions and closed his eyes. Lucy, fierce-eyed and dramatic, and surely a little ridiculous, appeared behind the lids.

He saw her again that evening after dinner. She stopped beside his table. She wore a dark blue sleeveless linen dress which accentuated the darkness of her skin. The fat man who had talked about being shown the ropes was by her side. 'There is a little party going to the casino this evening. If you'd like to come along you will be welcome.'

'Thanks. I'll think about it.'

The fat man said, 'Don't worry about losing, Lucy's coming as our mascot. Can't lose with her.'

'I don't give any guarantee. You might lose the shirt off your back.' Her tone was almost coquettish. 'We meet at eight-thirty, in the entrance hall.'

What am I doing here, he asked himself, what am I thinking of? He felt nothing more in relation to Lucy than the mild sexual interest natural for a man in his forties who has received instead of making advances, or so he told himself, but at eight-thirty he was in the entrance hall.

He was not attracted by the idea of winning a quantity of dinars which, as notices made clear to him and as Lucy emphasized, could not be taken out of the country, but in any case he lost small sums steadily. When he was a couple of pounds down he stopped playing and watched the others. The fat man, whose name was Briars, reacted to every drop of the ball with shrieks of laughter in which his wife joined him. It was as though they were applause machines at a TV comedy show.

'There's ten dinars down the drain,' Briars roared. 'Ten smackers right down the plughole.'

'No dear, I'm *winning*,' his wife said. 'Three times now I've won on red, what do you think this time.'

'You've been winning on red, I've been losing on black,' Mr Briars cried in an ecstasy of mirth.

Nails dug into the palm of his hand. Lucy said, 'Not having fun?'

'I shouldn't call it exactly gay.' He indicated a particularly grim-looking croupier who was pushing chips towards one of their party. 'He might smile.'

'It is against their principles, you see. They think gambling is wrong, but they want dollars and pounds and German marks, so they allow it. But it all has to be respectable and dull, don't expect them to smile.' Her forefinger explored his palm, curled round his own index finger, moved gently up and down, was withdrawn. She moved away.

'How's it going, old man?' He turned to confront Painter. 'Made your fortune yet? You don't have to tell me, nobody ever made a fortune here. Where's the better half?'

'My wife is not here.'

'On your Franchot Tone? I tell you what, young Milo in my office here told me of a little place in the Old Town where you can see a bit of life. What do you say?' About Painter's confiding beaky look there was something manic.

'I've had me chips.' Briars had two chips left, one red

and one white. He stuck them over his eyes and whined, 'Can anyone spare a dinar for a poor blind man?' Heads were turned, a group of muscle-bound Germans spoke to each other and laughed. They're saying it's the English, Gilbert thought, not the mad but the poverty-stricken English who don't know how to lose a few dinars.

Briars dropped the chips out of his eyes, caught them neatly. 'Let's get away before they take me shirt. Lucy, I thought you were going to be our mascot, I thought you never lost.'

Lucy's smile was slightly foxy, it made her look wary and showed her small even teeth. 'I never lose because I don't bet.'

General laughter. 'Got you there, Tom,' said Mrs Briars.

'There's a café by the water where you can get slivovitz. Or a cup of tea,' Lucy announced. A chorus of joyful yelps greeted these last words.

'How about it?' Painter asked. 'Might have some fun, bring on the dancing girls kind of thing.'

'No, thanks. I'm really with the hotel party.'

'I expect you're right.' He sank from manic to depressive in a moment. 'Bound to be a washout here, girls dancing in a blanket. Dead and alive hole.' As Gilbert moved away he called, 'Give my regards to the trouble and strife.'

Tea at the café was approved, it was agreed that Lucy knew her way around. Gilbert found himself next to Briars.

'Very very nice little kid. No flies on her, either. Man in one of those shops in the what d'ye call it, main street, tried to overcharge the wife, she was on to it, you should have heard her. Of course she's clever. Father's a diplomat.'

'Really?'

'She told Mrs Craxton. Somewhere out in the Far East. Hong Kong is it? You can see she's got class.'

Had she got class? Watching her talking easily to the party of a dozen men and women, keeping them amused, responding with apparent pleasure to the idiotic jokes of the men and listening patiently to the women as they talked about their homes in Woking or Bromley, he wondered if that was the right word and decided that it was not. She had a feral quality, there was something uncontrolled about her, she gave the impression of playing a part. In the café he was content to sit and let the waves of conversation roll over him. His body felt anaesthetized so that a pin stuck in it would have remained unperceived, and as they left the café in a noisy group and went on making their ugly English noise as they walked through the quiet town, he seemed to be removed from any conscious sensation. On the way back Lucy did not acknowledge his individual presence in any way. In the entrance hall they parted, with assurances that it had been a good day.

'So tomorrow is this place called Kotor, is that right?' asked anxious Mrs Strong, or perhaps it was Long, because confusingly there was one of each in the party.

'No. Tomorrow is Lokrum, an afternoon trip.'

'But what shall we do in the morning?' Mrs Strong/Long asked. 'I mean, there's not much to *do*, is there? Will you be here?'

He left half a dozen of them talking in the hall, with Lucy in the middle of them. In his room he put away his clothes tidily as usual, got into bed and fell asleep at once. The sleep must have been light, for it was only twenty minutes later that he was wakened by a gentle tapping.

He opened the door which he had locked. She moved quickly inside and stood with her back against the wall, looking at him. The room was still in darkness and he could not see the expression on her face as she said 'You certainly took your time.'

'I'm sorry, I didn't realize.' He abandoned that sentence. 'I fell asleep.'

She began to laugh.

CHAPTER TWO

The Second Day of Love

Is THERE a technique of seduction? Books have been written about it, but it often seems that they are evasions rather than discussions of reality. Many couples have the *Kama Sutra* on their shelves, but how many practise the activities described in it? Few significant variations of the sex act are possible, the refinements are elaborations of a central theme. This at least would have been his view if he had been compelled to formulate it. Certainly he performed no physical act with Lucy that he had not undertaken at some time with Mary or Virginia. Yet the sensations he felt were unlike anything he could remember.

It was four-thirty when she said, 'I must go.'

In the dawn light he looked at the dark hair hiding her face, pushed it aside. 'Love,' he said, and repeated the word questioningly. 'Love?'

'I've got to go.'

'We must talk.'

'What about?'

'We haven't talked.' This was not literally true, but their conversation like that of most people making love had been partly specific, about what they were doing, and partly inane.

She ran her hand over his body, then touched his face, fingers wandering about nose and eye sockets. 'I don't know what it is about you, some bloody thing. I think it must be that you're like my father, don't you?'

'We ought to talk about things. I've got a wife, I told you that. I don't know anything about you.'

'I've got all the right things in the right places. What else do you want to know?'

'Everything. I want to know everything about you.'

'I think—'

'What?'

'Nothing.' She rolled over on top of him, found his mouth, bit his lip. 'Christ, I do fancy you. I'd better get out of here.' She dressed nervously, almost angrily, while he lay in bed and watched. 'I look a wreck.'

He got out of bed and moved towards her. She averted her face.

'I never kiss goodbye. Bad luck.'

'When am I going to see you?'

'I'll be busy most of the morning. You saw what it's like. Half past eleven or as near as I can make it. On the terrace.'

After she had gone he opened the french windows and stood on the balcony, looking at the city in the pearly light of early morning. It was already warm, but when he got back into bed he was shivering. The shivers were pleasurable, they ran through his body as though created by fingers. His lips felt twice as thick as usual, the soft tissue inside them was swollen when he ran his tongue over it. His body felt as though it had been bruised by hers. Was he deceiving himself in thinking that his feelings had little to do with sex, when they were so firmly grounded on it? He embraced this contradiction, although he had no idea of how it would be possible to phrase what he wanted to say. 'What begins as sex ends as love'—something like that? The feeling of well-being he had, as though his body had been simultaneously drained and satisfied, was no doubt sexual in origin . . .

It was nine-thirty when he woke again.

Conflation of red and green umbrellas, blue sea, brown or white bodies, grey of city walls. A mess of colours. Conflation also of shapes, forked people, circular tables, wedge shaped concrete nose pushing into the sea. A mess of shapes. Colours and shapes merging into one. Down the steps strode Mr Kornaro, incongruous in black jacket and striped trousers, the Yugoslav manager's wear.

'Telephone. For you.'

How long ago it was that he had sat in Mr Kornaro's office. He looked at the receiver standing on the table with disquiet. What did its blackness contain?

'Mr Welton. I thought you should know that—'

'Who is that?' The voice was completely strange.

Silence, then outraged tones. 'This is Miss Pinkthorn. Mr Welton, is that you?'

No one of that name or character known here, disappeared I'm afraid, Mr Welton has disintegrated, the phrases went through his mind but were not on his tongue. 'Hallo, Miss Pinkthorn. I didn't recognize your voice.'

'Are you enjoying yourself? Did you find Mrs Welton quite well?'

Both questions were unanswerable in Pinkthorn terms. A simple affirmative seemed proper and he gave it.

'I thought you should know that we've had another cable from Mr Bomberg. He is at the Hotel Europa, in Sarajevo. He wants to get in touch with you. I haven't given him your address, because I didn't know if you'd still be there.'

'Yes.'

'What shall I do then? Shall I give him your number, or will you telephone him?'

'Yes.' The affirmative repeated.

'Mr Welton? Mr Welton, what would you like me to do?'

He ran his tongue round swollen tissue. 'You can leave it to me.'

'You'll get in touch yourself?' He did not reply. 'Are you there?'

'Certainly, yes.' *And how is every little thing in your life,*

Miss Pinkthorn? 'And how is everything, Miss Pinkthorn?'

'Mr Welton, can you hear me properly?'

'I have to go now. Wanted here. Urgently. Keep in touch.' He put back the receiver. How easy it is to cut yourself off from the boring and disagreeable, how easy after all to make a new start. He laughed at the thought. Mr Kornaro laughed with him. The slivovitz bottle was produced. There was a little joke about the Hotel Splendid being splendid, an inquiry about his wife. He said that he would stay another day, perhaps two.

She was sitting on the terrace drinking Cinzano and soda, with an open folder in front of her. She put away the folder.

'I'd forgotten what you looked like. Your eyes. I've never seen eyes so blue.' She did not acknowledge the remark. 'There are lots of things I wanted to say. For me this kind of thing is not—not casual.'

'I don't know what you mean. Nothing is casual.' She took a sip of her drink. 'You want to know about me.' He had meant to talk about himself, but he listened. 'My father was a Jew, did you know that? I told you I was brought up on a kibbutz.'

'Yes, you said that. It must have been interesting.'

'Awful. I ran away when I was fourteen. They found me and brought me back. When I was sixteen I ran away again. For good.'

'To school in England?'

She took out a packet of cigarettes, lighted one, talked between puffs. 'The kibbutz, do you know what it does to you? You aren't a person any more, you do what everybody else does, you're part of the group. The collective ego, they call it. You want to break something, you don't do it because it's anti-social. You want to make love, you don't do that, because that might be anti-social too, it would disturb the group. Love, it just doesn't exist, it isn't there. Do you know what I wanted more than anything else when I was eight? For my mother to tuck me up in bed at night. In my kibbutz it wasn't allowed, mothers weren't allowed to be possessive.'

He remembered Mary's indifference to Matthew. 'Sometimes mothers don't want to have much to do with their children.'

'All right. But in the kibbutz it wasn't *allowed*. It broke my mother's heart, she died when I was eleven. He was a bastard.'

'Who?'

'My father.'

'Somebody told me he was a diplomat.'

'Yes. He gave it up, joined the kibbutz.'

'What sort of diplomat?'

'Consul. In Hong Kong.'

'And you said he was a super person.' He found *super* a difficult word to say.

'I said he was a good man. He just had this thing about permissiveness, the kibbutz way of life and all that. I'll never be part of any group, I'm a separate person.'

'You're unique.' Idiotic, idiotic.

'But are you separate too?' She did not wait for him to reply. 'Are you coming to Lokrum after lunch? Over there.'

She pointed to an island covered by pines that spread over it like a green helmet. He wanted to ask if it would be possible for them to be alone there, but did not do so when she added that of course it would be with the hotel party. He said that he would go. Simply to be near her, to watch her, would be a pleasure.

'Super.' She opened the folder, made a note.

'Lucy.' He wanted to say that their talk had been inadequate. Instead he asked, 'What's your other name?'

'Spandrell. That's what I call myself here. I took it out of a book. By Aldous Huxley.'

'Lucy too?'

'Yes, she's in the book too.'

'But why? What's your real name?'

'Too hard to pronounce. You can call it Anna.'

'After Karenina?'

She laughed. 'As a matter of fact, yes. I've got to go. See you.'

On the short boat journey he sat next to the brawny Irma, nowhere near Lucy whom he now thought of as Anna, and as soon as they stepped ashore she was surrounded by the hotel party, talking, making crude jokes. Accompanied by hairy-legged Englishmen wearing shorts that came down to their knees, and trailed by their wives, she set off up a path through the pine woods without so much as a glance at him. He stood sulkily waiting for her to turn and suggest that he should join them, but she did not look back. Instead Irma pounced on him.

'Mr Welton, you will come along with me.'

'I was with the other party.'

'I am going to better places. And I have not so many.'

Unwillingly he joined her cortège, which was German instead of English. All the men carried cameras, the formidable thighs of the women strained their tight shorts, their brawny shoulders reddened like meat in the sun. She strode along, arms swinging like a sergeant-major's, talking all the time in German. He left them and went down a path on his own.

For the next three hours he wandered through pine woods, scrambled down from one of them into a small bay in which he swam, and then lay on his back in the sun thinking about Anna. Had she been telling him the truth about the kibbutz, was her father ever consul in Hong Kong, what was she really like? One part of his mind fastened on these questions while another was aware of their irrelevance to his feelings. Most of us under the stress of passion are capable of believing two different things at the same time. So Gilbert was now able to build an image of Anna which ignored oddities of speech and behaviour.

On the beach at Lokrum he constructed a relationship between them which involved Starting Again. The idea was not only possible but easy. By selling out to the American he would have enough money to live on for at least ten years. They would settle in a small English country town, he would open an antique shop, selling only things that he enjoyed seeing and touching. In time he would become in his own small way celebrated, people would say, 'You can be sure that anything you buy from Gilbert Welton will be marked by his own impeccable taste.' Anna would go on fancying him. A satisfied vanity took possession of him as he dwelt on the fact that at the time he married Mary, Anna could not have been born. To have slept with her was a kind of triumph, although their sexual contact was only the beginning of the unsuspected tenderness that he felt opening out in him.

When he returned to the landing stage she was the first person he saw. 'Where the hell have you been all this time, where have you *been*?'

'Sunbathing. Swimming. On my own.'

'You knew I couldn't come with you. Don't tell me you thought we could go off on our own. I'm conducting tours to Paradise, remember?'

He smiled and said that he knew it. On the way back in the boat he sat next to Craxton, a puffy man whose forehead and legs were turning beetroot colour. 'You missed a most interesting tour, very instructive. This island, Lokrum, belonged to the Archduke Maximilian, the one who was killed in Mexico. I saw a film about him once. Did you get to the park?'

'No, I didn't.'

'Very keen on plants, he was, Maximilian. I've got quite a collection myself, but there were some I'd never even heard of. She knew, though, knew all the names.' He pointed

123

to Anna, who was talking to Briars and his wife in the stern. 'Of course she ought to.'

'She'd learned them, you mean?'

'Her father was a botanist, spent a lot of time up the Amazon. Took her with him when she was so high, taught her all the names.'

What can be more conventional than an account of the second day of love? Passion has been succeeded by reflection. Will the pleasures you enjoyed be repeated, did they ever happen at all or were they partly imaginary? Gilbert lay in his bed staring at the dark ceiling, the door this time unlocked, and by midnight was convinced that she would not come to him. Ten minutes later she was in his bed.

The physical transports of the second day of love, how are they to be described, and what is the point of describing them since inevitably they repeat the first? The uses of mouths, hands, penis, vagina, were all as they had been before. There was a difference for him, however, in that he felt the tenderness that had pervaded him upon the beach at Lokrum. He spoke the word love to her, said positively *I love you* for the first time to the black hair spread out beside him and the turned-away face. She did not reply.

'I love you, Karenina. Anna Karenina.'

'It's sex you're talking about. What about your wife?'

'She's gone.'

'What do you mean, gone?'

'I don't know where she is. But it doesn't matter. I thought it did, but it doesn't.'

'I know the name for you. The man who lost his wife.'

'No, that's not the name.'

'What is, then?'

'The man who found himself. I want to live with you.'

'How would we live? Tell me.'

He told her about Gilbert Welton, the man who had made a first foolish marriage and thought that he wanted to be a bookseller, and then married again and lived in St John's Wood and ran a publishing firm in which he was not interested, the man whose tedious skin would be sloughed off when they started again in the English countryside. He talked about the antique shop and the selectiveness with which they would choose the things that they cared to stock.

'I don't know anything about antiques.'

'I should teach you.' That would be part of the pleasure in their relationship. He said easily the kind of thing he had never said before to any woman. 'You are so beautiful that you would be certain to love beautiful things.'

'Wouldn't it all be like what you did before? With your first wife, I mean?' It seemed sufficient answer to say that she was not Mary. She yawned. 'It might be rather a drag. But you're sweet, you know that?'

'I don't like sweet. It means old. I like "I fancy you." '

'Age has nothing to do with it,' she said vehemently. 'I hate young men, they're boring.' She touched his face. 'I don't much fancy the country, not in England. Couldn't we live in Italy, I'm mad about Italy?'

'Perhaps,' he said doubtfully. 'As long as you're with me. We'd have enough to live on anyway.' He turned her head with his hands so that she faced him. The shutters were open, her wide eyes looked into his own. 'Do you want to be with me, Anna Karenina?'

'Yes. I can't really speak Italian, only a few words. Could I have a poodle?'

'What?'

'A poodle. I do think they're super dogs, I'm mad about them. So artificial, and still they're real.'

'You can have what you like, as long as you go on fancying me.'

Their conversation went on like this, conventional, repetitious. She sighed when he asked if her father had been a botanist, and said he had been fifty different things. 'We'll go away from here then, go together? You'll give up Paradise?'

'They won't like it.'

'I thought you didn't care about that kind of thing.'

'Hell, no, why should I? Let's go straight to Italy.'

'I ought to go back to England first. But I want you to come with me.' He felt that once out of his sight she would disappear.

She left him again at half past four, but before doing so she woke him up. 'Something I wanted to say. We're separate people. I don't like the way you try to make us the same.'

'Separate people,' he said drowsily.

'You're not responsible for me, I'm not responsible for you. I do what I want.' Her voice was shaking with emotion. He agreed. She kissed him, dressed, briefly touched his face again with her lips, left.

This time he did not fall asleep.

CHAPTER THREE

The Last Day of Love

IN THE MORNING he felt the need of action, action that would make the happenings of the night irrevocable. Boats must be burned, bonds cut. He ought to speak to Coldharbour, speak to Max, tell them that he wanted to accept the American offer and was going to resign from the firm. A shrinking from action went with this desire for it. He felt that if he let the past come into contact with the present it would destroy the world in which he was going to live with Anna. It was with reluctance that after breakfast he made a call to Max in Sarajevo, with relief that he learned that all the lines were engaged. Afterwards he looked for Anna, and found her in the foyer with Briars, the Strong/ Longs and half a dozen others. The English contingent was in a rebellious and inharmonious mood. Fat Briars, no longer jolly, was their spokesman.

'It's a bit much, don't you agree? One of the best hotels in the place, or supposed to be. You would think they might make an effort.' He appealed directly to Gilbert.

'What sort of effort?'

'Eggs and bacon. Bacon and tomato. Something more than the old bread and marmalada.'

'You must understand that they don't eat things of that kind for breakfast,' Anna said patiently. 'You can have boiled eggs, or cheese. They won't offer anything else.'

'Cheese for breakfast, I ask you,' said Mr Strong/Long.

'I'm not blaming this little girl.' Briars patted Anna's shoulder. 'She's doing a grand job, as they say. But you take the trip this morning to—what's it called?'

'Cilipi. They wear local costumes.'

'On our booking it says tours included.'

He listened to her explaining that some trips were included, others had to be paid for. She barely looked at him, and in the end he called her aside, and asked how she could bear to go on with this. She gave him what seemed almost a hostile glance.

'Why not?'

'You know what we talked about.'

'Yes.'

'Why don't you say you don't care what they do?'

'Are you asking me to go away now? This morning?'

'Not this morning.'

127

'All right. This morning I shall take the party to Cilipi. Are you coming?' He shook his head. 'All right then. You don't have to come.' She went back to Briars and the Strong/Longs.

He turned away, to be confronted by a smiling Kornaro. His call to Sarajevo had come through. It was strange to hear Max's voice.

'Tremendous news.' He spoke as if they were continuing a discussion begun half an hour ago. 'Eugene is excited, he wants very much to join us.'

'Eugene?'

'Eugene Ponti, *The Tigress*, you remember. The thing is you're here, it's an ideal chance for you to meet him and clinch the deal. Can you get here today?'

Are you asking me to go away now? This morning? 'I don't know if I can manage today. I'll let you know later on.' Why should Anna not come with him? 'Perhaps today. Or early tomorrow.'

'Terrific. For you to meet Eugene, that will be the clincher. We'll see him tomorrow, OK by you?'

'Yes.' Perhaps the last problem of the old world could be disposed of. 'How's Virginia?'

Silence. Then Max's voice, less bouncing than usual, said 'I thought she was with you.'

'She's not here. She said something about going on to Sarajevo.'

'Is that so? Where's she staying? I sure would like to see Virginia.' The voice had taken on Max's mock American intonation.

'I thought she might be with you.'

Silence again before Max spoke, his voice perfectly clear. 'I can hardly hear a word on this damned line. It's just hopeless. Look, my dear, did you say you were coming tonight?'

'I'm not sure. Tonight or tomorrow.'

'All right then, I'll fix—' The click of disengagement.

Had Max been cut off before saying goodbye, or had he replaced the receiver?

He sat on the terrace of the Gradska Kavana, at the Ploce end of the town, a small cup of bitter coffee in front of him, thinking about the past night and understanding for the first time the phrase, *You're getting under my skin*. Anna was not perhaps under his skin, but it seemed that his skin was impregnated with her. When he sniffed his hand what he smelt was her body. He had always disliked what he thought of as the fleshy scent associated with lovemaking, but this smell was not disagreeable. It was a long way removed from anything he had felt after making love to Virginia. These impressions occupied his mind, although they could not have been classified as thinking. He tried to visualize Starting Again with Anna, but could think of nothing but his desire for her and his tenderness about her.

He drained the coffee cup and thought, I must go back to England, I must see Max in Sarajevo, I must find out what Anna is really like. Of these, only the last seemed important. He closed his eyes.

'Snatching a spot of shut-eye?' Painter stood by the table. He wore very tight dark blue trousers and a shirt striped in blue and green with a cut-out panel in the centre which said ILUVIT. He sat down. 'How's everything? Feeling a bit Harry groggers myself, you should have been with me last night. Les girls. Something about old King Sol that gets them. But I forgot, you were otherwise engaged. How's the wife?'

'Not here.'

'You didn't meet her?'

'She's gone on to Sarajevo.'

'Sarajevo. Going there myself. What about joining forces, two's company. Shake up the office there, they don't know their arse from their elbow. Do you know what the chap servicing our Topline cars here used to be? Guide to the jolly old Rector's Palace there.' He pointed to the Renaissance portico of the building beside them. 'Calls himself an engineer, looked down at his feet when I asked if he'd checked the brake linings. Read this?' He laid a paperback book on the table, *The Monkey's Puzzle.* Gilbert shook his head. 'This chappie has a monkey, trains it to fix a gadget on a lift so that cyanide gets pumped into the cage, kills the chap inside. Works with a kind of bellows effect, little nozzle in the lift connected to some tubing. Monkey sets it going, pulls out the tubing afterwards. Dead clever.'

Two large glasses filled with red liquid appeared on the table. Painter's large nose pointed questioningly. '*Koliko?*'

'*Dvadeset jedan,*' said the waiter.

'Twenty-one, that is. Daylight robbery, but it's a good drink. Try it.' He put down some notes and waved away the change. The drink was strong and sweet. 'And the accounting system was all to pot as well. Yes, I can tell you I've put a bomb under their backsides here. Going to do the same at Sarajevo, then Split, then Zagreb. Then home. How about it?'

'How about what?'

'Bit of a burn up to Sarajevo. You said your wife was there.'

For some reason he found himself almost unable to speak. 'The thing is—' he said and stopped.

Painter looked at him. 'All right, old man? You look as if the sun's knocked you a bit skew whiff.'

'I'm all right. The thing is, I'm not sure, I may have someone with me.'

'Plenty of room in the old jalopy.' He looked at Gilbert again, gave a cackle of manic laughter. 'Don't tell me it's a native damsel? Slipped her a length, have you? You want to watch it, old man, they're very sniffy about these things here, her Montenegrin boyfriend'll do you.'

'Nothing like that.' The need to confide in somebody was

intense, and he gave way to it, aware of his foolishness. 'My wife and I have parted, she's gone off with someone else. I've met a girl here.'

Painter whistled, long and low. 'You're a quick worker, old man. Never have thought it. Why Sarajevo, though? Having it out with your wife there, if I may coin a joke?'

'I'm not sure. I have to go there. On business.'

'Say no more. Mine not to peek or pry and all that.' He winked. 'This deserves another. Hey, what's your name, *gospodin*.' The waiter came over. 'What the hell's two?'

'*Dua*.'

'Dua more of the same then. Give you and your girl a lift, no trouble at all.'

'The thing is, I'm not sure about the time. It might—' He was already regretting what he had said.

'I tell you what, old man. I'm at the Imperial, I told you, old-fashioned sort of place, just outside the Pile Gate. You come along there. This afternoon I'm reading the riot act again to the clot here who calls himself a manager, then I'll have a zizz. Be ready around four. If you're not there by six I'm off.' He drank what remained in his glass, refused another. 'This stuff's stronger than it looks, you want to watch it. I'll have the other half tonight.'

'I'm not sure I shall be able to come.'

'OK, old man, leave it flexible.' Painter picked up his crime story, tapped the message on his shirt. 'Don't do anything I wouldn't.' He moved off down the Placa. The panel on the back of his shirt asked: 'DO YOU?'

Climbing up the steps of the Ulica od Sigurat towards the ramparts, houses overhanging menacingly from both sides, he approached a figure in green stepping daintily down. The identity and even the sex of this figure remained uncertain, and it was uncertain also whether Gilbert or somebody behind him was being acknowledged with a wave of the arm.

At half a dozen steps' distance the figure was identifiably masculine—a long white face, a faint smile—and recognizable also as somebody he had met, but who was it? The eyes were hidden behind an owl's dark glasses, a camera hung loosely over one shoulder.

'Hallo.' They stood beneath a stonework balcony. 'What a delightful surprise.' The voice was thin and slightly fluting.

'Hallo.'

'Isn't this place simply *spectacular*? But exhausting. Are you going round the ramparts?'

'No, just filling in time.' He turned and they went down the steps together. *Filling in time*, a curious phrase, which covered all the recent years of his life. And what was he doing filling in time here? Perhaps he should have gone to Cilipi with Anna or taken her away this morning, perhaps he had failed some vital test set for him. As they moved downwards his unidentified companion, picking his way as delicately as if he were moving on stepping stones through mud, talked on.

'I mean, what can you do with a place like this? It's all too much, don't you think so? It just *is* a picture postcard. Though I must say I was tempted.' They emerged into the Placa. The green clothing was revealed as a two piece in tussore silk, the jacket hanging loosely, the trousers voluminous. 'It's just not my scene. This little beauty believes that life is real and earnest, she's truly at home in Whitechapel or Saint-Denis.' He patted the camera. The gesture brought recognition. This was Felix Perkins, the photographer.

'We met at that night club.'

'The Out Going, yes.' Perkins turned and looked back up the steps. A child stood looking at them, fingers in mouth. 'I think I must succumb.' The camera clicked and clicked. Perkins said apologetically, 'Ridiculous, but I just couldn't resist.' They walked up towards the Ploce Gate. Heads were turned to look at the green silk. 'You simply vanished that night, very wise. I was in rather a state, I know, Richard became *so* offensive. At the end I got into one of my rages. Would you like a drink?'

'No, thanks. I ought to get back to my hotel.' He felt a consuming meaningless anxiety. 'You're not here on an assignment, I take it?'

'Oh no, *quite* the contrary. By appointment you might say. Journey's end, you know.' He giggled. They crossed the bridge to the Ploce Gate and walked up the Put Frana Supila into the hotel courtyard. Perkins stayed with him buzzing away with speech, a harmless but irritating fly. He was talking about a book of East London pictures he had coming out in the autumn, a book for which somebody whose name Gilbert didn't catch had written a scrumptious text, when the buses drove in. The Briars got off and the Strong/Longs, but where was Anna? Again anxiety paralysed him. Everybody got off the bus. Then he saw her blue dress, and realized that of course she would see the rest of the passengers away first. Now she looked around, saw him, waved, smiled, began to walk towards him. He felt his heart distinctly flutter.

What happened after that was a passage of corny film comedy. Her smile widened as she approached, she said 'Hallo,' and moved into Perkins's green tussore silk arms. He took off his glasses and spoke reprovingly.

'Naughty, naughty little Dolly.'

'What super gear.' She stepped back and looked at him. 'Fantastic.'

'Do you like it? *Really*?' He turned to Gilbert. 'Dolly's my wife. Dorothy Perkins. Well, that's her name, though she's been calling herself Lucy lately. Did she tell you her name was Lucy?'

Gilbert stared at her and she looked back at him, frowning. 'You two know each other, do you? That's a bit awkward. I've been having rather a thing with him.'

'And after you'd written to me too.' He spoke to Gilbert. 'You know you can't believe a word she says, don't you?

She's just a naughty Dolly Perkins, you can't *rely* on her. I do hope you haven't been relying on her? Oh dear, I'm afraid you have. You remember my saying I was madly unhappy because she'd gone away? In the Out Going, you must remember. Well, being on her lonesome didn't work out, did it, Doll? So she sent a veritable *cri de coeur* to her loving husband. And out I flew.' He waved green arms. 'But the point is, she's so unreliable, I didn't know for sure she'd be here. She might have taken off.'

'You didn't say you were coming.'

'You know if I had you'd have flown away.' He went on flapping his arms.

Gilbert said ineptly, 'Why didn't you say you were married?'

She did not look at him. Perkins said, 'I do assure you she is. Off and on anyway. Now I think the thing to do is to leave this picture postcard scene as soon as possible and get back to reality. If all the bugs are out of your head, that is.'

'They are for now.'

'Then let's take the first plane back, Dolly darling.'

'What about my job?'

'You know very well you don't care about your job, you're only playing.' He said to Gilbert, 'She's very good at playing.'

'Don't you even want to go in the sea, now you're here?'

'Dolly darling, why should I? I know it's wet.'

'You didn't tell me you were married,' Gilbert repeated. 'And you said your name was really Anna.'

Perkins replaced his dark glasses. 'Are we going to have a scene? I think I'd better leave you, I shall be in the way. I'll see what unspeakable concoction they're offering for lunch.'

'Sitting down is allowed,' she said when they were alone. They sat at one of the iron tables.

'Are you going back with him?' It seemed that he could ask nothing but foolish questions.

134

'He isn't queer, you know, or not very. And he's mad on me in his way. I'd never have gone back if he'd not flown out to get me, he's quite right.' She gave her foxy smile.

'How can you? After what we said.'

'What did we say?' She stuck out a leg, examined its burnished brown.

'You said you loved me.'

'It's what you say. I mean, how can you say anything else?'

'You lied to me, all the time.'

'Oh, come on.'

'Even your name. And all that about your father being an Australian diplomat and a botanist and so on, all lies.'

She swung her leg, looking down at it with her smile. 'Not all.'

'You mean about being brought up on a kibbutz?'

'It doesn't matter, does it?' She lighted a cigarette, puffed, met his gaze. 'This morning I would have gone away with you if you'd wanted, do you know that?'

'Suppose I said it now.'

'You always say *suppose*. Felix is here, no suppose for him. I'll tell you something. You're lucky, we both are. It would never have done, we'd have split in a week.'

'It isn't true,' he said hopelessly.

'You must know it is.'

'You mean you'd sooner be with him?'

She looked at the hotel. 'He's a person, I'm a person, he understands me.'

'And I don't?'

'You don't understand anything,' she said brutally.

He reproached her like an adolescent, the words bitter on his tongue. 'I don't understand people like you. You lie, you lie all the time. About everything.' Conscious of his own absurdity, of the game being lost, he cried 'You said you fancied me.'

135

'I did. I do.'

'Well then?'

'Well then what?'

'Didn't it mean anything to you?' He felt the old dislike of naming sexual parts and routines.

'Yes, it was fine. Put your hand on the table.' He did so and she covered it with her own. 'I get the feeling. You know. I get it with you all the time and I love it. But there's something about you I can't take.' Still with her hand covering his she said, 'You want it but you can't give it back. You're detached, but you don't want me to be. It's like sucking blood or something. I don't know what it is, but it makes me shudder.'

He snatched away his hand at the same moment that hers was withdrawn. She rose. 'That's it then. Ciao.' She went into the hotel. As she entered the foyer a shade in green silk rose to meet her.

'How about that? Isn't she a beaut?' Gilbert looked at an ordinary grey car and nodded. 'I'm a patriot, old man, but on the production line for the old combustion engine we have to give Jerry best over an awful lot of things.' He stowed the cases, unlocked the door. 'Hop in and let's get going. Listen to that, doesn't she purr? Like a three-month-old kitten.'

'Very nice.'

'I'll say. Very nice, she's beautiful, if she were a woman she'd be lying down for me. What happened to your little filly?'

'Her husband arrived. He's taking her back to England.'

Painter roared with laughter. 'The lady's husband arrived. And you and your wife have packed it in already. Forgive me, old man, but I find that funny, I've got a peculiar sense of humour.'

As the car moved out of Dubrovnik's dull suburbs Painter muttered to himself. The muttering emerged in a phras or two. 'Lazy buggers . . . no, not lazy . . . all of them . . . glad to be . . .' They reached the Adriatic Highway and he raised his voice. 'Goodbye, Dubrovnik. Sarajevo, here I come. Be another shambles I expect. Had much to do with them?'

'Croats, you mean, the people here? Not much.'

'You're lucky. Croats, are they, I'd cut their croats. I call them all bloody Slavs. They're not lazy like wogs, just inefficient. Work hard but don't know what they're doing. They can build a dam but they can't run an office. I'll bet I have to light a few more bombs under them in Sarajevo. They don't watch the clock, just don't know it's there. Like the country?'

'What I've seen of it, yes, very much.'

'Give me the Sussex Downs and the Lakes any time.' The car in front of them was slowing down. Painter sounded his horn. 'Come on now, don't play silly buggers.' He shot past, through the gap between the car and an oncoming lorry, braked sharply and cut in, then took a bend with a cry of tyres.

Goodbye Dubrovnik. How was it possible to be so greatly deceived, to hold the body of love at one moment and find yourself empty-handed the next? One of the tyres made a flicking noise, repeated over and over again, the sound formed itself into the pattern of two lines from Housman:

Possess, as I possessed a season,
The country I resign

The lines were inaccurate. Anna was a country he had never possessed, and he had not resigned from it but been expelled. Extraordinary to think that he had slept with her last night and that they had talked about Starting Again. He became aware that Painter had asked a question.

'What's that?' He realized that the question was about how long he had been married. 'Five years.'

'I've been hitched fifteen.' Taking one hand from the wheel he fumbled with a wallet in front of him, extracted a photograph. 'Moira. And the kids. In the garden.'

The snapshot showed a harassed-looking woman holding a watering-can, and two small boys, one in a paddling-pool. A suburban lawn stretched around them, the neighbour's fence could be seen to one side. 'David and Jonathan. Little devils, fight like tigers, but I wouldn't be without them. Got any children?'

'One son. But he's grown up. It's my second marriage,' he added to forestall further questions.

'I'd die for my family, you know that.' Painter half-turned to him, inviting contradiction. 'But a man wants his freedom. Different for a woman, but a man has to have it. I'm a free man, my own master, that's what I like about this job. Shall I tell you something? Most people don't know what to do with freedom, they stick their arses in the air and ask you to give 'em a kick. But not Jerry Painter. Last job I had working for somebody else, I was a car salesman. Do you know the boss asked me to wash a car one day. I said to him take that and stick it up your jumper.' He blew a loud raspberry. 'Did he look surprised! I was pleased when he fired me. Never been able to stick working for other people. In Topline I'm not just a rep, I'm a partner. And there are pickings on the side if you want them.' He glanced at Gilbert. 'Not saying I do, mind you, never step out of line. You wouldn't say they were free in this country, would you?'

'I don't know. There are different kinds of freedom.'

'Too deep for me, that is. Either you're free or you're not. Tell you something, I've been in France, Belgium, Holland, Spain, Italy, Germany, Ireland. Seven countries, and in every one of 'em I've dipped my wick. And I haven't paid for it either. Here's our turnoff.'

The sign said *Opuzen, Metkovic*. They ran across an

138

open plain, with a river on one side. Painter looked at his watch. 'The sixty-four-thousand dollar question is whether we stop the night at Mostar and look for local talent, or push on to Sarajevo.'

'I'd like to get there tonight if possible.' He wondered why he said this. What did it matter when he reached Sarajevo, or whether he got there at all?

'All right with your Uncle Jerry. They say the road's a bit rough later on, but she'll get through all right, won't you, my beauty?' He patted the steering-wheel affectionately. 'Been reading a very clever story about a car—*First Gear Murder.*'

'That isn't the one I saw you reading.'

'No, I get through three a day.' He went off into one of his gusts of laughter. 'Long as there's a body and some clues I'm happy. But this one really has something, it's about a chap who crashes into a brick wall when his brakes pack up. Thing is, you see, this other bugger, that's the local doctor, hates him because he cheated the doctor over a share deal when they were young out in Australia So he ups the bonnet, drains his brake fluid, brakes won' work. Trick of it is, the doctor's first on the scene, carries bottle of brake fluid in his black bag, tops it up again.'

'How does he get found out?'

'Detective, very bright geezer named Verity Glendenning, pinches the doctor's bag, examines it, finds traces of brake fluid. Can't think why you don't publish detective stories, you'd make a mint. Read another good one this week, *Open Wide Please*, about a dentist who gets patients to make a will in his favour, then knocks 'em off with a drug in the injection which doesn't take effect for the next half-hour. You're not listening.'

'I'm sorry.'

Painter was silent. Then he said, 'Funny thing, love, have you ever thought that? Doesn't matter how many times I

dip my wick, it's only the wife and kids who mean anything
to me. Don't you agree?'

'I'm not sure. I don't think I've had that much experience.'

'Believe me it's true. The one you poke isn't always the
one you love, not by any means.'

'I'm not sure I know what love is. It seems to me just a
word.'

'That's very true too, old man.' Painter sighed. 'Mostar
coming up.'

CHAPTER FOUR

The Hitch-Hikers

JUST OUTSIDE Mostar the plain ended. They began to climb
along narrow roads, through gashed and fissured moun-
tains, with the Neretva running fast in a ravine below them,
and beyond it the railway line stretching along like a toy.
Painter kept up a flow of comment on the scenery and the
road, comparing both unfavourably with the Lakes. The
heat of the day died, and he produced from the boot a black
and white striped blazer which he put on. A toy train, four
crawling coaches behind a puffer, passed along on the
other side of the ravine and vanished in a tunnel. Gilbert
drifted into a daydream in which he was travelling in the
train with Anna. It stopped often, and at one of the tiny
stations they bought grapes, bread and rough sausage. They
ate these in the carriage, sharing them with a Yugoslav
couple. No conversation was possible, but the Yugoslavs
made it clear that they thought Gilbert and Anna were man
and wife. Something about this made him uneasy, but he
did not know what it was. Perhaps the train was going to

crash, perhaps the man's friendly look would change to a snarl . . .

Painter whistled. 'Did you see what I saw?'

'What was that?'

'Two birds, two luscious birds thumbing a lift as I live and breathe.' He pulled up, opened the door and jumped out. 'I think we're in, old man, I think we're in. Here they come.'

The sky had become perceptibly darker, light was failing. Two long-haired figures with packs on their backs hastened towards them. Something about the appearance of one made him say 'I think—'

Painter realized it at the same moment. 'Christ, it's a man.'

The two reached them. They were both young, the girl a round-faced blonde, the boy darkly handsome with hair that came down almost to his shoulders. 'Are we glad to see you,' he said. 'Another hour and we'd have settled for camping out.'

'And there's some snake they warned of us around here. What do they call it, the poskok? Snuggles up to you for warmth.' The girl shivered. Like the boy, she was American.

In the fading light they confronted each other. Painter's big nose jutted out belligerently. The girl eased off her pack.

'You want to get your hair cut,' Painter said to the boy. 'You could get into trouble that way.' The boy did not reply. 'The boot's pretty full, I don't know if we can get all that gear into it.'

The boy seemed about to say something. The girl said 'David,' and he stayed silent. She went on. 'We'll get the stuff in somehow, it can go on our knees in the back if we have to put it there. If you can take us somewhere we can stay the night, we'll be grateful.'

The boot easily took the two rucksacks. The boy and girl got into the back of the car. 'Bloody hippies,' Painter whispered out of the corner of his mouth to Gilbert, and drove off with jolting energy. 'What's the idea then, what's it supposed to prove?' he shouted.

'I'm sorry?' That was the girl. Gilbert turned round. They were sitting very consciously apart on the back seats. The boy's dark narrow head was still, his eyes were watchful.

'Like my Aunt Agatha said when she produced quintuplets, in somebody else I'd call this excessive but when I've never been with a man it's just ridiculous.' There was no laughter from the back. 'I mean, jeans, long hair, you look the same, you dress the same, it takes the kick out of everything. Hell, maybe you are the same, maybe hippies just don't have anything down there.'

'We're not hippies.'

'You just want to look like a girl, eh? When I was at school we used to call that cissy.'

'Look, mister—' That was the girl again.

'Jerry, my love. Not to be confused with the homely utensil that used to be found under the bed. And this is Gilbert.'

'You don't have to give us a lift if you don't want.'

'Who said I don't want to? I stopped, didn't I?'

'We're not hippies, we're students.'

'Your boy friend said so. American university, eh? Which one?'

'Berkeley.'

'I might have known it.' Painter groaned. 'You heard of Berkeley, Gilbert?'

'I've heard of it, yes.'

'Where they write up four-letter words in the classrooms and call the police pigs. Anyway it's June, why aren't you at home?'

'We just dropped out for a year. David thought it was more culturally important to see things for ourselves.'

There was a sharp crack, the windscreen became blind. Painter jammed on his brakes, switched off the engine. 'Bloody *hell*,' he said, and opened his door. 'There's a torch in the glove compartment, let's have it.'

The torch revealed a windscreen still intact but split into a thousand opaque pieces. Painter went to the boot, rummaged, shouted : 'Don't just sit there, get out and do something. And watch it. We're only a few feet from the side.'

They got out. It was almost dark, a steep drop on the right was faintly visible. Warmth had gone out of the air. 'What happened?' Gilbert asked.

Painter threw the two rucksacks out on to the road and emerged with the car jack. He got inside the car and swung it twice. The splintered windscreen crackled out, with only a few jagged fragments left. 'Some flint on the bastard sodding road came up and hit the windscreen, what do you think happened? If you've got anything warm you'd better put it on. We're going to have a lot of mountain air blowing through and it's a long way to Sarajevo.' He chuckled, and began to sing 'It's a long way to Sarajevo' to the tune of 'Tipperary.'

The boy opened the rucksacks and asked, 'Babs, are the pullovers in yours or mine?'

'Babs,' Painter said. 'That's good, you look like a baby.' His hand moved out to touch the girl. She shrank back from him.

'Stop it,' Gilbert said. 'Just stop that.' He was surprised by the passion in his voice. David, bent over a rucksack, paused. Painter looked surprised.

'What did you think I was doing, old man? Believe me, all Jerry Painter wants to do is get to jolly old Sarajevo and get his head down.'

'Just leave her alone.' He had heard the remark in a hundred bad films, how did he happen to be saying it?

143

'Right you are. If the deadly snake comes slithering out of the rocks I won't—' He stopped and shouted, 'Look out. Behind you.'

The girl screamed, the boy pushed her aside and stood staring. Laughter welled up in Painter, rocking his body.

'If you could have seen, if you could just have seen your face. 'Ware snakes. Oh dear me.'

The boy and girl put on thick pullovers, and Painter found a pullover which went under the sports blazer. Gilbert wore his raincoat. Babs and David moved round the car. Painter opened the front passenger's seat and bowed gallantly. David got into this seat himself and Gilbert sat in the back with the girl. They drove on.

Round some bends they hugged the mountain, and bits of rock and scree lay in the road, occasionally the drop to the river could be seen on the other side. There was little traffic. Once a lorry passed them with much loud preliminary hooting. They were rising most of the time, and it became colder. At one point they bumped over a shaky-looking log bridge. A hundred yards beyond it the road narrowed so that it was impossible for cars to pass. Headlights showed in the distance, became brighter. Painter hooted and was met by a hoot in reply. He put on speed. The lights approached nearer, and were dazzling.

The boy spoke. 'What are you trying to do, get us killed?'

'Let 'em go back then.' Painter kept his thumb on the horn. The hooting from the other car stopped, the lights became less bright. 'That's it, my beauty, back you go.'

The other car backed for a quarter of a mile before the road widened and it was able to pull into the cliff side. As they passed a window was opened, shouts of abuse rang on the night air. Painter played 'Colonel Bogey' on his horn and roared back, 'And the same to you.'

'You could have gone back,' the boy said. 'The road was wide enough to pass after we'd crossed the bridge.'

144

'An Englishman never retreats. The Yanks may, they're a mongrel lot anyway, but an Englishman always goes forward.' With cheerful belligerence he asked, 'Do you mean to tell me they let you drop out and then go back again?'

'At Berkeley, yes. I'm majoring in European sociology and they agreed it would be useful for me to have a year in Europe. Mind you, I've got good grades.'

'Never went to the varsity myself. People couldn't afford it. You don't know how lucky you are.'

'The States is different. If you want to go, you go, just a matter of where.'

In the back seat the girl's leg pressed against Gilbert's with unerotic warmth, or perhaps he was no longer capable of being erotically roused. He tried to summon up thoughts of Anna. Supposing she was beside him now in this car, her leg pressed against his, would he feel different? The girl put her arm through his. She shivered, and whispered something.

'What's that?'

'Your friend? What's the matter with him, why is he so angry?' He thought of saying that Painter was not his friend, but before he could do so she continued. 'He shouldn't ride Dave that way, Dave's got a temper.'

'So has Painter.'

'Dave can be nasty, he doesn't like anyone trying to ride him. What do you do?'

Hardly believing it, he said, 'I'm a publisher.'

'I'm majoring in English, the twentieth-century novel.'

'We publish Bunce, Jake Bunce.'

'Well, what do you know?' She leaned forward, the whole upper part of her body touched him. 'Dave, this guy is a publisher, he publishes Jake Bunce.'

Dave said something, but with the air rushing through the gap of the windscreen it was not possible to hear the words. Only snatches of conversation from the front were audible, but they seemed reasonably friendly. 'I'm going to sleep,' Babs said. She curled up to him like a kitten.

In the front Painter was laughing. A good sign or a bad one? As he bent forward to hear, Babs accommodated herself to him.

'I'll tell you what I'd do,' Painter was saying. 'The first hundred I caught, they'd go up against a wall, then—' He made a clicking noise with his tongue. 'The next hundred I'd say do you want the same, or are you going back to work with your professors like good little boys? And I can tell you the answer.' Dave murmured something. 'Are you trying to tell me they're such democrats themselves? I'd say to them, I'd say to you, you've got a job to do, so get in there and do it.' Another murmur. 'I'm a free man, I'm one of the lucky ones. That's what free enterprise means, my son, those who deserve it get to the top.' His laugh boomed out, his head was turned. 'Jablanica, getting on now. Bloody great dam they've built somewhere around. Half-way there, I'd say. Everything okey-dokey there in the back, snuggling up to you is she?' He said something to Dave and laughed again.

The girl's hand was pushed inside his raincoat. She whispered complainingly, 'Dave, I'm cold.'

'It's not Dave.'

She pressed herself closer to him. Quite impersonally he considered what her reaction would be if he put a hand on her thigh. The idea surprised him. He did nothing.

While his mind wandered vaguely around such thoughts he must have dozed. He was aware of voices in the front, of the cutting wind, the noise of the car engine, the body beside him giving and receiving warmth. Then all this stopped. There was silence. Perhaps he was asleep? The silence was broken by Painter's voice cursing loudly, monotonously, repetitiously. Doors slammed. He reluctantly roused himself, pushed the sleeping Babs aside, opened the door and got out.

The night was full of stars. The silence had some quality —of depth, should it be called?—that was quite different from what one thinks of as silence in a city. At once, and ridiculously, he thought of Anna. Would she have understood the quality of this silence, would she have looked up at the stars, said *Goodbye Felix* and walked away with him? He rubbed a hand across his face as if it were a damp flannel, and was surprised to find the hand warm. Painter was shining a torch at the engine. Dave stood by his side.

'Why did I ever trust that stupid lazy bugger who called himself an engineer? Trust a Slav, I'd sooner trust the blind school.' He put his head inside the engine, grunted, leaned over, emerged and shone the torch on his blazer sleeve. Something dark showed on it. 'That's oil, how am I going to get oil off?' he said in an indignant whine. 'I ask you, how am I going to get oil off?'

Dave was leaning over too. 'Have you checked the distributor head?'

'You just get out of there. I don't want any American layabout fiddling with my car.' He put a hand on the boy's shoulder and pushed him away. For a moment it seemed that Dave would react, but he did nothing. 'If you want to make yourself useful get inside and try the starter.'

Dave got into the driver's seat and switched on and off half a dozen times. The engine did not respond. Painter glared at Gilbert, who yawned uncontrollably.

'Is there anything I can do?'

'You've done enough already.'

'I have?'

Dave was still trying the starter. 'Stop that, you bloody clot, you'll run the battery flat,' Painter shouted. To Gilbert he said accusingly, 'Who was it wanted to get to Sarajevo tonight? I could have been in Mostar drinking the old slivovitz if it weren't for you. And I wouldn't be lumbered with these deadbeat lovebirds either.' He gave the mudguard a kick. 'Bloody sodding rotten car.'

'Do you mean we're stuck here for the night?'

Painter smacked his forehead. 'God give me patience, what do you think I mean? What shall I do, ring up the nearest garage and ask 'em to send a breakdown van? This isn't civilization, it's Yugoslavia.'

'It couldn't be that you've run out of petrol?'

Painter stared at him, his great nose shining in the moonlight. Then he gripped Gilbert's arm, led him round to the dashboard and pointed. 'Three-quarters full. And don't say it might be empty. I filled up at Mostar, remember?'

'I thought you knew about cars?'

'Are you trying to be funny? I don't crawl about underneath 'em, I let the peasants do that.'

Dave joined them. 'I've checked the distributor head and the points. Nothing wrong there that I can see.' A car's headlights shone round a bend in the road and then showed dazzlingly bright as it neared them. Dave moved out waving his arms, jumped back as the car hooted and accelerated.

'Nobody's going to stop, they're all afraid of getting their throats cut,' Painter said. 'We're stuck till morning.' Grotesque in his blazer he stood glaring from one to the other of them. The absurdity of his appearance moved Gilbert to facetiousness.

'You're sure it isn't escaping brake fluid? Like *First Gear Murder*?'

Painter gave the car another kick. 'That stupid young devil in Dubrovnik, I'll have him for this. What the hell are you doing?'

Dave was taking the rucksacks out of the boot. He said cheerfully, 'Getting out the tent and stuff. I'll wake up Babs and we'll go and search for a bit of flat ground.' He shone the torch. 'Looks as if there might be something away there on the left.'

'Some people have all the luck. A nice bit of nooky in the sack, that's your name for it, isn't it? What's she like in the sack? Quite a handful, I should imagine.'

148

'I don't like the way you talk,' Dave said. 'I don't like you, I tell you that.'

'But you share and share alike nowadays, don't you? Seen her on the job with a dozen other boys, I expect.'

Dave turned abruptly away from them and went round the other side of the car. 'What are you trying to do, get him to hit you?' Gilbert asked.

Painter grinned. 'I'd like that. Used to be middle-weight champion in the Terriers.'

There was a shout. Dave came running round the car, got into the driver's seat, switched on. The engine started. He jumped out, thumbs up, grinning. 'Vacuum built up in the petrol-tank. Just thought of it, had it in another car once. Take off the petrol cap, she goes whoosh, and it's clear.'

'That's wonderful,' Gilbert said, although upon the whole he would have preferred to be left here in the limbo of a Yugoslav mountain rather than face the problems waiting in Sarajevo.

One of the car doors slammed, there was a noise. 'What the hell?' Dave said and left Gilbert, who followed him. Painter was holding the girl, Dave was pulling at him, Painter pushed her away. She staggered and slipped to the ground. Painter brushed away the vague swing that Dave made at him.

'Juicy, very juicy,' he said with satisfaction, and then spoke to Gilbert. 'Had to get her out.'

'What do you mean?'

'End of the road. Thought I'd kiss her goodbye.'

'You can't turn them out.'

'Who says? I like your face, I give you a lift. I don't like it any more, I say that's enough. My car, my privilege. Smarty pants here had got their gear out already, saved me the trouble.'

'You can't do it.'

He could not see Painter's face clearly, but he knew the grin that would be stretching it. 'You want to call a halt too, old man? Perfectly free to do that if you like, that's what freedom means. Expect you'd find it very snug, three of you in one sleeping-bag.'

The torch in Dave's hand shone on Painter's grinning teeth, flicked to Gilbert and then to the girl. His voice was still quiet. 'Get back into the car, Babs. Back seat.'

'Oh no you don't.' Painter moved forward.

'Look at my hand.' The words were still not loud. The boy's left hand held the torch, which shone on to his right. The right hand showed no stigmata, it was smooth and white in the torchlight, but the fingers were curled round a small revolver.

Painter laughed and moved towards the girl. 'All right then,' Dave said, and at the strangled note in his voice Painter's hand jerked back as though he had been burned.

'He would, you know. The little bastard means it,' Painter said to Gilbert. Then he spoke to the girl. 'You'd better do what Superman says, get back into the car and catch up with your beauty sleep.'

'Dave,' she said quaveringly. Gilbert became aware that Painter was close to him and had said something. It took a few moments for the words to penetrate, and then he realized that they had been something about rushing him together. Dave told Gilbert to get in the back seat.

Painter said conversationally, 'Are you going to let this little thug tell you what to do? If we rush him he won't have a chance.'

Gilbert did not answer him. He opened the car door. Dave's even voice said, 'I don't think we'll take you with us, I think I'll give it you now. After all, why wouldn't I? You know the kind we are, Babs is on grass and I'm on acid, we think it's shit funny when one of the pigs gets it, why wouldn't I give it to you?'

He held the torch on Painter, who was sweating. 'You heard him.'

With a confidence he did not feel, Gilbert said, 'He's kidding, don't worry.' As he got into the car he had the feeling of shutting out something disagreeable. What happened next he saw through the barrier of glass.

Painter cried out something and dived forward, in what Gilbert vaguely recalled as a rugger tackle. Dave must have been expecting something of the kind. He sidestepped and hit Painter with the butt of the revolver. Painter fell down.

Gilbert stared through the car window. The moon was obscured and the impression of things outside the glass was confused. The body on the ground appeared to shift slightly, but he could not be sure. Beside him Babs made a sound between a whimper and a giggle.

'He shouldn'ta talked to Dave that way, should he?'

The back door was flung open. 'Help me get him in,' Dave said.

'But he can't drive.'

'I'll drive.'

'He may be badly hurt.'

'Look, I've had all I can take. I could leave you both on the road, the way he was going to leave us. Is that what you want?'

They lifted Painter and put him in the front passenger seat. A trickle of blood ran from his scalp to his forehead. Gilbert wiped it away. Dave started the engine and ground the gears as he drove off.

He drove along the mountain roads with the headlights full on, never dipping them, and ignoring the hooting of the few cars they met. Glancing back occasionally over his shoulder he talked to Gilbert as though to himself.

'I don't want you to get the wrong idea. That's only the second time I've ever hit anybody, to hurt them I mean. The other was a boy I had a fight with at school. But a bastard like that, what can you do but look after yourself? It's you or him.' He said reflectively, 'Babs's father is

Judge Deeley, one of the best-known men in Northern California, isn't that so, Babs?'

'Daddy's famous,' Babs claimed. 'He's stuffy, you know, but kind of sweet.'

'He let you come on this trip.' Dave spoke earnestly, turning again to emphasize the words. 'And he let you come with me. He wouldn't've done that if he'd thought I was just a drop-out, don't you see?'

'You don't have to convince me,' Gilbert said.

'It's true though, isn't it Babs? Her father trusts me.'

'Daddy just loves Dave. He said to me, "I wouldn't let you go to Europe with just anybody but Dave's a fine boy. A little wild maybe, but I like a boy to have some spunk." And I tell you something else Daddy said. He said to me, "I reckon that boy loves you. If you love him too, then that makes it all right by me." And he gave me funds for the trip. Not too much, mind you.'

'He doesn't sound stuffy to me.'

'Some ways he is. I had to promise him I'd never drink wine, he said it would heat my blood and it was hot enough anyway.' She giggled.

'Her dad's a great guy.' Dave's voice in front was solemn. 'And what he said, you know that's true. We love each other. We're going to get married.' The word *marriage* jarred him like a dentist's drill touching a nerve. Dave negotiated a bend and went on. 'He said to me, "I trust you, you'll look after my daughter." This gun now, I'll tell you something funny, Judge Deeley gave me this gun. It's his. Just in case we ran into trouble. I guess he didn't mean this sort of trouble. He a friend of yours?'

'No. He just gave me a lift.'

'I don't reckon he's got any friends. Hell, he didn't have to give us a lift, he didn't have to stop. And then pawing Babs about that way. Saying those things.'

'I hope he's all right.'

As though at a signal Painter groaned and sat up. He put his hand to his head, looked at Dave and then round into the back seat.

'Dave,' the girl said. 'He's with us.'

'He hit me on the head, you're a witness to that.' Gilbert said nothing. 'And now he's driving my car. Without a licence, I'll bet.'

'International driving licence,' the boy said.

'You're driving without my permission. You can just stop the car and get out.'

'You'd never have got it started. And you're not fit to drive.' They crossed a bridge and came into a large village. 'What's this place, I didn't see?'

Gilbert peered out. 'Konjic.'

Painter's hands were clasped tightly together. 'I'll tell you what I'm going to do with you if you stay in the car. When we stop I'm giving you both in charge.'

'What for?'

'Stealing my car, kidnapping me, grievous bodily harm or whatever they call it here. And let me tell you, sonny, they don't like your sort. Nobody likes your sort.' Dave did not reply. 'You're in trouble up to your neck. Stop the car and get out.' He put his hand on the steering-wheel. 'Stop the car.'

Dave cut the engine, but left the headlights on. Ahead lay rock, scrub, the winding road. The moon was showing again and illuminated Painter's beaky profile turned towards Dave, the stripes of his blazer, the boy's flowing hair.

'Now, out,' Painter said. The boy rested his arms on the steering-wheel. 'I said o, u, t, out.'

Dave turned to face him. He had a look of surprise. 'So easy, that's what I can't get over, it's so easy. Just a little tap on the head and he falls down. You have a gun, you can do anything. Why don't I shoot them, Babs, what do you say? Take their money and then ditch the car. Why don't we do that?'

The girl made her giggling noise.

'Don't be such a clot,' Painter said. 'They'd have you in a few hours.'

'Why would they?' He turned to the back. His voice was still quiet and reasonable. 'I don't see it. Nobody was there when he picked us up, nobody sees us leave the car. We run it over one of these big drops, go on a bit and pitch our tent for the night, clean the gun and ditch that somewhere too, take the bus in the morning. I don't see anything wrong with it, it's easy.'

'I never know when you're kidding,' she said.

'I'm not kidding. At least I don't think so.'

Painter shouted something incoherent to Gilbert, leaned over and tried to pinion Dave's arms. Again he must have been expecting the move, for in a moment he had the door open and was standing outside with the revolver held loosely in his hand. The interior light came on, revealing Painter with his arms stretched forward. 'Don't you move, don't you try to get in that other seat or I swear I'll let you have it.'

Not since he was a young man, a quarter of a century ago, had Gilbert experienced any situation which placed him in physical danger. Now there seemed to be within him a block of some kind, a solid mass of material which precluded fear. He opened his own car door.

'You too,' Dave said. 'You stay where you are.'

'Why should I? You're not going to shoot me.' He felt an absolute confidence that this was true. Outside he breathed in the mountain air, invigorating and clear. A car passed on the way to Mostar, flashing its lights. They showed Dave's face, dark and desperate. 'I mean, you don't have any reason to.'

'It's so damned easy. They shouldn't make it so easy.'

Painter started to say something. Gilbert cut him off sharply. 'Be quiet, you've said enough.' If Anna saw me now she'd be surprised, he thought. 'It isn't easy, it's impossible. You'd never get away with it and you know you couldn't do it. You'd better get in and start driving. And give me that.' He put out a hand towards the revolver.

'No.'

'All right, keep it. But start driving.'

'Why can't I do it?' His voice now was petulant, appealing. 'He thinks we're drop-outs, why not?'

Supposing the gun were fired, the bullet would bounce back off the block within him. He felt impermeable to harm. 'Think about Judge Deeley. That's not why he gave you the gun.'

'He wouldn't ever know.'

'You're not like me, you've got something to live for.' In the night air his thought process seemed wonderfully clear. 'It doesn't matter to me. Or to him, all he's after is a quick lay in every country in Europe. We don't have a future, but you do and so does she.'

Painter said something. From outside the car he looked like a striped fish in a tank. He wound down the window. 'He left some native bit back in Dubrovnik, that's why he talks such a load of cobblers.'

About the glance that the boy directed at him there was something betrayed, something wounded. Out of some inner feeling that he had not known he possessed, Gilbert cried, 'Things are different for you, different for Americans.'

A long stare, then his words were approved by a nod. 'I guess you're right, they are.' He held out the revolver. In Gilbert's hand it felt small, cold, disagreeable.

'I'll be damned.' Painter began to laugh, a jarring nasal sound. He began to shift over to the driver's seat. Gilbert made an imperative gesture.

'Let him drive.'

'Christ, man, it is my bloody car.' But he made no further

protest when Dave got into the driving-seat. The engine buzzed. They moved away.

An hour and a half later they reached Ilidza, a few kilometres from Sarajevo. Hardly a word had been spoken during the whole of that time by Dave or Painter. In the back seat Babs put her hand over Gilbert's. 'You were so right, you know that, so right. I don't know what came over Dave, except he's got a temper, I told you.'

'Yes.'

'But I don't believe he'd ever have used that. I've never seen him that way before. It was kind of frightening. You know.' She shivered, and her shoulder touched his.

'I had a girl. In Dubrovnik.' He wanted to say *she was not much older than you*, but what would she care?

'Yes.'

'Nothing. I don't know what I wanted to say. She went off with someone else.'

'That's what made you talk the way you did. About not caring. Isn't that so?'

'Perhaps. I just don't know.'

'I like you.' Her mouth shaped itself towards him, he went to meet it, but found the kiss planted on his cheek. Her right hand, a warm hostage, remained in his left one. His right hand still held the revolver.

At Ilidza Dave parked the car in a small square beside a hotel. He got out, stretched himself, said 'Come on, Babs,' and unloaded their bags.

'It's all right if I drive my own car now?' Painter held out his hand for the keys. Dave dropped them into his palm.

Gilbert gave back the revolver. 'Thanks,' he said without smiling. He weighed it in his hand, put it into his hip pocket and said 'Thanks,' again.

The hotel said *Serbija* over the front. 'Are we going to be able to get in here?' the girl said. 'I'm pooped.'

'We'll soon find out.' He bounded up the steps, opened

156

the swing doors, disappeared. They stood about awkwardly without speaking. He came back. 'OK.'

'Well folks, it was nice knowing you,' Babs said. She kissed Gilbert's cheek again. 'Some of you.'

They passed through the swing doors.

Painter drove for a mile without saying anything. When he did speak his voice had the geniality of their early encounters. 'Very dicey there for a bit. The old tick-tick was working overtime. You handled him perfectly.' His tone changed. 'Bloody young psycho. He should be shut up.' The lights of Sarajevo could be seen now, blue and white stars ahead of them. Painter went on talking.

'Americans are two sorts like anybody else. Good and bad, and he's one of the rotten apples in the barrel. And that girl. Just a little tart. They'll find they can't muck about with Jerry Painter. Now that he's got the taste for it that boy's not going to stop. I got away with a crack on the head, the next chap may not be so lucky.'

'What are you going to do?'

'Just what I told them I'd do, old man. Go to the police, tell them what happened, the crack on the head, the way he stuck us up, everything. They can't say I didn't warn 'em.'

'No.'

Painter jerked the wheel in his surprise so that they skidded. 'What do you mean, no?'

'You'd need me as a witness. I wouldn't support you.'

'Wouldn't *support* me? What kind of weirdo are you, you like being threatened with a gun?'

They were coming into the outskirts of the city. Blue sodium lights were strung along endlessly in the middle of the road. On either side white cliffs of flats loomed up and were passed.

'You were going to turn them out of the car. That's why it happened.'

'And that means it was all right for them to hold me up?'

Behind the round neutral face of Babs he saw that of Anna. What were the last words she had said to him? He groped for them unsuccessfully, yet he knew that they had left an open wound. 'I shouldn't give evidence against them. Not in any circumstances.'

He was thrown forward joltingly, so that his face almost came into contact with the jagged bits of glass round the empty space of the windscreen. The car stopped. Painter turned to him a face violently red with anger. 'Then not in any circumstances will I have you in my car. You can get out and walk, and I hope you bloody well walk for ever.'

Gilbert opened the door, got out, bent to take things from the boot. A blow on the shoulder sent him spinning. 'Let my car alone.' He opened the boot, took out Gilbert's case and threw it on the ground. A shirt and pyjamas fell out on to the road. Painter laughed. His words sprayed saliva into Gilbert's face. 'If there's anyone I hate it's weirdos who're soft on crime. I don't wonder your wife left you, and your piece in Dubrovnik too. If you ever had one, which I doubt.' He put two fingers up in a Churchillian gesture, got back into the car and drove away. Gilbert knelt on the pavement, repacked his bag, looked at his watch. The time was half-past nine. He felt as if he had been in Painter's company for a week.

He walked a few hundred yards, and after waiting twenty minutes caught a bus which took him through wide anonymous streets into the centre of the town. At the Hotel Europa they understood and even spoke English. They told him that Mr Bomberg was out and had left no message, although he had given instructions that a room should be reserved for Mr Welton if he arrived. Gilbert became aware that he was hungry, and ate some kind of meal in the restaurant. Then, depressed and overwhelmingly tired, he went to bed.

CHAPTER FIVE

Max

WHAT VOICE was at the other end of the bedside telephone?
He envisioned it as Anna, saying that she was waiting in
the lobby. But of course it was Max.

'Hallo, my dear. The top of the morning to you. They
told me you were here, but I was late last night. I had fish
to fry. You know?' His laugh was warm and easy. 'Shall
we breakfast together? In fifteen minutes.'

Rosy-faced, euphoric, wearing a very thin suit of some
shimmering material, Max was more himself than usual.
'You have not been here before? A wonderful place in its
way. The Turkish quarter is terrific. The covered market,
do you know what the top of it looks like? Pressure cookers,
big pressure cookers. And the mosques, you just have to see
them. What's the matter, you don't look up to the mark.'

'I'm all right.' The sight of Max had dissipated the block
of indifference within him as though hot water had been
poured on to ice. Twinges of feeling that he had thought
dead moved into action with the painfulness of unused
muscles.

'You're angry because I've spent a lot of time on this?
But wait till you read *The Tigress*, it just has everything.
Adventure and sex and tenderness, and all—all *infused*
with such a perfect historical sense.' He touched his finger
to his lips. 'We meet Eugene for drinks before lunch today, OK?'

'Yes.' He did not mention Virginia, but remembered another reason why he should be angry with Max. 'I had a
call from a man named Melvyn Branksom. I don't appreciate your conducting negotiations behind my back.'

'The silly devil.' Max seemed genuinely annoyed. 'I wasn't conducting negotiations, just having a chat. But I told him he must on no account talk to you before I had a chance to see you.'

At another time he might have left it at that, but irritation made him go on. 'I should think half London knows about it. Somebody in the club spoke to me.' Something in Max's open face, something un-put-down-able in his bouncing optimism, pushed him further forward. 'It's not what I expect. If you're going on like this we've come to the parting of the ways. You'd better realize it.'

'My dear, what's up?' The open-eyed astonishment seemed ingenuous and genuine. 'If I've offended you I'm very sorry. I apologize. I shoot off my big mouth, I know I do, but what I said to Mel was in confidence and he should have respected it.' He paused, but Gilbert did not express forgiveness. Max flung out his arms. 'I apologize, it won't happen again, what more can I say? You know me, I'm impetuous, I rely on your judgment.'

He said, 'All right,' feeling the response to have a schoolboy's sulkiness. He was right, but in some way Max had put him in the wrong.

'You're not yourself. Do you want me to put off seeing Eugene, shall I see him alone and make your excuses?'

'No.'

'He has a villa near the top of Trebevic. Marvellous view. You can go up in the funicular, but we will use my little hired car. So sad that Eugene cannot see the view, he is blind, you know that?' Max spoke with his usual liveliness, but Gilbert sensed that he was being watched, assessed. 'You told me you would send a telegram.'

'I didn't have time.'

'And you mentioned something about Virginia. I thought you said she was with you.'

Enunciating carefully he said, 'I don't know that she

is even in the country any longer. I don't know where she is.'

Max made no reply. Looking at him, catching what seemed to be a quickly-suppressed smile, Gilbert knew that he was concealing something, and that the something was connected with Virginia. A moment later Max took out a handkerchief and blew his nose. Gilbert recognized the handkerchief. It had on it a strongly-marked pattern in light blue and dark blue, and Virginia had given him half a dozen of these handkerchiefs on his birthday last year, telling him that they could be bought at only one shop in London. With the production of the handkerchief there came also the powerful odour of her new scent. The smell lingered, but was much less strong, when the handkerchief was replaced.

The sight of the handkerchief, the smell of the scent. It was these things, combined perhaps with what had happened on the drive to Sarajevo, that made him think of killing Max.

They spent the morning wandering round the Bascarsija, the old Turkish quarter, and in the Brusa Bezistan, the covered market whose semi-circular domes Max had likened to the tops of pressure cookers. The immense quantity of carved wooden ashtrays, salad servers and small wind instruments in the market reminded Gilbert strongly of Heal's, and the tumbledown shacks outside in the doors of which tailors sat cross-legged stitching at unidentifiable garments, or metal and leather workers added a burnish to some undistinguished bit of metal seemed to him merely sordid. Max, however, was in transports of pleasure. He haggled lengthily over the price of some broad copper pans, left them with a regretful shake of the head and bought a wedge of sticky pastry which he ate with the greatest relish. He forced a small piece on Gilbert. The nuts and syrup were cloying in his mouth. He gulped the rest of it and felt sick.

Max drove the car, a Morris, with characteristic dash, and kept up a flow of chatter as they crossed the shallow lively Miljacka and went out through the suburbs.

'Bistrik,' he said. 'Austro-Hungarian. The mixture of Muslim and Frank Joseph is interesting, don't you think? Some of this, you know, it's what I was brought up in.'

'Here, you mean?'

'No, but the old building was the same everywhere, heavy, dignified, but not graceful. Like old Franz Joseph himself. Though I've been here. My father was a construction worker and he spent six months in Sarajevo before the war. Of course I was a child then, and it was winter. In winter it's cold here. This is the gipsy quarter, they call it Dajanli.' They passed through steep winding streets where the little wooden houses clung to each other for support and muddy streams ran along between the narrow alleys. The houses were filled with small lean children and hungry-looking cats. 'Muslims,' Max said. 'They never kill cats, you know, they say that Mahomet cut off a part of his robe rather than disturb a cat who was sleeping on it. Not much like England.' He glanced at Gilbert.

'No.'

'In a way I love all this, in another way it's what I wanted to get away from more than anything in the world. Being poor in central Europe, that's no fun. You wouldn't know about that.'

'I suppose not.'

'In England everybody is a gentleman or they pretend to be. When you know you're not one it gives you an advantage. But this is where I belong. I've got away from it, but it says something to me.'

'You're not a Muslim?'

'My mother was. Half-Turkish. By religion, you mean?

I'm nothing.' They moved out of Dajanli, up a corkscrew hill. He moved into lower gear, gunned the engine. 'I'll never understand you, Gilbert. People like you.'

They went up and up. The scenery changed to scrub, with occasional pine trees. They then moved out of this, the landscape opened, Sarajevo was spread out below them, the domes of two dozen mosques gleaming in the sunlight. 'That's something, isn't it? But barbaric, you'd call it barbaric.' He turned a bend at a right angle, came almost to a dead stop. A lorry was in front of them, the driver on the road changing the wheel. A car shot down the hill going too fast. The Morris pulled over to the left, towards a hundred-foot drop, came with shuddering uncertainty to a halt. 'Damn' thing pulls over if you have to make a quick stop. Needs new brake linings.'

As Max spoke the word 'brake' Gilbert remembered *First Gear Murder* and what Painter had said about brake fluid. You let out the brake fluid and the brakes just didn't work. 'Suppose you had no brake fluid,' he said almost before he knew he had spoken the words.

'Then I should just have the hand brake which is distinctly dicey.' Max grinned at him. 'Like everything about this car. You know I don't mind that, I like taking chances. But it might be goodbye two members of old-established English publishing firm, one a foreign upstart. Are you wishing you'd taken the funicular? Not much farther now, but most of it in first.'

The road went round and round as they climbed. Five minutes later they stopped at a pair of elaborate wrought-iron gates which said 'Villa Garibaldi'. A bent old woman wearing drab clothes came out of a small stone building, said, '*Dobre danya*' and opened them. They drove into an enclosed courtyard to the front of a sprawling villa, whose generally Italianate style was blended with Moorish arches. Max jumped out and spread his arms.

'We have arrived. It's OK, don't you think?'

163

'Somebody's here before us.' An Alfa-Romeo stood by an open garage at one end of the courtyard.

'Flavia's. She uses it to go down into town.'

The effect was rather what Gilbert thought of as Hollywood architecture, and this was for some reason enhanced when a maid wearing a white cap and frilled apron led them through a dark large hall with a green and white terrazzo flooring into a large drawing-room full of books and Italian china, opened french windows and stood aside to let them pass.

'I thought this was a Communist country, hard-living and high-thinking.'

'Not for Eugene. He is a sympathizer, an honoured guest.'

From the wide stone-flagged terrace the ground dropped steeply away, so that you had the impression of the terrace being built on air. Below it Sarajevo shone, the Miljacka running through it like a vein in a hand. Three people sat out there, a white-haired man talking into a tape-recorder, a dark girl who sat at a table reading a set of proofs and a blonde in a bikini wearing dark glasses stretched flat on a sun bed. The man switched off the tape-recorder as they approached, and stood up. The white hair was disorderly around his powerful head. Max said formally, 'May I present my managing director Gilbert Welton, Signor Eugene Ponti.' They shook hands. 'And this is Janet Ponti.' The dark girl looked up from the proof. 'And Flavia Orsini.' The girl in the dark glasses took them off, looked at him and put them on again.

'A perfect view, isn't it, Mr Welton? Unhappy for me that I cannot see it, and yet I know this view because Janet has described it to me. It is printed in here.' He touched his forehead with a hand flecked by liver spots.

'It's marvellous. Your English is very good.'

'I learned it in the best possible way, among Englishmen. In the war. I was your prisoner.' The proud head reared up, the white hair looking like a cock's crest.

They sat down. The smiling maid came out with a tray of drinks and then left them. Ponti said interrogatively, 'Janet?'

'Why the hell doesn't she do it, I'm working.'

Ponti said something in Italian to the blonde girl, who answered him with a couple of laconic phrases. 'You do it, Janet.'

'She's too busy, I suppose.'

'She will have letters to type later on.'

'She can't speak English, she doesn't know enough French to correct proofs, she has only one talent.' She slapped down the drinks in front of them. A little spilled on to the table.

Ponti raised his glass to them. He drank only Perrier water. 'I am happy to learn that you will publish my book.'

'We are honoured,' Gilbert said. Something about Ponti's manner made this kind of tone obligatory. 'Do you want to discuss the terms in detail? I understand we deal with you direct.'

'I have done with agents. The terms content me perfectly.' They had contented Gilbert too, when Max outlined them. For an author with so high a reputation Ponti had asked for surprisingly little money. 'But I must mention the translation.'

'Eugene was dissatisfied with his English translation,' Max said easily.

'I was disgusted. Have you heard of Abraham J. Cohen?'

'I have explained that that was an American translation. Ours, now—' Max sucked in his breath to show the stylistic purity and academic correctness of the translation they would sponsor. Ponti looked directly at Gilbert. The look was not comfortable to meet, because his eyes had apparently an assessing gaze. The whites were clear, the irises a vivid blue.

'You understand that money no longer is of importance. My life is simple, my wants are few.'

165

'Just a house outside Amalfi, a flat in Rome and this villa for the summer,' Janet Ponti interjected. Ponti gave no sign that he had heard.

'I am an old man now, I have lost my sight, of what importance is money? My life is over, it is time to contemplate what is eternal.'

Janet drew back her chair, the noise harsh on the stone. Her pale skin was blotchy. She gave Max a single glance, then her feet made a rattling sound as she went back into the villa. Ponti looked inquiring. Flavia said something, and Max for a moment appeared to be about to protest but stayed silent.

'You must forgive my daughter.' It was almost as if he were a priest forgiving sins. 'Your partner here tells me that the translator will be Angus Wilson. That is satisfactory.'

Max gave Gilbert an enormous wink. He was too stunned to do more than repeat feebly, 'Angus Wilson.'

'I was speaking to Angus just after the last PEN Congress,' Max said smoothly. 'I think I told you that he has the greatest possible admiration for your work.'

'I was gratified. I have read his novels with interest.'

Recovering a little from the shock, Gilbert decided that he must be firm. 'I must make it clear that at present it is impossible to say who will do the translation.' Rather lamely he went on, 'We shall certainly get the best possible translator, and he will be most carefully chosen.'

'Exactly. You've really hit the nail on the head,' Max agreed heartily.

'You spoke of Angus Wilson.' Ponti's voice was accusing. 'Who are you speaking of now?'

The blonde got up and stretched like a cat, then walked delicately across the terrace. She halted by the easy chair in which the old man sat, kissed the top of his head and put one hand on his knee. She ran this hand up his thigh until it reached his crotch, where it deliberately lingered.

Bending over, she murmured something into his ear, then went inside the villa.

'We are speaking of the very best,' Max said earnestly. 'You want the best translator, nobody else is good enough, we understand that. If it is not Angus Wilson, it will be somebody of equal distinction. Perhaps Iris Murdoch.'

When Ponti stood up it seemed natural for them to stand up too. 'I shall have to consider. I regret that my household arrangements make it impossible for me to ask you to stay to lunch.'

'Eugene—'

'Mr Bomberg, I shall have to consider. I have said this, I repeat it.'

'May I call on you later—this evening—to discuss the whole thing. And make other suggestions. I assure you that we shall give you a translator of your choice, a real interpreter. Like Scott-Moncrieff with Proust.'

'I shall be happy to see you.'

'Would eight o'clock be all right?'

'My appetite is that of a sparrow, but if you wish you may come to dinner. The food will be the simplest.' With a noticeable lack of warmth he added, 'Mr Welton, if you are free, I shall be happy to see you.'

'Too bad you've got that date this evening,' Max said. With a feeling that he was being rather weak, Gilbert agreed that he had a date.

Ponti moved uncertainly towards the french windows. Max put out a hand to help him, then withdrew it. Janet appeared as though she had been waiting, and took his arm. He shook off her hand. Max and Gilbert followed them through the sitting-room and out to the hall. At the bottom of a curving staircase Ponti shook hands with them ceremoniously. Flavia appeared and said something. Slowly he moved up the stairs. The audience was over.

As soon as he was at the top of the stairs Janet turned on

them. 'Do you know what will happen now? He will make my life miserable for a week. Why did you do it?'

'Do what?' Gilbert asked stupidly.

'Let him think that Angus Wilson is translating his book, what does it matter? Who is going to tell him anything different? Me? And I'll tell you something else, he hates the English anyway.' She turned and went through a swing door which evidently led to the kitchen.

By the time they had driven out through the iron gates Max had recovered his bounce. 'An unusual household.'

'Ghastly. How long has he been blind?'

'Oh, quite a while. His wife was English, you know that? She left him twenty years ago when Janet was a little girl. That was her misfortune.'

'How do you mean?'

'For someone like Eugene it is unthinkable that a woman should leave him. He sent Janet away to school in England, to get her out of his sight. Then he brought her back here to work for him. Fortunately as you saw she is ugly, not like her mother. She has not left him. Eugene has, you know, a certain reputation with women. His wife insulted him, and he takes it out of Janet. With Flavia, and no doubt others.'

'How do you know all this?'

'I have my methods, Watson, as old Sherlock used to say. And then he is very mean, you gathered that?'

'We are going back a different way.'

'Ah ha.' They went through a small pine forest and came out almost at the top of Mount Trebevic. Max paused for a moment to admire the view, which he seemed to regard proprietorially. 'Isn't that just something?' he asked. Then he drove on to a small restaurant near the top of the cable railway. 'Have you ever eaten roast boar? Then you will do so today.'

The roast boar was flavoursome but tough, rather like venison, and it was Max's attitude in relation to it, his central European air of instructing the ignorant, that was the immediate cause of their quarrel. Or perhaps it was the powerful locally made red wine that they drank with it. Sitting under the restaurant awnings, looking at yet another unquestionably magnificent view and remembering the scent on the handkerchief, he felt hatred for Max.

'When you go up there this evening I want it made perfectly clear that all this talk about Angus Wilson or Iris Murdoch translating the book is nonsense. Neither of them is a translator as far as I know.'

Max nodded, smiling. He took out a cigar case, offered a cigar to Gilbert and when it was refused lighted one himself. With the large tube rolling between his red lips he looked, Gilbert thought, like an East End Jew who had made it.

'After all, they may not even know Italian,' Max offered. He rocked with laughter. 'A joke. You should have seen your face. But actually, my dear, you have made what might be called rather a balls-up of the whole thing.'

'*I* have?'

'Precisely. Now look. That girl is perfectly right. All we want from Eugene is a piece of paper with his signature on it. It is one of our standard agreement forms. Oh yes, I have brought one with me. It gives terms, publication price, advance and so on. Everything we have discussed. He signs it, I come home, and we have a best-seller.'

'But our agreement says nothing about a translator.'

'Precisely,' Max said again. 'As Janet said, how would he know?'

Gilbert felt rising in him a full-blooded anger worthy of E.R. Did it spring from sexual jealousy, the Anglo-Germanic syndrome, a knowledge that Max would always succeed with women while in the end he would always fail? Was it hatred of all that Max represented, his unEnglish gift of easy friendship and his unEnglish vice of easy adjustment to dishonesty? He managed to keep his voice quiet.

'We could never do anything like that, surely you must realize it?' Max shrugged. 'To cheat a poor old blind man, with the help of his daughter because she hates him—that's plain disgusting fraud.' Max did not stop smiling and Gilbert fleetingly wondered, *Does he hate me as I hate him?*

'Eugene isn't poor, he's rich. He's not a poor old man, he's a tyrant who sleeps with his secretary and makes life a misery for his daughter. But what you don't understand, what you most don't understand, my dear, is that this is a game he is playing. Eugene is not a fool, he knows quite well he will not get Angus Wilson to translate his book, he simply wants to make sure we understand his importance. It is a game, he enjoys it.'

'It's fraud. It may be the kind of thing you have done before, perhaps it is commonplace for somebody with your background. You may as well understand that I should never consent to it. If you come back with an agreement I shall want a specific letter signed by Ponti to say that the choice of a translator is left to us.'

Max stubbed out his cigar and rose from the table. He paid the bill. They did not speak on the drive back. The Europa car park was full, and Max put the car in a back yard where bricks and bits of concrete lay scattered about, looking as though they were part of a simultaneous process of building and demolition. In the hotel lobby Max spoke.

'I shall go up there this evening, and I shall come back with an agreement.'

Gilbert could not stop his voice from rising. The clerk at the desk, the one who knew English, looked amused.

'You know what I said about that. I mean it.'

'But I am not so foolish as to think you have insulted me because of that. There is something wrong with you, and you connect it with me.'

He turned away. Gilbert gripped his arm. 'I connect

you with Virginia.' He shouted the next words. 'What have you done with Virginia?'

'Take care. People will look at us, you would not like that.' And in fact the clerk was now watching with fascination this uncharacteristic, unEnglish show of temper. 'Virginia would love you, if you would permit it. That is my opinion. I can't be responsible for your delusions. But I want to say this. I intend to remain in the firm. You won't find it easy to get rid of me.'

Would he not find it easy? You unscrewed two nuts near the front tyres, was that what Painter had said? He bent down, looked and saw nothing. It occurred to him that he ought to open the bonnet, which had a spring catch arrangement. Peering in, he saw that there did seem to be some nuts beside the wheels, but he had no idea whether they were the ones Painter had meant. In any case, how did you undo them? Nothing had been said about that, but presumably there must be a spanner among the tools. He rummaged hurriedly in the boot, found an all-purpose spanner and fitted it to the nuts. They turned easily. One turn, two turns, three turns. Should he make it half a dozen? He had no idea. Were there similar nuts at the back? He had no idea about that either.

He stood in the empty yard, surrounded by builders' rubble, trying to decide whether he should look for nuts at the back of the car and undo them, or tighten up again those he had loosened. There was a sound. Somebody was behind him, somebody had disturbed the rubble. He closed the boot, straightened and walked away. A black cat came out of the rubble and stared at him, then ran off. He saw nobody as he came out of the yard and returned to the hotel.

In the hotel room he wondered whether he should go back and try to screw up the nuts again. He decided against it.

What would he say if Max found him bent over the car? What idiotic feeling had possessed him, that he should try to tamper with a car about which he knew nothing in a way derived from a ridiculous crime story? It seemed to him impossible that Gilbert Welton could have done any such thing.

While he washed his hands he remembered Max's last words, something about Virginia loving him if he would permit it, and he suddenly realized that if she had returned home and was trying to reach him she would be unable to do so. He put in a call to his house and lay on the bed for half an hour, to be told that they had not been able to get through. Had the number actually been rung, or was it not possible to make the London connection? There was no point in staying any longer in Sarajevo, or indeed in Yugoslavia. Nor was there any point in seeing Max again. He had made his position about the translation clear, and another meeting would no doubt end in another quarrel.

He went down to the lobby, and discovered that it was impossible to fly direct from Sarajevo back to England. The best connection was via Zagreb, with a four hour wait, and he made a booking on this for the morning. With all this done he went out, partly to avoid seeing Max. As he walked past the yard the car still stood there, with two others now beside it. A man and a woman got out of one of them.

At half past nine he was in a nightclub called the Bosna, in a narrow street off the long Marsala Tito. He had found it by wandering about the streets, after eating in a fish restaurant a good but rather expensive lobster. It was not much like what he thought of as a night club, and certainly resembled very little the Out Going. Young men and women danced what he recognized as a local version of the twist, in a manner both more whole-hearted and more decorous than anything he had seen in England. The musicians played an adulterated version of Western pop songs, with occasional solos of quite a different kind, languorous and passionate. There was a sprinkling of tourists, mostly German but with one or two American couples. They did not speak to Gilbert, and he sat alone at a small table. Once he asked a girl to dance, but she smiled and turned away her head and a moment later her escort appeared. He was a fierce-looking young man who wore earrings, and under the strength of his glare Gilbert went back to his table.

He sat there drinking something called prepecenica, which he had picked at random from the list offered by a bald, gloomy waiter wearing dark trousers and an embroidered waistcoat, topped by a fez. The first glass seemed to burn away the lining of his throat. He drank a second to see if it could really be as atrocious as he had thought, and discovered that it was comparatively agreeable when accompanied by Turkish coffee.

'What ho, we meet again.' The voice was unmistakable, but his eyes needed to confirm the evidence of his ears. Jerry Painter stood beside his table, wearing a shirt of which the whole front was in the pattern of the Union Jack. He was smiling broadly. A small girl hung on to his arm as though she might lose it.

'International collaboration.' He turned and revealed that the back of his shirt showed the Stars and Stripes. 'Bright but not gaudy. And I've beeng doing a spot of the old fraternizing. This is Maria. Maria, meet Gilbert. She's an assistant in our Topline office here.'

'I am sorry, my English is not good.' The girl smiled.

'We use the old sign language.' Painter patted her bottom and sat down. 'Mind if we park here? I owe you an apology, old man. Those weirdos drove me round the bend, I don't mind admitting it. I apologize, I grovel, I bow my head before you.' His head touched the table top. 'Two Englishmen in a strange land. Mustn't quarrel. Shake on it. What's your poison?'

In the club, in St John's Wood, anywhere in England

he would have got up and walked away. Even here he did not touch the hand held out to him but placed in it his empty glass, at the same time saying accusingly, either to Painter or to the girl, 'You left me to walk into Sarajevo, he dumped my case in the road.'

'How could I ever have done such a bloody rotten thing?' He said to the girl, 'It was these weirdos, I told you the boy held us up with a gun. You know I don't think she believed me if she understood what I was talking about at all, but it's true, isn't it?'

'You told me you were going to report them.'

The girl had been sniffing his glass. She said gravely, 'Prepecenica, not good.'

'If Maria says it's not good it must be terrible. Her stomach's made of cast iron. I know, I've felt it.'

'Did you report them?'

'What do you take me for? Anglo-American solidarity for ever, that's what I say. Let's drink to that.'

Gilbert asked Maria to dance. He found with surprise that standing up demanded a good deal of his attention. They staggered about on the floor.

'Jerry is a funny man. He makes me laugh. He is an old friend, yes?'

'No, we met out here. Not a friend at all really.'

'You think he is hard? I think he is very hard. He has booted here a lot of people.'

'Booted? Oh yes, I see.'

'The order of the boot, he said. I think it is an idiom?'

'Yes.'

'Here in Sarajevo it was very bad, Topline, sometimes we send out the cars and they are very bad. Jerry gives the order of the boot.' A couple bumped into them. He lurched and almost fell. Her arm was raised to hold him, and he saw the dark hair in the armpit.

'I should like very much to go to England, do you think

he will take me? He says yes, perhaps.' He was about to express scepticism when he stumbled again. 'Perhaps we go back.'

'Isn't she the most wonderful little thing you've ever held in your arms?' Painter asked as they returned.

Gilbert sat down heavily. His head was clear although his movements seemed not perfectly co-ordinated. He felt a militant dislike of Painter, a desire to insult him. 'She says you're talking about taking her to England. I was going to tell her, want to tell her, don't believe a word he says.' Painter looked injured.

'Maria knows I'm a man of my word.'

The prepecenica went down easily this time, although he was glad to have finished it. Then disconcertingly, mysteriously, his glass was full and he felt bound to raise it again. He heard the girl say something about leaving, and although he hated Painter and wanted to insult him, he wanted also to keep them there, not to go back to his hotel. He remembered his plane booking.

'Flying back tomorrow. To Zagreb. Got to wait at Zagreb. Glad to get out of the country.'

Painter leaned across. The Union Jack glared at him. 'I agree, old man, but I shouldn't say it too loud. Not here. You don't know who might be listening.'

'Bloody rotten country, it's brought me no luck.' The lines of the Union Jack wavered, he blinked to keep them straight. 'Good books lately, read any?'

'I think we'd better get you home. Which hotel is it?'

He could see the flecks of broken blood vessels in Painter's nose. 'Any more first gear murders?'

'I don't know what you're talking about.'

'Know what you said about me, a weirdo who was soft on crime. Never do anything, you said. Well, I've done it.'

'Of course you have. Up you come now.' His hands were on the table. Painter's hand was placed over one of them,

175

tried to disengage what turned out to be his grip on the table. With his other hand, made into a fist, he smacked down on it. Painter yelped and let go.

'Your brake fluid nonsense, I've done it all. Doesn't mean a thing, any of it. Just books. Bad books lately.'

'*Jerry*,' the girl said. 'Jerry, I must not have trouble.'

Painter wrenched away Gilbert's left arm from the table, pulling him up. Almost instinctively he struck out with the right. He was astonished to feel the flesh of Painter's face, delighted to see blood appear in the nostrils of his detested nose. A couple of drops went on to the Union Jack. A look of rage replaced the amiability of Painter's expression, he said some inaudible words and one of his fists—or was it both?—came forward. Gilbert felt a blow in his stomach and then a grinding pain in his mouth as though all his teeth were being shaken in his head. Then he knew nothing more.

CHAPTER SIX

The Interrogation

HIS HEAD ACHED, he was lying flat on his back, two commissionaires were looking at him upside down. He closed his eyes to take away this illusion and when he opened them again the faces were the right way up. They had been standing behind the bed on which he lay and now they had moved round to the head of it, that was all. They wore rather pretty blue uniforms, and at their waists were holsters from which the handles of revolvers protruded. The revolvers settled the question of identity. They were not commissionaires but policemen.

176

He was prepared to take the presence of police officers quite equably until he saw a blue passport in the hands of the younger one, a fresh-faced boy who looked as if he should have been in a school choir. He sat up and pointed at the passport. A searing pain split his head through the middle. He became aware at the same time that he was fully dressed except for his shoes. With a great effort he moved his head and saw that the drawers of his dressing-table had been opened, and that his bags were open too. The other policeman, a grizzled man with an unfriendly expression, held up his keys. They must have been taken from him while he slept. He pointed at the keys.

'How dare you take my keys and open my bags?' The words came out in a croak.

The grizzled man held out a hand for the passport, which was given to him. Slowly and disdainfully as a strip dancer he removed dark gloves, looked at it, and said, 'Jil-bear-vel-ton.'

'That's right. But what are you doing with my passport?'

'Zasto posjecujete Jugoslaviju? Sto je svrha Vase posjete Sarajevu?'

Unintelligible. 'Give me my passport,' he retorted. Grizzle stared at him contemptuously, flicked open the passport again and then put it in his pocket, taking care not to crease his jacket.

'Navedeno je da ste Vi izdavac. Da li je Vasa posjeta u vezi publikacije?'

'I don't understand you. Speak English.' The pain in his head became too great to bear and he sank back, groaning. Grizzle snapped something at his youthful partner, who came across and held out one hand with a boyish smile. Gilbert unwisely took it, to find himself briskly hauled to his feet. For a moment he thought he would faint, and for another that he would be sick. Then he recovered, and actually standing up made him feel better.

'I can't understand a word you say, and you can't understand me. Why don't you get some linguists in your police?' he asked.

Grizzle stared at him and then spoke rapidly to Round Face, who went out of the room. Gilbert looked at his drawers and case. Everything appeared intact, and indeed what was there that might have been taken? Then he saw his wallet, which lay open on a small table beside Grizzle. He moved towards it. Grizzle divined his intention, picked up the wallet and calmly slipped it into his other jacket pocket.

It was not until the desk clerk appeared from down below, looking apologetic and nervous, that it occurred to him to wonder why the police were searching his room. As soon as he thought about it he knew the answer. There had been a row last night which had involved the police, either in the Bosna or at the hotel.

'Did I cause trouble last night?' he asked the desk clerk. The man stared at him. 'When I came back, perhaps there was a fight. If so, will you say I apologize.'

'Your friends brought you here. You were—' He mimed unconsciousness and then discovered the word. '—sleeping.'

The trouble had been in the Bosna then, and perhaps that was worse. He started to ask about this, but was interrupted by a spate of questions, or perhaps accusations, from Grizzle, which seemed to startle the clerk. Gilbert waited until this fusillade of phrases had subsided and then asked, 'What did he say?'

He could not hear the reply, because Grizzle started again. '*On ce poci sa nama*,' he said, and added as an after-thought, '*Sad*.'

'He wishes you to go with them.' The clerk had become pale.

'To the police station, I suppose. What for?'

'Naturally, to answer some questions.'

He looked at his watch. It was on his wrist, but the glass had splintered and the hand was not moving. He had no

178

idea of the time, and as always this disturbed him. He spoke with a sharpness that was the product of uncertainty.

'Tell him that I am ready to answer questions here, but I do not wish to go with him. And tell him that whatever happened last night, it does not justify his searching my room and taking my wallet and passport. Do you understand?'

The desk clerk shrugged and shook his head, although Gilbert felt certain that he understood. 'I want my wallet,' he said loudly and angrily. The clerk said something. Grizzle put a hand on his revolver holster, then seemed to change his mind and held out the wallet with a shrug.

'That's better,' Gilbert said. He looked at the wallet. His money was intact.

Grizzle said, '*Gospodin Velton molim podjite sa numa da odgovorite na neka pitanja.*'

'He says you must accompany them to the police station.'

'This is absurd.' The throbbing in his head had lessened, but now it became suddenly worse again. He sat down on the bed. Grizzle made a sign and Round Face heaved him up, started to pull him towards the door.

Gilbert pointed a shaking hand at the desk clerk. 'You are a witness that they are taking me away under protest. I shall complain to the British consul. And I want to know what this is all about.'

'*Sta on kaze?*' This was evidently a question. The clerk made a long speech to Grizzle and then said to Gilbert, 'I do not understand.'

'You mean you don't understand what I'm saying? Nonsense.'

The man wiped his forehead and said pleadingly, 'If you will go with them, please. I am sure it will not be for long.'

He gave up. 'Perhaps at least they'll have somebody there who can speak English.'

179

The desk clerk smiled in relief and nodded emphatically.

He sat in the back of a little black car, with Grizzle in the front seat and Round Face by his side. The driver might have been Round Face's brother. They crossed one of the bridges over the river into an area that looked like Bistrik, although he could not be sure. After ten minutes' driving the car turned into the courtyard of a large grey building. The driver got out and opened the front passenger door for Grizzle, then the back door for Gilbert. He looked up to see the sun almost directly overhead. It must be about midday. He walked between Grizzle and Round Face through swing doors, and followed Grizzle into an office where half a dozen men sat at desks. They did not look like policemen, or like anything except clerks. Grizzle spoke to one of them, who made a note.

'*Ovamo*,' Grizzle said, and beckoned. They went in convoy, Grizzle in front and Round Face behind, along a passage with doors at either side. There were no names on these doors. Grizzle stopped suddenly in front of one door, and Round Face moved from behind Gilbert to open it. With a trace of a smile showing beneath his clipped moustache Grizzle made a gesture indicating that Gilbert should precede him. What was waiting for him inside the room, a man at a desk waiting to question him? He hesitated momentarily, and a hand on his back gently pushed him inside. The door closed.

There was no desk, and nobody else in the room. It contained a bed, a chair, a small table, a curtained recess. A window set high up in the wall had bars on it. There was no handle on the door. He was in a cell.

Or at least he was shut up. Looking at the furniture, which was of light oak and rather similar to the utility furniture made in Britain during and immediately after the war, and discovering behind the curtain a lavatory, wash-basin and towel, he had the impression that he was in a rather low-grade hotel. Or perhaps in a waiting-room from which, after a few minutes, he would be called to some disagreeable appointment of an orthodontic kind. This impression was enhanced by the fact that the toilet recess had in it a shelf containing half a dozen books, most of them Marxist classics in Serbo-Croat, but including a Penguin edition of Evelyn Waugh's *Decline and Fall.*

Its presence was a kind of reassurance, implying as it surely did an English visitor, somebody who had spent an hour or two here and, his spirit enlivened by Llanabba Castle, Captain Grimes and Margot Beste-Chetwynde, had thoughtfully left his copy of the book to entertain other possible English readers. He opened it and read the name 'Frosic' written on the inside cover in a neat cribbed hand. Looking at the chapter headings he saw one that said, 'Stone Walls do not a Prison Make,' and turned to it:

The next four weeks of solitary confinement were among the happiest of Paul's life. The physical comforts were certainly meagre, but at the Ritz Paul had learned to appreciate the inadequacy of purely physical comfort. It was so exhilarating, he found, never to have to make any decision on any subject, to be wholly relieved from the smallest consideration of time, meals or clothes, to have no anxiety ever about what kind of impression he was making; in fact, to be free.

He put back the book on the shelf, feeling intense anxiety. What nonsense it all was. There were no stone walls, this was not the Lubianka, but the light oak and the lavatory did not conceal its identity as a prison. He was shut up and could not get out, how could anybody possibly identify that as freedom?

He stood on a chair in an attempt to see out of the window, from which a gleam of sunlight shone, but was unable to reach the bars. He felt a need to urinate in the wash-basin instead of the lavatory, did so, and was at once ashamed and alarmed. Was this what happened to you in prison, was his need like that of the housebreaker to defecate on valuable carpets, slash pictures, scrawl obscenities on walls? He sat on the bed, which creaked beneath him, and tried to concentrate on images from the reality of his past life, Virginia, Coldharbour, even old Langridge-Wood. They were only names, which summoned up no pictures of any kind. He got up, went to the door, banged on it and then kicked it. Nothing happened for a minute or two and then a slot which he had not previously noticed was pushed aside. A voice said, '*Sto zelite?*'

He went to the grille revealed in the door and looked through it. An eye, bloodshot and rolling, stared at him. 'How long am I to be kept here? I demand to see somebody in charge.'

'*Mirujte,*' the voice said.

He felt the frustration of somebody unable to make himself understood. The alien character of this fragment of Europe had been hidden from him by his situation as a tourist, smiled at and agreed with by hotel managers and waiters. Now it seemed to him that he might as well try to make himself understood by a central African tribe.

He continued to look through the grille until the bloodshot eye disappeared and the gap was decisively shut. The little wooden panel closed over it perfectly from both sides, so that the join was almost indiscernible. He lay down on the bed, but found that various twitchings were taking place in the calf of his right leg and arm that he was unable to control. He walked about the cell, noting that he covered it each way in three strides, so that the area must be approximately nine feet by nine. He seemed to have read that this was the size of an English prison cell, although of course in England there was no curtained-off lavatory. It occurred to him that the curtaining off, presumably to conceal the prisoner on the lavatory seat from the warder's eye, was a surprising piece of prudishness or carelessness. Suppose you tried to commit suicide by putting your head in the lavatory bowl? The thought was slightly cheering, for it seemed to imply that these were cells for only temporary habitation.

The sunlight had gone from the window when the grille moved again. He stopped pacing and looked at it. The door opened. Two men stood there, one in uniform who was no doubt the warder, and a younger fair-haired man wearing a grey suit. This man beckoned him with one finger. Gilbert stepped out of the cell and they began to walk down the passage, in the opposite direction from the way they had come.

'Where am I being taken?' he asked. 'I demand to see somebody in charge.'

The fair-haired man said, 'You will see the President himself.'

Did that mean he was being taken to see Tito? His bewilderment made it seem possible.

Upstairs, along a corridor, over an internal bridge that joined his building to another, at last to a door with a name written on it that he had no time to read. The fair-haired man tapped on the door and they went in.

He was seeing at last a man behind a desk, a man looking at papers. He put them aside, and made a motion for Gilbert to sit down. The fair-haired man also sat down at a smaller desk near the door. Gilbert did not sit down. He asked, 'Do you speak English?'

'Pretty well, yes. Do you smoke—English cigarettes?' The accent was only slight.

'I won't smoke. I want to know why I was taken forcibly from my hotel, brought here and kept in detention for several hours.'

'Forcibly, Mr Welton?' He took a cigarette and drew on it. 'Was force used? I gave no such instruction.'

'Against my will, then. And without an explanation.'

'Let me introduce myself. Ivan Radonic. I am the President of Police.' Radonic had a large smooth face. He wore heavy horn-rims. His expression was mild, even friendly. 'I really should advise you to sit down. You may be here some time.'

The maintenance of an indignant attitude is always difficult for an Englishman. Gilbert sat down.

'Your name is Gilbert Welton, you are the director of an English publishing company. Why are you in this country?'

A strong sense of his own rights had returned to Gilbert with the relief of being able to make himself understood. 'I have no intention of answering questions until you have told me why I am here.' Tapping in the corner distracted him. Radonic followed his glance.

'He is making a note of your interrogation, that is all. An old English custom. Perhaps we have a more up-to-date machine, than those in your country.'

'I've told you, I shan't answer questions—'

'You do not understand the situation. Or perhaps even my own position. I am the President of Police. That means I am in charge of this district. I am like—oh, say, one of your Superintendents, although my powers are a little wider. You will have to talk to me.'

'I don't see why I should. You've had me brought here against my will, why should I say anything. I refuse to say anything at all.' He folded his arms.

'You are angry as well as ignorant. I am trying to make excuses for you, but please do not make it too difficult.' He went on, speaking more rapidly. 'You are not in England now. Do you know the old saying that a foreigner who drives a car in this country has one foot in prison and the other in the grave? A foreigner in trouble with the police is in a worse position. If he behaves himself he will never

184

see us, except occasionally in the street on traffic duty, but if he comes here to commit a crime we dislike that very much. *I* dislike it, Mr Welton. I do not like our own criminals, but I like much less those who come from another country to commit their crime here because they think we are foolish. I take pleasure in showing them—yes, I take pleasure, Mr Welton—that this is not at all the case.'

He said with genuine bewilderment, 'I don't know what you mean. I'm not sure what I said last night, or who got mixed up in the little fight I had—'

'Do you really think that for just a fight we should search your room, look at your passport?' Radonic took off his glasses, pinched his nose where they had been, and spoke gently. 'Mr Max Bomberg is your partner, is he not? You went with him yesterday to see Eugene Ponti, the distinguished novelist who makes his summer home in our country. I have to say to you that we are delighted for Signor Ponti to visit us. We are concerned for his welfare. I, personally, am concerned.' He put on his glasses again. 'And I have also to give you the sad news that your partner Mr Bomberg is dead. His car went off the road coming down Mount Trebevic last night and it fell a hundred feet or more. He and his companion were killed immediately.'

'His companion?'

'Her name was Flavia Orsini. She acted as secretary to Signor Ponti.'

'But why was she in the car?'

'She was your partner's mistress. She had stayed in his hotel room the past three nights, returning in the morning. The hotel staff knew this, but of course she did not care. And we knew it too, but we also did not care. We are used to the immorality of foreigners and we tolerate it.' Radonic's mouth turned down at the corners. 'It is natural for you to be surprised, Mr Welton, but why are you so disturbed?'

Two thoughts emerged from the confusion in his mind.

He had committed a double murder, he had killed a woman utterly unconnected with him. And the murder itself had been pointless. It had been committed in error, for if Max had taken Flavia back to his room for the last three nights, Virginia could not have been staying with him. Perhaps she had never even come to Sarajevo. He closed his eyes.

'Mr Welton.' The fair-haired young man was holding out the national receipt for all ills, a glass of slivovitz. He drank it in two gulps and felt better.

'You see we do not practise the third degree.' Radonic slapped the table with his hand. 'Now I will tell you what is the matter, Mr Welton, why you are here. You were expecting this, were you not, it is not a surprise to you at all. You are only surprised to be caught.'

He stared dumbfounded at the large smooth face across the table. Radonic said, in a lowered voice, 'There was a brake failure. That was something you arranged. You know what I am talking about, don't try to pretend.'

'I don't understand.' He felt a desire to confide in the man on the other side of the table. Was not confession followed by submission the way to grace? Radonic had about him the kind of benevolence, the air of tolerance towards more fallible human beings, that is said to have been possessed by the Spanish Inquisitors who were truly sorry that those who came before them should be so foolish and so unrepentant. About the knowledge he possessed there seemed something miraculous. Why should Gilbert have been linked at once with the brake trouble on the car? But when put to the point Gilbert, like other modern men, did not believe in miracles, and it was for this reason that he repeated, 'I don't understand.'

'Then this will take even longer than I thought.' He picked up a telephone and spoke in a low voice. A dumpy middle-aged woman came in carrying a tray which she put on the desk. It contained a teapot, two cups, a milk jug,

186

and four thin biscuits on a plate. Radonic smiled. 'A dish of tea with biscuits, English style. I shall be mother.'

The tea was thin and weak, the biscuits tasted like straw. Radonic watched him steadily as though the way in which he drank tea would in itself provide the answers to questions. 'The tea is refreshing, is that the right word?'

'Yes.'

'Very well.' The tray was pushed aside. 'So you don't understand. Well, fortunately we have the rest of the day, we have many days. You might say that we have all the time in the world, although the time will pass more slowly for you than for me. Do you admire my English? I was in your country during my naval service. Edinburgh, Liverpool, fine places.'

'Very good. Your English.'

'You had a quarrel with your partner yesterday.'

'I did? Certainly not.'

'At the Vjdikovac Restaurant, on Trebevic. Ah, I see you remember. Why did you quarrel?'

'I'd entirely forgotten. It was nothing.'

'That is not what I was told by Lieutenant Andric. What did you quarrel about?'

'It was an argument, not a quarrel. About what translator we should get for Ponti's work.'

'A literary matter. Not about your wife?' He stared at Radonic. 'Your wife's name is Virginia?'

'Yes.'

The President of Police laughed. 'Do not look at me like that, I have no supernatural powers.' He read from a paper in front of him. 'Statement of Janos Vujic, desk clerk. "I saw the two Englishmen in the hotel lobby at about fifteen-thirty hours. The taller one was shouting at the other. It was something to do about his wife—with his wife, I am sorry. At one point he shouted out, 'What have you done with Virginia?' I think that was the name, it was a difficult English name." That is part of his statement. Correct?'

'Yes. I'd forgotten.'

'Two things you had forgotten. But I should not have thought you were forgetful, I should have said you were a careful man.'

'It meant nothing.'

'I should not have thought you were a man who said things that meant nothing.' Radonic got up from his chair and began to walk about the room. He was a big man with a slight limp, which made his walk seem eager and predatory. 'This fight you say you had last night, tell me about it.'

'It was in a night club.'

'The Bosna, yes.'

'You know about it already.'

'Just tell me.' He stood looking down at Gilbert. 'Believe me, it will be best to tell me. Tell me everything. Your position is not comfortable.'

'I'd had too much to drink. Well, not so very much, but it affected me. I was with a man named Painter and we had a row. I don't remember every word.'

'Did you say you would be glad to be out of this country?' He laughed at the look on Gilbert's face. 'Do not worry, my friend, we are used to the rudeness of foreigners. There is freedom of speech for everybody in the Yugoslav Republics.'

The words were spoken with infuriating smugness. In England, far away, he would not have been moved to reply. Now he said, 'Including Milovan Djilas?'

'*Ovo nemoje da zapisujete.*' The tapping stopped. 'Do not make things worse than they are. You have nothing to do with Djilas. His pronouncements are political.'

'So freedom of speech doesn't apply in his case.'

'You have a gift for making enemies, Mr Welton. I do not advise you to make one of me. Be thankful that I have not had your remark noted.' He nodded to the fair-haired man. The tapping continued with the next question.

'I repeat, we are tolerant. You are not here because you insulted my country in a public place, although you would be unwise to do so again. Tell me what else happened in the Bosna.'

'You know it all.' And indeed it did seem to him that Radonic had traced with impossible speed and accuracy his words and movements. 'I had a fight with Painter. I hit him and he hit me. After that I don't remember.'

'You were both asked to leave. Then your friend brought you here. If he is your friend. The night porter got you to your room.' The President spoke absently, as though his mind was on something else. 'What else did you say to Painter?'

It was then that he remembered (although had he ever really forgotten?) that he had said something to Painter about *First Gear Murder* and brake fluid. If he told the inquisitor, what would happen? The urge to confess was so strong that he did not trust himself to speak. He shook his head and stared at the floor. He felt a hand placed beneath his chin, and strangely this gave him comfort. His head was lifted. Radonic was squatting beside him. Behind the thick horn-rims brown eyes looked into his own. A hand patted his head. It was a moment of comradeship so poignant that he could have cried.

'No third degree. A pity in a way that we are civilized, not like the gangster Americans.' He stood up again, loped round to his chair. The moment had passed. 'I shall be frank with you, why should I be anything else? We are efficient, but in spite of appearances we do not work miracles. I do not care for this whole affair. We have here Autoservis and Putnik, why did your friend have to hire a car from these people called Topline? I am speaking of your friend Bomberg. It was because of this that we talked to Mr Painter. He calls himself a *trouble-shooter*.' With heavy irony he added, 'I should rather call him a *trouble-maker*.'

'I see.' Like all conjuring tricks this one was disappointing when revealed.

'We talked to him. And he talked about you. He had already made a complaint about—' He looked through the papers. '—two American tourists. That they held him up with a gun. In his car. An extraordinary story.'

'I was with him in the car.'

'So he said.'

'It's not true. He behaved badly to them. He is a very unpleasant man.' When had he told so many lies in so short a time?

'I thought he was your friend. He took you back to the hotel.' Gilbert shrugged. Radonic tapped the papers. 'Here is an interesting thing. Andric talked to him early this morning. He told us then something you had said about interfering with the brakes, some nonsense about a detective story.' He paused on an interrogative note. '*After* this we checked the brakes, and found that the controlling nuts had been loosened. How do you explain what he said, if he was not telling the truth?'

'It is not for me to explain it.' Almost happily he said, 'He still had the hand brake.'

'No doubt he tried to apply it. There were skid marks on the road. The point is that Painter told us this story *before* we checked the brakes. Do you suggest that he interfered with them himself?'

'I don't suggest anything.' From some point outside himself he listened to the answer and was pleased by it. Was it a totally new Gilbert Welton who spoke, one who had relinquished the past? Or was it a game he was playing, based on his reluctance to face reality?

'I see.' Radonic sighed, perhaps a little theatrically. 'You are not being helpful.'

'I'm sorry.'

'Perhaps you do not understand the difficulty of my

position. You thought I should say "your position," no doubt, but I am an open person, not a deceiver. There are several aspects here, the affair is not simple. One, we—and I am speaking not of our Sarajevo commune alone but of important people in Belgrade—are anxious that nothing should disturb Signor Ponti, our distinguished visitor. Any kind of scandal would be regretted. Two, an Englishman has died violently, and his woman companion also. It would be unfortunate if this appeared to reflect on the state of our roads, if any local negligence were implied. Three, I have the statement of your friend—I know you say he is not your friend, but you were travelling and drinking with him—your friend Mr Painter. If I pursue what he has said, there will be some undesirable scandal, if I do not, perhaps scandal will be caused also. This Flavia Orsini, she was well connected. A whore, but well connected,' he said without heat.

'There is also the question of justice. That seems to have escaped your attention.'

'Naive.' The President sounded irritable. 'Justice is not an abstraction, Mr Welton. Juries in your country reach their verdicts on the basis of bourgeois prejudice, judges pass sentence to protect their own kind of society. The sort of justice you are speaking of does not exist. The question is, where is the balance of advantage?' He spoke to the young man, and then said to Gilbert, 'I have told him there is no need to record this, it is merely conversation.'

There was a switchboard beside Radonic, and now a green light showed on it. He picked up one of three telephones in front of him and talked for a couple of minutes, giving an occasional speculative glance at Gilbert. With the receiver replaced he said, 'Very well. Thank you.'

The fair young man stood up. Gilbert stood too. 'We've finished?'

'We have finished.'

'And I can go?'

'I did not say that. We shall resume our conversation later.'

'Then I want to see the British consul.'

'Later. Perhaps it will not be necessary.'

'What do you mean?'

'This is a chat, that is the English word. No more. But in this chat you have not told the truth. Be quiet, listen to me. We shall talk again. If I am satisfied with your story, very well. If not, you will appear before the examining magistrate. When that is decided, is the time to see your representative.'

'You were talking about the balance of advantage. You mean you've made up your mind what it is?'

'I did not say that. You have not been helpful.'

'I want to see the English representative, somebody official.'

'Later.' Suddenly Radonic seemed cold, unfriendly. He pushed a button on his desk and a buzzer sounded.

Back in the cell he realized how confidently he had expected to be set free, and how little that expectation was justified by anything Radonic had said. There might be two, three, a dozen interrogations, and if the balance of advantage appeared to justify it they would end by his being placed on trial. No doubt the British authorities would intervene, but in practice what could they do? He faced for the first time the prospect that this cell might for the next several months be his home. The prospect did not alarm him. Perhaps Paul Pennyfeather had been right after all.

The room became darker, an electric light behind a wire casing was switched on from outside, he was inspected through the grille and a plate of food brought in. It was some sort of stewed meat with vegetables. He ate it all with relish, and drank the mug of thin coffee that came with it. As he chewed the stringy but by no means tasteless beef he wondered why he did not feel distress and guilt. He had been responsible for killing a man because of the mistaken idea that the man was his wife's lover, and also for the death of an absolutely innocent woman. Yet he felt no responsibility for this, remained quite unworried by it. Had the local air created a man anaesthetized to Western ideas of liberal justice because of what he had been through, his ludicrous but still agonizing affair with Anna and the incident with the American hitch-hikers?

What would he have done if the boy had carried out his threat and killed Painter? Contemplating it quite coolly he knew that he would have done nothing, and that his inaction would not have been caused by fear but by what Radonic called the balance of advantage. Perhaps the boy and girl were now in prison because of the complaint that Painter had sworn he did not make. If that was the case, would he prefer that they had killed Painter? He decided that he would. Everything that had happened to him in this country was a contradiction of the ideas he had lived by for at least a decade. Shut up in this small box he did not worry about where Virginia was, or about the crime he had committed, or how long he would stay here. He took down *Decline and Fall* from the shelf again, lay on the bed and began to read it, but found himself too sleepy.

The thought of going to bed filled him with pure unsensual pleasure, and he was indignant to find that he had no pyjamas. Had they been left at the hotel by accident, or was this an indication that he was not expected to stay the night? He banged on the door with one shoe and managed to make the warder understand what was needed. The man returned with a large coarse nightshirt which Gilbert put on. The rough texture of it was comforting. He had his toothbrush and now slowly brushed his teeth and got between the blankets of the hard bed. He felt affection for Radonic, who had been fatherly and kind, and was sorry that he had been a disappointment by his unhelpfulness. Tomorrow, or at their next interview, whenever it was, he would tell Radonic everything and leave him to work out which way the balance of advantage rested. He took off his watch, as he always did at night, and put it on the floor. It was for some reason a comfort that the watch did not work, with its implication that time had been permanently stopped. A feeling of luxuriant emotional ease spread through his body.

He stayed in the cell for another thirty-six hours before being called again to see Radonic. During this not precisely happy but certainly contented time he ate and slept well, re-read *Decline and Fall* and asked his guardian for a Serbo-Croat dictionary with which he tried to puzzle out a few words in the other books. He also prepared in full detail the statement he would make, so that he could hardly conceal his pleasure when he was taken again along the corridors. Radonic awaited him, plump and smiling. The fair-haired young man was in his place.

Gilbert began immediately to make his statement. He said that he had reason to believe that Bomberg was carrying on an affair with his wife, and described briefly his inexpert tampering with the braking system. The statement was quite short. It ended with an expression of regret for what he had done, and with praise for Radonic. 'I should like to thank President of Police Radonic for the courtesy with which he has conducted my interrogation, to apologize for the trouble I have given him by not making this statement before, and to emphasize that everything I have said has been entirely voluntary.'

He finished almost on a note of triumph, but something was lacking. What was it? The stenographer's fingers were still, the tapping sound was missing. He said appealingly to

194

Radonic, 'You said before that I was not helpful. You can't say that this time.'

Radonic raised his eyebrows. 'Can I not?'

'I have told you everything, everything I know.'

'You have told me a story, but is it the truth?'

'Of course it is.'

'The motives of people like yourself are often obscure to me, but a desire to confess to crimes that have not been committed is not unknown. This is done to gain attention, to impress. There is also the desire to be loved. Such confessions, for such reasons, are rare in our country but not in bourgeois society. They express a wish also to suffer, they are a compensation for social guilt.'

'What I said—you didn't even have it taken down.'

'It was not necessary.'

Outraged, he cried, 'How dare you say that?'

'What you have to say is no longer relevant. A good word, is it the right one?' He smiled. 'We had learned the cause of the unhappy accident in which your partner and Miss Orsini lost their lives. The steering of the car was faulty, very faulty indeed. It was by this defectiveness that the accident was caused. This our experts have established.'

'But the brakes. You told me yourself about them.'

'A statement based upon a mistaken assumption, correct that, I should say a preliminary examination.' The tapping faltered, was resumed. Radonic looked at Gilbert, but sounded as if he were addressing a meeting. 'In fact it is true to say that the level of the brake fluid was low, but this did not cause the accident. There was very little lining left on the brakes, it was dangerous to drive this car in any circumstances, even along a straight flat road. The basic reason for this tragedy was the use of a car hired from a foreign agency whose vehicles did not conform to the standard of efficiency demanded in this country. The English representative of this agency, the Topline, is at present under interrogation.'

He felt dazed, deprived. 'You mean he may be charged with negligence, something like that?'

'It is dependent upon the result of his further interrogation. There is also a question of currency offences with which he may be charged.' Radonic almost twinkled across the desk. 'For you, Mr Welton, it remains for us to thank you for your co-operation with us, to express very great regret for the trouble caused you. This trouble was caused by the misleading statements of the man Painter.'

'You don't want me any more, I can go?'

'At any time. And thank you.' The twinkle became a smile. His passport appeared. He took it angrily.

'The balance of advantage you talked about, this is an example of it?'

Again the clicking stopped. The President regarded him tolerantly, almost with pity. 'You assume too many things, you feel too much and think too little. Everything one says is not to be taken seriously. Some things are for effect, isn't that the phrase?' He came round his desk, laughing. 'Come now, you will make me think you are sorry to be out of here. We are friends, isn't it so? Put your passport in your pocket.' They shook hands. 'There have been some messages, isn't it so, Paul? Here they are. From your office somebody rang, Miss Pinkthorn—is that the name? And Mr Bunce—is that also correct?—wished to speak with you. I think your firm had told him that you were here in Sarajevo.'

'How did they know—' He did not complete the sentence.

'They did not of course know that you were our guest. The hotel said simply that you were not available.'

'Nobody knows I've been here?'

'Helping the police with their investigations, isn't that your English phrase? We still have much to learn from the English. Shall we try to reach your office for you, now? It is Monday morning.' He shook his head. It seemed to him that he would never again have anything to say to Miss Pinkthorn. 'Your partner's death has of course been reported in the English Press. Paul.'

The fair-haired young man had already poured glasses of slivovitz. 'Your health, Mr Welton. I hope we shall meet again on a happier occasion.' As they put down the glasses he said, 'One thing more. The burial of your friend is this afternoon. You will no doubt wish to attend. Signor Ponti would like to see you afterwards. I believe you have reached agreement to publish a book of his. Isn't it so?'

'It's not finally fixed. He was arranging it.'

'I should like you to see Signor Ponti.' For a moment his look was stern again. 'He is a good friend of my country. I very much hope that nothing happens to disturb Signor Ponti.'

CHAPTER SEVEN

The Funeral

PAUL ACCOMPANIED HIM to the cemetery. The driver misunderstood the instructions, so that they went first to the Jewish cemetery Alijakovac, and when they reached the new cemetery in Jukiceva they were late. Paul got out and walked along not exactly with him but just behind, like an old-style Oriental wife. They went through a maze of gravestones, some with crosses, others with pictures of the dead under glass, flanked by artificial flowers. He thought this too might be the wrong place until he saw a little group at the far end of one of the long avenues.

From a few feet away he saw that a service was being conducted at the graveside. Perhaps this was the wrong funeral? But on the other side of the hole in the ground into which the coffin was at this moment being lowered he saw Janet Ponti, looking pale in a black dress and hat. She glanced up at him and then lowered her head. He joined the group and bent his own head. A voice beside him whispered, 'There you are.' It was Coldharbour.

He whispered back. 'What are you doing here?'

'Somebody had to represent the firm. We spent a *fortune* trying to get in touch with you, most inconsiderate.' As his voice rose the priest's rose also, soaring over it in some beautiful incomprehensible incantation. Appropriately to this image of soaring, his arms waved like a bird's wings.

'But why?'

'Why *what*?'

'This service. Max had no religion.'

'We were in touch with Louise. She thought he was a Catholic.' Louise was Max's divorced wife, but whatever Coldharbour had been going to say about her was checked by a harsh 'Quiet,' spoken by somebody on the other side of him. Leaning forward a little he saw that the word had been spoken by Bunce.

Earth was thrown on the coffin, the priest crossed himself, the service was over. A group of what appeared to be official mourners—for surely they could have had no connection with Max?—accompanied the priest as he moved slowly away.

'Gil, it's good to see you.' Bunce shook his hand. 'It's moving, don't you find that? There's something about putting a body in the ground that gets you, it has meaning.'

'Mr Bunce wanted to accompany me when he heard that I was flying out. That is, after we were unable to contact you.' Reproachfully he said, 'I was sick on the plane.'

'It isn't that I wanted to intrude,' Bunce said earnestly. 'Just to pay my little tribute to a good guy, is all. Most people, you know, they're just nobodies from nowhere, but Max was really somebody.'

'Excuse me.' Paul had gone over to Janet Ponti and was

saying something to her. He introduced her and said, 'This is Paul.'

Paul shook hands with them both and clicked his heels slightly. Gilbert said, 'I think Signor Ponti is expecting us. Max was negotiating about our publishing his book, *The Tigress.*'

Coldharbour sniffed. He was looking at Paul in a speculative way, and it occurred to Gilbert that a Christian name introduction was no doubt odd. 'Mr Coldharbour is one of my co-directors, would your father mind if—'

Before she could reply, Paul spoke. 'Signor Ponti is very tired, I think he wishes only to see you.' He turned to Coldharbour. 'Perhaps another day.'

Coldharbour's shrug conveyed that to be deprived of seeing Ponti was in accordance with the treatment generally meted out to him. Bunce asked, 'You his secretary or something?'

'I have not that honour.' They were approaching the cemetery gate.

'Then just you button your mouth.' Paul looked mystified. Bunce said to Janet, 'Miss Ponti, I'd be honoured to meet your father, speaking personally. He's a traditional writer, you might say out of date, but I respect him.'

Outside the cemetery two cars were drawn up, both with drivers, the black car they had come in and a large red Fiat behind it. The drivers got out and moved like automata to open the passenger doors.

'I'm sorry,' Janet said to Bunce. She got into the Fiat and Gilbert followed her.

Coldharbour said, almost in a wail, 'But where shall we see you afterwards?'

'I will arrange,' Paul said. He pointed to the black car. The Fiat was away.

They passed again through Dajanli and began to climb. Janet looked out of the window. He said, 'Why does your father want to see me?'

199

'He made an agreement that night with Mr Bomberg. He wants to make sure it holds good.'

'If it was made under false pretences it doesn't.'

Now she turned. The black dress made her more unattractive, accentuating the coarseness of her skin and the blotches on it. 'You are a fool, you still don't know what it's about, do you? I should have thought that policeman—'

'Radonic, you mean?'

'I should have thought he would have told you. They said you'd been talking to him.'

'Told me what? I don't understand.'

'This is where they went off the road, just here.' It was on a sharp bend. To the left there was a steep drop, green slopes succeeded by pine trees. He thought of the car turning over and over, and looked for skid marks on the road or a scar on the green lushness, but saw nothing. Then they were round the bend.

'That bitch. Flavia Orsini. Her father is the Minister for Export Trade.'

'I thought she was Italian.'

'In Italy, of course. Now do you see?'

'I'm afraid not.'

'There is some big trade deal going on between this country and Italy. Supposing there were an investigation and questions were asked about what Signorina Orsini was doing as a permanent guest of the famous novelist Eugene Ponti, why she spent half her nights in Sarajevo and who she spent them with—you don't suppose your friend was the only one, do you? And do you see now? There must be no trouble, everything must be hushed up, it does not matter what lies are told.' From her tight throat there was wrenched a single dry sob.

'Radonic knew all this?'

'He has been up at the house talking to my father. My father is old, he does not care what happens as long as he gets what he wants. At the moment he wants this agreement. He is like a child. It will make him happy and then he will cause no trouble. Radonic wants that. I suppose you will be happy too.'

What about the steering, he wanted to ask, had it been faulty or was that just a convenient invention? But she would not know what he was talking about. Only Radonic knew, and whatever Radonic said was not to be believed. He would never know the truth.

'I don't see why you're so concerned. You can hardly have been fond of Flavia.'

She was looking away from him again as they went through the wrought iron gates. 'No, I was not fond of her,' she said as they stepped out into the sunshine. He remembered that single long look she had given Max, and understood. As he followed her out to the terrace he wondered again what quality it was that made a man like Max a sexual magnet, no matter what he said or how badly he behaved. And why was Gilbert Welton anti-magnetic? Thoughts of the Anglo-Germanic syndrome passed across his mind like thunder clouds. Then he was again in Ponti's presence, and the white cock's crest was turned to him.

'Come and sit. Beside me.' There was a chair close to his. 'Sit and enjoy the view.'

'Wonderful.' Much the same thing had been said when he came up here with Max. With conscious banality he spoke about a terrible tragedy.

'The old get used to tragedy, they understand that it is the meaning of life. When I lost these, that was tragic.' He touched his eyes. 'Tragedy is the nature of life, death is a commonplace. It has no power to disturb me. I confront human tragedy with the power of art.'

To this rotund wisdom Gilbert did not reply. Ponti's rich voice changed from complacency to complaint. 'What does disturb me is to be woken in the middle of the night, to be asked questions by police officials, impertinent questions about my life.' The liver-spotted hands quivered, he broke into a rush of Italian. Janet, who had been sitting a few feet away from them looking at a magazine, got up, came over and spoke to him. Her pale face contorted with anger. She said to Gilbert, 'I have said to him do not worry, you will find another secretary, there are plenty like her to fawn around famous men.' She went into the house.

Ponti listened to her retreating footsteps. 'Tragedy and ingratitude, an old man is used to both. But the official stupidity and the, what is the word, is it prying?—that must not be tolerated. Their inquiries! I could say things, I could say many things that would cause trouble.' His lips puffed in and out. The maid brought tea things. Janet reappeared, poured the tea and offered biscuits, placed an envelope between them on the table and went away again. 'She thinks she can be a tyrant now that I am alone, all human beings wish to be tyrants, but I shall not submit. I do not like tyrants.' Yourself excepted, Gilbert thought. The old man took a biscuit, crumbled it, put pieces in his mouth. Without faltering he placed a hand on the agreement. 'This is the paper I signed. Will you read it to me?'

Gilbert opened the envelope, began to read. It was their standard form of agreement for translation. Ponti stopped him after a few lines. 'Tell me about the name. Does it name Mr Angus Wilson?'

He turned the page. Inserted in typewriting were the words: 'The translation shall be undertaken by Angus Wilson, if that is possible and he is agreeable, or if not by another translator of the publisher's choice, who will make a true rendering of the original into the English language.' It meant nothing at all. But what had Max said and promised?

'It names Angus Wilson.'

'Very well. I have signed it. Are you prepared to sign also?'

He remembered Radonic's last words: 'I very much hope that nothing happens to disturb Signor Ponti.' He was not sure whether he loved or hated Radonic, but he knew that he did not want to sit again on the other side of the table from the President of Police who did not use third-degree methods, with Paul tapping in his corner. His confession, what seemed now his stupid and astonishing confession, had not been typed, but perhaps it had been recorded on tape. What the old man thought he was getting was ridiculous, but the result of saying no to him might be unpleasant.

'I am prepared to sign it.' Ponti looked for a moment almost disappointed. 'But I must tell you that the name of Angus Wilson inserted in the agreement means nothing. I don't know what my partner said, but this is the full clause.' He read it.

There was silence. Ponti's hand slowly stretched for another biscuit, put it on his plate, broke it. Crumbs fell to the ground. Then he threw back his head and laughed. His chair tilted perilously backwards and righted itself. Gilbert looked at him in bewilderment.

'A test,' he said. 'I was testing you. Give me the agreement.' Gilbert handed it to him. 'Now the envelope.' He put the agreement into the envelope, handed it across the table. 'It is yours. You have the right to publish Eugene Ponti in Britain.'

'I don't understand.'

'Your partner, Max Bomberg. I liked him very much.'

'I know.'

'But I did not trust him. I knew he was playing a trick on an old man. I do not like you, Mr Welton. But I trust you.'

'I think I am entitled to ask for an explanation,' Coldharbour said. It was raining. They sat in the large lounge of the hotel and watched the rain fall on the terrace. 'The office has been turned really *upside down*. It was quite inexcusable not to let us know where we could find you. When I received the news from the Yugoslav Embassy—'

'The Yugoslav Embassy?'

'They got in touch with me through the caretaker at Max's flat. I naturally supposed that you would handle the matter since you were in Sarajevo. You had said that you would be getting in touch with Max.' Coldharbour rustled a little. Obviously he had made no concession to the local climate. 'Anna has been very worried. And upset.'

'Anna?'

'Miss Pinkthorn. She has been a tower of strength. I can't imagine what you've been doing in the last forty-eight hours, why you didn't get in touch.'

'Let's have a drink.' A waiter bore down on them, smiling. They were back in the world where the tourist was deferred to. Gilbert found that the thought of slivovitz revolted him, and ordered beer. Coldharbour drank mineral water, which he sipped cautiously, eyeing Gilbert as though he were a wayward animal. 'Where's Bunce?'

'He went off. To look at the Turkish market, he *said*. I must say I was glad to be rid of him. Do you know, on the plane he became very familiar with a stewardess? I am afraid Americans are lecherous by nature.'

'Not all of them, surely.'

'Perhaps not. Who was that man?'

'What man?'

With a slight smirk Coldharbour pronounced the name. 'Paul.'

Foolishly unprepared for this question, he improvised. 'He's something to do with an official department, the Home Office I think.'

'Bunce said he was a policeman, that he had all the signs of being the law.' He sniffed. 'I thought myself that he was rather nice.'

'Yes. Quite nice.'

'Gilbert, what have you been doing, why did you just turn up at the funeral? I think I have a right to know.'

For this question he was prepared. 'We have an agreement with Ponti for publishing *The Tigress*. Max and I arranged it. Really it was Max's doing,' he said truthfully. He drew out the agreement, but Coldharbour was not to be deflected.

'And then?'

'How do you mean?'

'After Max had his accident, where were you? Why couldn't the hotel find you?'

'I went off on my own for a short time, I only learned about it when I got back.'

'But how did Paul—' Coldharbour began, obviously dissatisfied. He was checked by the appearance of Bunce, exhausted but enthusiastic.

'What a town, what a wonderful little town. It's where history began. I've been standing in the assassin's footprints.'

Gilbert was startled. 'What's that?'

'The assassin or the hero. Princip, the guy who knocked off the old Archduke and got things moving. They've got footprints let in the pavement. You know they named a bridge after him and put up a museum. He had small feet, mine fitted exactly. Something symbolic there.' Somehow Bunce had obtained a glass full of what looked like whisky. 'Max would have appreciated it, he was like me, he had a foot in both worlds, the old and the new. A great man, Max. It's a hell of a thing to die, but that's the way to go if you're going.' He raised the glass. 'Max.'

They drank. Bunce relaxed in his chair. 'What are you doing here, Gil? I'd have thought you'd be with Virginia.'

'With Virginia?'

'I quite forgot.' Coldharbour wriggled uncomfortably.

'She rang the office, wanted to get hold of you. I told her you'd be here. With Max.'

'You've spoken to her, you know where she is?'

'If you hadn't done so much chasing about and going off on your own, you'd have talked to her yourself.'

'Where is she, Denis?'

'There's no need to look like that,' Coldharbour said pettishly. 'She rang from Amsterdam. She's staying with your son.'

PART III

Wife Found

CHAPTER ONE

Matthew

OUT OF THE BIRD's belly at Schiphol : the return to reality. The feeling was strengthened when he saw his son in the reception hall. A strong handshake, a hand lifting his baggage out to the car.

'Good to see you.' Was this square man in a double-breasted suit really his son, anybody's son? Matthew lighted a pipe as they got into the car, tamped it down, got it going. From adolescence he had been a pipe-smoking man. 'Got your telegram,' he said as he started the car and they drove on the exit road from the airport.

'I couldn't reach you on the telephone.' He hesitated to ask why Virginia had not come to meet him.

'Sorry to hear about your partner. Rotten business. You flew out to clear things up, I suppose.' At a traffic light Matthew gave him a glance. 'You knew Virginia was here?'

'Yes. You mean she isn't with you now?'

'Flew back yesterday. You haven't spoken to her then?'

'No, we haven't been in touch. I've been trying to find her.' It seemed to be the understatement of his life. 'How is she?'

'Fine, fine. I gather she's been in Yugoslavia too.'

'Yes. How's Miriam?'

'Couldn't be better.' Matthew removed the pipe. 'You're going to be a grandfather.' He put back the pipe.

For a moment he did not take in the meaning of the circumlocution. Then he said, 'That's wonderful news. Congratulations to you both.'

'We're very pleased. Virginia was pleased too.'

Miriam was waiting in their apartment on the Herrengracht. When he saw her, small, dark, not pretty but elegant, and conspicuously foreign, he wondered as he had done before how Matthew had come to marry this rather exotic plant. It occurred to him that he had never speculated on the attraction Matthew held for her. He had always automatically assumed that British stolidity had its charm for the butterfly foreigner. Was this an indirect product of the Anglo-Germanic syndrome, or was Matthew really an entirely different person from the tractable child and adolescent who had grown into the solemnly boring young man now telling him in detail about the firm's turnover increase in the past six months? He wondered about this while he drank a single glass of sherry and ate a delicate lunch.

Miriam waved away his congratulations. 'It's going to be a bore really, because I'll have to give up my job.' She was secretary to the director of an industrial trust and, he felt sure, very competent. 'But Matthew thought we ought to have a child while we were young.' Was Matthew young? It seemed hard to believe. 'I shall have to leave in another couple of months but then I shall go back when Reuben is at nursery school. They have wonderful nurseries here.'

'Reuben?'

'It was my grandfather's name.'

'Suppose it's a girl.'

'It won't be. Matthew says it will be a son, and he is always right.' The look she gave her husband was so melting that something within Gilbert twanged like a piano wire. 'If you will forgive me, I have to go back to work now. But I shall see you later, you'll stay with us of course.'

'Thank you, but I must get back to London. I really have to talk to Virginia.' He had already made a telephone call and heard that discouraging double ring going on and on.

'She is so delightful, so gay. I like her very much. By the way—'

'Yes?'

'Reuben's other name will be Gilbert.' There was a smile, a quick brush on the cheek. Then she had gone, and he was alone with his son.

'More coffee? Glass of port? Or try some of this Dutch liqueur, Van der Hum they call it, don't know if it is Dutch really.' Tiny liqueur glasses sat in a cupboard along with sherry glasses, wine glasses, brandy snifters, everything was in its place. 'Glad of this chance to have a chat.'

It struck Gilbert that their roles were reversed, and that Matthew was speaking to him like a father, or perhaps like a housemaster at school. The feeling was heightened when they took their drinks to the small room that Matthew (but of course) called his den, and he said, 'Everything all right?'

'How do you mean?'

'Virginia said she'd been off on a bit of a holiday. On her own. That seemed rather funny to me. And then you being out there too. If anything's going on I'd like to know.'

'Of course nothing's going on, as you put it.'

'Because we're fond of you both, Miriam and I. We'd be very sorry if anything was wrong.' He took out his pipe, looked at it, laid it to one side with a gesture appropriate to a TV serial. Then he picked up the pipe again and began to fill it slowly, still in the best televisual manner. 'She didn't stay long, Virginia. Just the one night. Then she rang the office to find you and somebody told her about your partner's death. After that she went back.'

'Was she upset?'

'What about?' Matthew gave his father the young executive's inquiring glance.

'Max's death.'

'I didn't notice. Should she have been?' He did not wait for a reply to that. 'She was jolly pleased about Reuben, I can tell you that.'

The walls of the den were covered with photographs in the manner of a housemaster's study. Or were housemasters' studies now covered with pictures of the Rolling Stones and Julie Felix? And for that matter school photographs like these, groups rock-climbing in the Lakes, Matthew in the school play, a photograph of his prep school soccer team, were not generally preserved by schoolboys but by their parents. It was with a shock that he saw a family group below a picture of Matthew in the tennis team, Mary, Matthew and himself. It must have been taken after Starting Again, on a desperate and unsuccessful family holiday in Devon. Mary was sprawled on the sand in an ungainly fashion, he was bent over digging with a tiny spade, the child examined them with an astonished expression. He had not thought of Mary for days. Now he said, 'You got my letter. About your mother.'

'Yes. That was what I wanted to have a word about.'

He turned from the photograph. Matthew's square face, set in the solid and reliable lines that would deepen with the years, the hair already thinning a little, looked up at him from the chair. He felt and controlled a spasm of irritation. 'About Mary? I told you she died in a friend's flat where she'd been living. Sleeping tablets. You probably saw the details in reports of the inquest.'

'I only read the Dutch papers now. If you're living in a country you ought to read their press.' He felt another spasm, more intense. 'I had your letter, yes. But I'd already heard.'

'What do you mean? I know I didn't write at once, but how could you have heard—'

'From Mother. She wrote to me that night, before she took the pills. She wrote to me. She told me she'd seen you.'

He sat down and looked at Matthew. He wanted desperately to see the letter. It seemed to him that it contained the answer to the whole of his behaviour, the things he had done and the things that had been done to him.

'She must have written it, posted it straightaway and then gone on drinking and swallowed the pills.' His tone was matter of fact. 'It was pretty maudlin. And very scrawly, she must have been extremely drunk.' He sipped his Van der Hum.

'Where is it?'

'I only saw her a few times after leaving school, but she wasn't an unhappy person, was she? I think she was a happy person, though I don't remember her that way.'

'You mean I made her unhappy?'

'Oh no. I only know—I never minded going back to school, that's all. She was rather feckless perhaps. I suppose that's why you didn't get on.'

Gilbert looked at him. He was amazed that Matthew had ever thought about his father and mother at all. 'Can I see the letter?'

'No. I destroyed it.'

'Destroyed it!'

'What was the point of doing anything else? Drunken ramblings, that's all.'

The final answer had been denied to him. He was angry, yet behind the anger lay fear of what he would have found. 'She must have said something important, something about why she was going to do it.' Matthew shook his head. 'She was my wife, you should have sent it to me. Or kept it for me.'

'She was your wife, she was my mother, but that was all a long time ago. When she wrote that letter she was just a drunk. A good deal of it didn't make sense.'

'She said something about me. I want to know what it was.'

'I told you, nothing important.'

'What was it?'

'She said she'd met you somewhere, she'd been to see you, you'd turned her out. There was a lot about not wanting to make a mess of your home.'

'What else?'

'Nothing I remember. I shouldn't have mentioned it.' His word-searching manner became more deliberate than usual. 'But there's one thing. You must have asked her back to the house. You saw the state she was in. Why did you turn her out?'

The serious ponderous face carried only inquiry, not condemnation, but he could not endure his son's company or stay in the apartment any longer. 'I must go. I'll get a taxi to the airport.'

'Why don't you ring Virginia again?'

'No, I must go.'

'I'll drive you there. If I've said something to upset you I'm sorry.'

'It's what you are that upsets me,' he said in a rare moment of openness. 'And what I am. I'll get a taxi.'

'No no, please let me take you.'

In the end it was less trouble to let Matthew take him. On the way out to Schiphol Matthew said what a pity it was that his father could not stay and have a look at the pleasures of Amsterdam, the canals, the shopping in the Kalverstraat, the night life. He wanted to wait, but Gilbert refused to let him. They shook hands at parting. There was a flight to London in three-quarters of an hour, and he got on to it with a standby ticket.

CHAPTER TWO

Virginia

IN LONDON lances of rain struck at the pavements. His sense
of moving from one life to another was enhanced. On the
way to St John's Wood in the taxi he wondered whether he
would be permitted to return.

Light showed in the hall, filtered through the drawn
drawing-room curtains. He walked up the path in the rain,
opened the front door, and stopped when he heard voices.
The last voice he had heard here was Mary's: *It's upsetting for women when men don't know what they want. I feel
sorry for Vir-Virginia.* Grotesque thoughts passed through
his mind. Would he find Mary and Virginia talking in the
drawing-room, would Max be there? He put down his suit-
case and turned the handle of the door.

Virginia was in there with the Sutherlands. She got up,
came over and embraced him. He noticed at once that her
scent was fresh and mild, 'Darling, did you have a good
flight?'

'You were expecting me?'

'Matthew rang and said you were on your way. Are
you mad with hunger? John and Sandra are staying to dinner, isn't that nice? Now you're here I won't have to pour
drinks.'

'I hear you and Virginia have been following each other
round Yugoslavia,' John Sutherland said. 'Very similar
thing happened to me in Greece, damned funny.' He told
a long story about a time when he and Sandra in a
motorized caravan had arrived a day late to meet friends
in a village near Athens, and had spent the next fortnight

213

narrowly missing them. 'Of course communications are bad in these countries.'

'I always say that's part of their charm.' Sandra could be relied on for the safe confirmatory remark. 'You must be pleased to be home.' He said that he was, and when John said that it was terrible about Max's death he agreed. They went on asking questions.

'I saw him out there, the afternoon before it happened. We went to see an Italian novelist, Eugene Ponti.'

'Oh yes, about the book you were so keen on,' Virginia said. 'You told me about it.'

Had he told her? He could not remember it. He asked if she had seen Max.

'No, I didn't even know he was there. Anyway, I never got to Sarajevo.'

'At the Dubrovnik hotel they seemed to think you were going there.'

'I thought about it, but never went. We're ready to eat.' She linked her arm in his and whispered, 'I'll get rid of them as soon as I can.'

This was not very soon. They talked about the relationship between soft drugs and violence, the connection of pop groups with American protest songs, the limitations of comprehensive education, where the Sutherlands might go for their summer holiday, about a new theory that autistic children could be helped by leaving them entirely alone for long periods at a time. It was an average evening for their class, age and income group, one that he found exhausting, although he would have taken it in its stride in the past.

'They're nice but boring,' Virginia said when they had gone. 'I wouldn't have asked them if I'd known you'd be back. I didn't actually know you were going away.'

'I flew out to Dubrovnik because I wanted to see you.'

'It was dull there, so I left. If I'd known you were coming—'

'I telephoned. Or tried to. Where did you go?'

'Oh, all over. A couple of the islands, Korcula and Brac, then to Split. Up to Lake Bled, that was heavenly.'

'But not to Sarajevo.'

'Not to Sarajevo.'

The showdown, the final explanation he had been looking for, where was it? It seemed that there was nothing to explain.

'Did you do what you wanted, make up your mind?'

'Yes. I don't know what I was thinking about. A woman's place is with her husband. I mean, she should live his life, not the other way round.' It crossed his mind that this low-grade magazine wisdom could have been obtained without going abroad, but he did not say so. 'Gilbert.'

'You?'

'Something has happened to you. Did you have an *adventure*?' Her eyes sparkled with pleasure.

'I didn't go looking for adventure. I was looking for you.'

'Don't be stuffy, I was joking. Let's make love.'

As they lay in the bedroom afterwards, she said, 'How was that?'

'Fine.' How was it compared with Anna, how had it really been? 'Marvellous.' He kissed her shoulder.

'I was sorry about Mary, I heard when I got back.' Why had she chosen that precise moment to mention Mary? 'She was a lush at the end, wasn't she? I shall never be like that.'

'You won't go away again?'

'Only with you.' She stroked his hair. 'Are you pleased you'll be a grandfather?'

'I don't think I mind either way.'

'Miriam wrote and told me, that's why I went to see them. I wish I could have had a child.'

'Matthew was quite enough.'

'Hold me.' He held her, nipples pressed against him, legs wound over his. 'Something happened while you were away, I feel sure it did.'

215

'Did anything happen to you?'

'No. I had a boring time.'

'Nothing happened to me either. I'm the same person that I was when you left.' He broke from their interlocking grasp, took her by the throat. 'You have to believe that.'

She pulled at his hands. 'You don't have to strangle me. Whatever happened—'

'I've told you, nothing happened. Nothing at all.'

'We're the kind of people to whom nothing ever happens. That's what you wanted me to say, isn't it?'

'It isn't just what I wanted. It's true.'

'Yes, it's true.'

Just before she turned out the light he saw the inside of her raised arm. It was perfectly smooth and white.

CHAPTER THREE

Da Capo

ON THE FOLLOWING MORNING he looked at the exterior of the house and felt his usual small but distinct sense of pleasure at its elegant lack of ostentation. This was a kind of test, which he passed successfully. He savoured the mild orderliness of England in walking to the office through Regent's Park. The day was warm without a hint of heat, an old man wearing a very long tattered sweater fed the ducks.

At the office everybody seemed genuinely pleased to see him. Even the lugubrious Paine smiled and said, 'You're back, Mr Welton.' It was as though he had been away for months, not a few days. Miss Pinkthorn (Anna) charged in head down and planked on to his desk a thick wad of manuscript. It was *A Welter of Gore*.

'*Mr Bomberg* was responsible.' She spoke as though he were in the next room and not under earth in Sarajevo. 'He gave it to J. Wilson Arkwright to read without saying a word. Not a word to anybody.' Pause. 'He seems to think it's good.'

J. Wilson Arkwright, a barrister who had found writing about crime more profitable than the law, was a name to conjure with. His enthusiasm for *A Welter of Gore* seemed total, his view of its prospects was optimistic. Gilbert dictated on the spot a letter to Dexter Manhood accepting the book.

'Very sad about Mr Bomberg,' Miss Pinkthorn said after they had disposed of the rubbish that had accumulated in his absence. 'Mr Coldharbour said he saw you at the funeral, though I don't suppose it was anything, being in an atheist country. He should have been brought back.' Gilbert suggested that Max wouldn't have minded. Miss Pinkthorn glared at him. 'Did you enjoy yourself?' It was impossible to say anything but yes. 'And I hope you found Mrs Welton well.' He said that he had.

'We shall miss Mr Bomberg. He had some funny ways but you couldn't help liking him.' She brushed away a tear.

He lunched at the club and received more condolences. After lunch he went to a sale of jewellery at Christie's and bought a diamond necklace. In the evening he took Virginia to the theatre. The play was a sexy comedy, at which they both laughed. When they returned he gave her the necklace. It was the most expensive present he had ever bought her, and she said she loved it. On the following day she made arrangements to invite to dinner an ex-Minister whose book about his resignation from the Government was being published by the firm. Getting together politico-literary guests to meet him was a problem that she seemed to face with relish.

The telephone call from Mel Branksom came a week later.

'Hi there. I should have called before, but I've been in the States. I wanted to say I was just horrified, and I mean horrified, to hear about Max. It was one of those goddam stupid things that just shouldn't happen. A man like that, he had flair. You might call it genius. It must be a blow.'

'We're carrying on.'

'I've had conferences with our parent company. When are you free for lunch?'

Coldharbour also came to lunch, in a restaurant called the New American, which as Mel said lacked English dignity. There, in his own words, he laid it on the line. Branksom Associates would either buy out the existing directors completely, or they would take a fifty-one per cent shareholding. In this case they would want financial but not editorial control. The terms proposed were generous. He showed Gilbert a report from their financial advisers which said that the firm was under-capitalized. The Spatial Realists were mentioned. Mel was enthusiastic, he was an enthusiastic man.

'Why not? I hear these Spatial Realists are the latest thing. And how about a book on the erotic art of the East, Indian temple paintings, old Chinese work, some of the Louis Fifteen stuff? You think it's too near to our old image, maybe you're right. But we ought to do half a dozen art books, make it a series. You'll edit them, won't you, Denis?' Coldharbour wriggled with pleasure. 'This is a great deal, one of my lifelong ambitions fulfilled. I'm only sorry Max is not here to see it. He was a genius.'

Coldharbour nodded in solemn concurrence.

Virginia arranged a dinner-party for Mel and his wife, who wore pince-nez and chainsmoked. She found some people to go with them.

Perhaps Max really had been a genius. The film rights of *The Way They Get You Going* were sold. It was said that Richard Burton, Elizabeth Taylor and Dustin Hoffman were to star. An offer for the paperback rights was received which staggered Gilbert. He queried the offer and it was immediately increased. Welton's got nothing from the film but a great deal of money from the paperback.

The calligraphy had a bold flourish, the postmark said N.W. 6. He read the letter at the breakfast table and put it into his pocket. Virginia looked at him with eyebrows slightly raised.

'Pass the marmalade.'

She did so. 'Bad news?'

'No news at all.'

'You looked rather—I don't know—the way you looked when you first came back.'

'It's a man who pestered me before. Now he's writing to me at home.'

A half-truth he reflected, as he read the letter:

Hallo there!

Saw a bit in the paper about some merger or other you were in with the Yanks, pity we can't keep anything British these days but that's the way it goes. Anyway, couldn't resist writing a line to tell you that I'm back in the Old Country safe and sound, after a spot of what they call interrogation because of a little bother over some Swiss francs. Least said soonest mended! The old tick-tock was going pit-a-pat, I can tell you. A couple of sessions with that cold-blooded police chief and anybody would be feeling a bit Harry groggers. Gather you got some of the same, afraid I said a couple of things I shouldn't in the heat of the moment, but all's well that ends well, as the bard put it.

In the end they decided to let me off with a caution, after trying to put the blame for that accident on Top-line. Trust the foreigners for that. However, the upshot was we've closed down our operations in a certain country, and yours truly can't say he's sorry. Must say, though, looking back I enjoyed our trip together and that little night club session—what a dump! Nice little piece, Maria, keen on me too. I'd have dipped my wick if unforeseen circumstances hadn't intervened, as they say. Back with the wife and kids now, a good thing too.

Well, here's hoping we'll meet again one of these days. I move around a good deal, as the girl in the newspaper shop said when the man asked if she kept stationery, but if you give a tinkle to the office number they'll always get a message through. All the very best.

Jerry

When he had read the letter again he tore it up and flushed the pieces down the lavatory.

'Gil.' Bunce had been swanning around unreachably in Europe when the paperback deal was made, but his voice on the telephone was warm and fresh. 'Gil, how are you?'

'We've been trying to get hold of you. Where have you been?'

'Crete, Minorca, up in Castile, pretty much every place I guess. Oh, and I forgot, Algeria, the boys there are really something. Now I'm going back to Mother.'

'To Mother?'

'My only Mother, the tart New York and the virgin Kansas, the mother country.' He sounded a little high. 'Gil, I'm at the Ritz. Come up and say goodbye.'

It turned out that the highness was natural Bunce, a euphoria engendered by anticipation of his return. 'Saks and Macy's I can't wait to get my arms around you, Yorkville you dreary old German slut I love you,' he said. 'Honestly Gil, Europe's finished, sucked dry.'

'That's not what you were saying a few weeks ago.'

'That could be. But whatever number you use to dial

the future it'll be America who answers. How about that for the title of my next book?'

'Rather long.'

The bedroom in the suite opened and a girl came out of it. 'This is Hedda. She's coming to the States with me. Hedda, say hallo to my publisher. Hedda, Gil.'

'Hallo, we've met.' It was Anna. She had had her hair cut very short, almost a skinhead crop.

Gilbert said, 'The hair and the name were different, but we've met.'

'She's married to some half-arsed photographer named Perkins. He calls her Dorothy, but her name's Hedda all right. She was born half-way through a performance of *Hedda Gabler*, that's how she got it.'

'She used to call herself Anna. After Anna Karenina.'

'Oh, for God's sake,' she said.

'She's a temperamental girl,' Bunce said seriously. 'What we all need is some brandy.' He sent down for a bottle and they drank quite a lot of it. Anna and Gilbert hardly said a word to each other, but that did not matter because Bunce talked all the time. Gilbert said an affectionate goodbye to him. He had become fond of Bunce. At the last moment Anna, or Hedda, came up and kissed him on the mouth. Her lips were hot, the effect slightly repellent.

'You've made up your mind then,' Virginia said. 'About the offer.' She was in a nightdress at her dressing-table, preparing for bed.

'Yes. They can have their fifty-one per cent. Coldharbour agrees. There'll be a couple of Americans breathing over our shoulders, but I don't think that matters.'

'You won't sell out altogether?'

'No. What for, what should we do?'

'I think that's right.' She said with her air of stating a profound truth, 'A man needs an occupation.'

'Virginia.'

221

'Yes?'

'Whatever it was made you go away—it's all over now?'

'Of course. I told you, I needed a change. To think about things.' She patted her cheeks. 'You must have thought too. You know, you're different.'

'In what way?'

'More considerate, I suppose. Something like that.'

'Virginia.'

'Yes?'

'If I said I'm still not sure what happened, what would you say?'

'I don't want to talk about it any more, do you mind?' She turned on her chair. 'I love my necklace.'

'Good.'

'Gilbert, can I have something? Something I want.'

'I expect so, what?'

'A dog. I'd take it for walks in the park.'

'A poodle?'

'No, I hate little dogs. A retriever or labrador, something like that.'

'All right.'

The next day he bought a new hat. It was a Russian-style fur hat. Mr Clapperton thought that he looked very dashing in it.

When he got home a golden retriever puppy jumped up and licked eagerly at his hand.

'Max,' Virginia called. She came out into the hall, smiling. 'I'm calling him Max. In memory,' she said.